KARM

Aditya Mukherjee is the author of the bestselling novel *Boomtown*. He is an alumnus of IIM Bangalore. After working as a strategy consultant for several years, he has now co-founded a start-up aimed at children's entertainment. He has written several features for the *Deccan Herald*, ranging from travelogues and articles on economics to various social issues. He also created a half-page comic strip for their New Year's Sunday edition in 2008.

Arnav Mukherjee has spent his last three years in three different continents, and he's stayed in more than fifteen cities since childhood. He has spent a lot of time in Turkey, Japan, South Korea and the US. *Karm* is Arnav's first novel, which he has co-written with his brother. His deep interest in film-making and screen-writing helps bring a cinematic flavour to the thriller.

KARM

Aditya Mukherjee
Arnav Mukherjee

RUPA

First published by
Rupa Publications India Pvt. Ltd 2015
7/16, Ansari Road, Daryaganj
New Delhi 110002

Sales centres:
Allahabad Bengaluru Chennai
Hyderabad Jaipur Kathmandu
Kolkata Mumbai

ISBN: 978-81-291-3470-7

10 9 8 7 6 5 4 3 2 1

First impression 2015

The moral right of the author has been asserted.

Typeset by SÜRYA, New Delhi

Printed at Thomson Press India Ltd, Faridabad

To my beautiful and brilliant wife,
who supports me in all my endeavours—Aditya

To my beautiful and brilliant laptop,
that supports me in all my endeavours—Arnav

AUTHOR'S NOTE

This book is intended as a homage to the vigilante genre made popular by graphic novels, but it is also a critique of the same. The story is, of course, fictional, and no similarity to anyone, living or dead, is intended.

PROLOGUE

'In the end, we're all just stardust.'

His father had said that once, when he'd asked where people go when they die. He often thought about that now. It gave him some solace. He would look up at the few stars that managed to twinkle through Mumbai's city lights when he managed to sneak into the balcony. It wasn't easy to get away. Munimji and the police would keep him hidden indoors all day long if they could.

'He's just a child...' they would say, 'Just eleven...We have to keep him safe.' He had begun to wonder if it would always be like this from now on. The sprawling house had begun to feel suffocating and prison-like. The curtains were always drawn. Light had to steal inside like vermin. It was always grey-blue or grey-yellow, shades of longing and empty rooms. He wondered sometimes if he was going blind, unable to see any other colour. It seemed like evening all day long! He touched the walls as he walked about the house, his small, stubby fingers tracing the roughness of the stone. He realized there were photos of his parents everywhere.

'There must be no photos,' he told Munimji gravely. 'None at all.'

Munimji looked at him with pity. He was getting used to the expression.

Sometimes he would hug Munimji's long legs, and then they would both cry. But that wouldn't do early in the morning. That wouldn't be right.

'There must be no photos,' he repeated, his voice small, and then ran away, as fast as his little legs would carry him and stopped only when he had reached the other end of the sprawling house. He longed to fly away, run away, escape into the edges of the world. He curled up against a stone wall in the furthest, smallest room, and felt his tears hot against the coolness of the surface.

The funeral was two weeks later. He had given express instructions that they were to be buried. They wouldn't be given to the sky, as was the custom of his people. They would not be food for crows and vultures. Not even to satisfy the circle of life.

'Their souls will not rest in peace,' his uncle thundered. 'What does this child know? How can he decide?'

But Munimji did not fail him. 'Would you take away even this from the boy?' he said, 'He is suffering what no child should suffer.'

'But the soul of my brother…'

'Find the killer!' Munimji shouted suddenly, his voice ragged, 'Find him! Get him hanged! Do this for your brother's son and then talk about his soul!'

But no one seemed to be able to do that. Every two days the inspector would come over. He would bring sniffer dogs, as if the killer was hidden in their own house. Munimji would shout and plead, command and discuss, but day after day, week after week, there was no arrest.

The story hit the headlines in every newspaper, every news channel. Munimji wouldn't let him see those, but

Munimji was always busy—fixing the will, meeting the family, finding a school. He had plenty of opportunity to watch all the TV he wanted.

The news people said that the man was a hired gun. An assassin, like in the movies. It made him sick in the stomach with guilt—remembering all the times he'd watched movies like those, how he'd loved them. He puked all over the Persian carpet on one of the days when he suddenly came across such a movie. He had to get the maid to clean it discreetly, so that Munimji didn't find out.

The police finally arrested someone in the third month. He was called in to identify the suspect. It was a wet day, just like the one when it had happened. The monsoons hadn't yet passed. Horizon to skyscraper, the firmament lay covered with a sheet of thunderclouds and the world looked much like a wet dog, tired of the incessant rain. The roads had been cleaned and then mucked up by the downpour. Drains were overflowing. He saw people running helter-skelter, trying to cover their head with handkerchiefs or flimsy umbrellas that threatened to blow away in the strong winds.

There was a crowd in front of the police station, braving the rain and protecting their cameras. The crowd roared like a mad animal as his car pulled up. They rushed towards him, as if to devour him, and the police tried to push them back. Munimji put his spindly arms around him, but he could still feel their hands, grabbing him like spirits of the dead. They were shouting. What were they shouting about? He wanted to run, to scream. He wanted to hide. But that wouldn't do.

The man the police had caught was so thin, his cheek sunken in and his eyes dead to the world. There were bruises on his face and arms and he trembled as he was made to stand before them. Munimji frowned when he looked at him.

'Is this the man, chotte sahib?' the police inspector asked, breath smelling of betel leaves and supari, red flecks on his lips.

'You have beaten him,' he said, looking at the accused and his sleepess eyes.

'Shouldn't we have done so when he killed your father?' The inspector leaned over to him and pointed at the thin man. 'It is him, isn't he? He's the man. He has confessed.'

He couldn't say. He couldn't remember. He just remembered the gun and the scream of his mother and his father jumping at the gunman to protect them both. He remembered the spreading red stain on the back of his father's shirt. He didn't remember the man's face. Surely, he'd been thin. Thin with sleepless eyes. But there were so many of those.

'I don't know,' he said finally.

'You must identify him, chotte sahib,' the inspector said, 'You must, or how will we hang the bastard? He killed your parents, chotte sahib! You must recognize him!'

He could feel tears welling up. Hot, treacherous tears that had no right to be there. They were clouding his vision. They were confusing everything. He wiped them away angrily with his sleeve, but there were more. The thin man swam in front of his eyes, his face blurred. He felt Munimji's hand on his shoulder.

'Come, let's go. There's nothing for us here.'

'He has to identify the suspect,' the inspector insisted, 'He's an eyewitness.'

'He's a child,' Munimji's voice sounded like it rose from a

grave. 'And this is some poor soul you've beaten a confession out of.'

When he next managed to steal a look at the news, later in the day, he saw that the police had taken the man to court. The judge had set the date for hearing two months hence.

One morning, Munimji called him over and knelt before him, holding him by his shoulders. The man's eyes were red and swollen.

'You've found a school for me,' he guessed.

Munimji said nothing, just nodded.

'I want to stay with you,' he said, though he already knew the answer.

'It will do no good,' Munimji replied. 'You need to get away from this place—from everything.'

'I can't.' He could feel his voice starting to break. It wasn't right. His body always failed him.

'Life goes on,' said Munimji. 'They would want you to move on. You have your whole life.'

'You will leave me,' he managed to say, between difficult breaths. 'Who will pay you now?'

Munimji frowned. Then his long arms enveloped him and he could feel the warmth of the man's embrace.

'I'm not your father,' Munimji said. 'He was a great man, and I'm not. But everything I am has been because of him.'

The boy felt a wave of relief sweep through him. He knew what those words meant. He knew he was safe, and the terrible worry that had grown in him was baseless.

'I will come back,' he said softly, his voice now back under his control. 'To this house…'

'I will wait for you,' Munimji promised.

The case dragged on for six years. He had pimples by the

time the verdict was announced and the man was let go. He hadn't cried for four years but he broke down that day, sitting on the floor next to the phone.

'It was never him,' Munimji said on the phone, his voice old and tired. 'It wasn't him, the poor man!'

ONE

A city built on a train track. That's what Mumbai felt like. The station reeled under its morning burden. The platform seemed to sway with a tide of people awaiting their deliverance.

It was a hot, sultry day in the month of May. That last, final period of waiting when it seemed like the monsoon would answer all prayers, fix everything.

Empty promises for empty wishes, Navkar mused to himself.

Sudhir Navkar was a man of medium height with a lean build. He was in his mid-twenties. He was wearing aviator glasses and carrying a fake Gucci sling bag, bought from Colaba. He stood at the edge of the platform, absolutely still, eyes closed, almost as if in meditation. He could hear the whistle of train approaching the platform. Navkar could sense the chattering of the platform grow louder. Worshippers chanting for their god. He could smell a hint of smoke. Was it from the train? The friction on the tracks? The moongphaliwaala?

Navkar felt a tug on his T-shirt and heard someone call his name. It was Mr Chawla, his daily travelling companion. A morbid little doctor who had taken this train to his little rundown clinic in a forgotten bylane for the past twenty years. Navkar had never seen him smile.

'The train,' Chawla said, 'Navkar, the train.'

Navkar felt a strong gush of wind on his face, pushing his hair back from his face. He opened his eyes in reaction. Metal thundered past before him, inches from his face. He felt the pressure of the crowd behind him swell and grow. For a moment it felt like he would get pushed forward, but the swell never burst. The platform waited as the train came to a stop. Then came the push, and he was carried forward in a wave of office-goers.

When the train moved again, Navkar found himself underneath the AC vent. The local trains had installed air-conditioning the previous year, in the 2018 municipal elections. They didn't work. All they did was blow freezing columns of air right below them, and anyway, the temperature dissipated immediately in the heat of humanity and sultry air blowing in from open carriage doors. Navkar felt the cold air creep down his spine, making him shiver. He looked for a way out, but the carriage was choked with passengers. You couldn't move an inch, as if the city had a death grip on you.

'Are you okay?' Chawla asked. He'd managed to find a place next to Navkar inspite of the rush during boarding.

'Yeah,' Navkar lied. He wasn't. It was a black day.

'A man was killed last night. On the 12.30 local,' Chawla said. He seemed to spend half his day following crime stories in the papers. Navkar could see he didn't have many patients.

'The cleaners found him,' Chawla continued. 'Gunshot wound in his chest, blood pooled on the seat behind.'

'Not today, Chawla,' Navkar muttered.

The train took speed, rattling like the last stages of whooping cough. Sunlight lost its way through the small windows and the spaces between people. The world was reduced to a worn down metal cave filled with the backs of others.

'It's the fifth this week,' Chawla continued, leaning against one of the sealed windows.

'It's a bad day,' Navkar said ambiguously. 'Bad day. Maybe bad week. Always has been.'

Chawla dug into his backpack that he was now holding to his chest and retrieved a packet of biscuits. He offered one to Navkar and began munching silently.

'You should cover these murders,' Chawla said, ignoring his companion's mood. 'They're really interesting—a municipality guy, a party worker, a contractor.'

He shoved the newspaper towards Navkar adding, 'The last one was a taxi union guy.'

'I'm covering a flower show,' Navkar replied, pushing the paper away.

Outside the dust-smeared window smudged skyscrapers marched backwards, as if disappearing into the past. The train would reach his stop soon. He would get out of this crowd and stench and have his ten minutes.

The kids next to him started listening to football commentary on their phones. Nobody around seemed to notice. Their voices grew louder to compensate.

'I think there must be some connection between all of them,' Chawla persisted.

Navkar didn't bother replying. The train began slowing down and he waded past the incoming tide of passengers. He stepped out, exhaling their scents and made his way out of the station. There, outside his office building, lay the swelling, silver-grey wreath of the sea. Navkar hurried to the edge of the embankment, feeling the wet air slap against him, and listening to the hiss of the wind. His hair flying, he looked out and finally took in his first real breath of the day.

Everything was fine as long as there was the sea. Even bad days!

He reached into his pocket and took out his wallet. He unfolded a newspaper clipping and looked at it for a silent moment, as he did every year on this day.

It was May 14, 2019.

Another year had passed.

~

From this height, the sea looked blue or green or both, vast and open as far as the eyes could see. All the buildings and people at its edge seemed so meagre in comparison. Just pebbles on a beach.

Inside the city, there were no horizons, but up here, Tara could feel the weight of that word, the taste of it. *Horizon*. The boundary of your world. The higher you were, the wider it became.

That explained a lot.

There were sparks of silver tearing across the black line where the sky met the sea. She could imagine the sound, though she heard nothing—a storm was coming.

She stood there silently, suddenly feeling chilly though the air conditioning in the room was mellow. Her hands traced the slight bruises on her body where he had gripped her; her hips, her thighs and stomach. Beneath the gentle, almost pained softness of his eyes, there lay a streak of violence.

She knew he was upstairs, in the garden on the roof. It was his favourite place, his sanctuary. The garden at the top of the world.

Tara gathered close the bedsheet she had draped herself in, and made her way to the elevator. She did not have to bother clothing herself. The penthouse and the garden were for his private use and there was no tower high enough closeby from where people could see them. In a city like Mumbai, privacy was only in the clouds. The elevator took her through several seconds of darkness. There was a space of about five storeys above the penthouse that was packed with soil—all for creating that one spot where she knew she would find him.

It was a Bodhi tree; a stately thick-trunked peepal with gnarled roots that spread deep into the soil and spread its branches wide. Its canopy was low and wide, protecting the centre of the rooftop, its large, heart-shaped leaves shading the mound of grass it grew on.

The entire roof, on the seventy-second floor, was covered in wild grass. There were no tamed roses or lilacs, no flowering shrubs carefully groomed, no shy plants well kept. It was just soil, transplanted and scattered with grass, fed by the rain.

But over time, that had changed. The few clumps of grass had multiplied. Wildflower has spread in vast stretches, heaped together in thorns and explosions of purple or white, small, vicious, wild, beautiful things. Waves of the ferns had grown, their white crowns glinting, catching the sunlight. It was like a small field, 20,000 square feet in area, its only occupants birds and one man. And in the centre, reaching up to the sky, stood the Bodhi tree.

Vishnu Rustomjee Mistry sat on its lowest branch, clad only in Bermudas, his muscled body painted with shadow and sunlight. He was talking on his mobile.

Tara clutched the sheet to her body, as the ever-present

wind up here threatened to disrobe her. She walked towards him slowly, letting herself revel in this moment, letting her hips sway and and her jet black tresses whip her face and bare shoulders. Her naked feet felt the coolness of the grass underneath, the wetness of the morning dew. She wondered whether the monsoon clouds would be low enough to touch from here.

He turned to look at her with those green-grey eyes, nearly inhuman. He could stare without blinking for a long time. It scared her sometimes. She'd noticed that he never kept his eyes on anyone for long though, as if he was afraid of them looking back.

Vishnu spoke on the phone while she waited at the foot of the tree, looking up. She held back her flying hair with one slender hand, while the other bunched the sheet over her. He took a few minutes more and then jumped down from the branch. There were shadows under his eyes, as always but he seemed pleased.

'When did you get up?' she asked.

'A while back,' he said, lightly.

'You don't sleep much.'

He smiled, 'A bad habit!'

She wanted to kiss him. Her fingers ran over the lines and planes of his torso. He seemed to be laughing. Was he laughing at her? He put his heavy arm around her shoulders, urging her to walk with him. They now stood at the edge of the roof, a single railing separating them from nothingness.

'How much did it cost? This garden?' she asked.

He didn't seem to be listening. His eyes were intent on his city below, as if he was trying to peer down into the smallest of lives on the streets.

She repeated the question.

'I don't know,' he said finally, 'I'll have to ask my accountant.'

'A few crores?'

'Ten-twenty, yes.'

'It could've built schools. Hospitals.' She was looking at him, looking for his reaction.

He didn't even turn. 'You disapprove?'

'I'm just wondering how you think.'

Now he turned to her, his hand cupping her chin. There was an amused expression on his face. 'Most women, when they're up here, prefer to flatter than wonder.'

His thumb traced the deepening crease running beside her mouth that had started giving her face a severe edge.

'This line wasn't here ten years back,' she said.

He chuckled. 'I don't think I would have liked you ten years back.'

She brought his hand lower, to the rise and fall of her body.

'There will be a big announcement at the symposium tomorrow,' he said distractedly, 'The chief minister too will be there. Bring lots of people.'

She didn't answer, but let her other hand drift to him. The wind carried the sheet away.

TWO

The office felt particularly gloomy today. The electricity was playing truant and the building, enclosed in glass and steel, was sweltering in the heat. The editor sat in his creaking chair, fanning his face with a notebook, its pages flapping in discontent. Rivulets of sweat ran down his face, collected at his French beard, and dripped down like melting icicles. It was not a good time for this conversation.

'Pronounce it for me,' he demanded.

'Flower show,' Navkar muttered.

'Louder!'

'Flower show.'

'My god!' the man puffed angrily in Navkar's face. He beat the notebook against his head. 'Flo-WER show…WER. Not flour show! Do you understand?'

'Yes, sir,' said Navkar dutifuly.

'Do you know what flour is? Flour is atta! You've been telling the whole country about the exotic varieties of atta!'

'Sir, I'm sure they'll understand. There was no atta there, sir.'

That was apparently the wrong thing to say. The editor slammed the notebook on the table. 'Everything is a joke to you, huh?' he shouted, eyes bulging.

'I just don't think it's that big a deal, sir...my pronunciation, I mean,' Navkar replied, though he knew he shouldn't.

'That's your problem, Navkar! Nothing is a big deal to you!' The man shook his head in exasperation, 'They just hire anybody these days.'

He glared at Navkar again. 'Listen, son, I'll tell you one thing. You're not going anywhere with this attitude. To reach somewhere you have to have some pride in your work. The pride of a craftsman.' His hands cupped the air to express his emotion. 'You have to treat it like your karm. Not just some job your dad got you.'

'I got the job myself, sir. I'm a gold medallist.'

The editor's eyebrows rose. 'In what?'

'English literature.'

The man stared at him. 'How is it that you're calling flower flour?'

Navkar shrugged, 'All the exams were written.'

The man said nothing. He just breathed in and out like a buffalo in heat. 'Just go,' he snarled finally.

Navkar walked out into a chorus of confusion and chatter. His first reaction was that of irritation. Then he remembered that today was the government-industry symposium hosted by the Rustom Group. Half the television staff seemed to be running around Tara to cover it.

It was official now. Tara Verma was dating Vishnu Rustomjee Mistry, the heir to the Rustom Group, a man worth fifty billion dollars. He was six feet one, an Asian Games shooting champion and so eligible a bachelor that a few magazines more or less survived just by writing about him. The whole situation was causing hysteria among the staff.

Everybody hated Tara. Too many loved her.

'Oye Navkar, get Ma'am's equipment,' someone yelled from the wall of commotion, 'You can't just stand around all day looking confused.'

'I'm confused?' Navkar yelled back. 'Who set up the fish market here anyway?'

On his way to the equipment room, Navkar crossed Tara's cubicle. Apparently, he had been assigned to go with the crew to the symposium, to help out with the set-up. He couldn't help run his eyes over the sparse contents of her cubicle as he passed it. She was not one of those women who adorned their workplaces with photos and stuffed toys. She was the star presenter of the news channel he worked for, but her cubicle was as empty as his own. It just had one picture—a cutout from a magazine featuring the first soap ad she'd appeared in, sporting a dazzling smile, short, curly hair and a fake beauty spot just above her upper lip. Behind the picture, almost hidden by it, was a small piece of paper with scribbles on it. Navkar couldn't help glancing over to read it.

Go then and act your tragedy, but I will not do so. You ask me, 'Why?' I answer, 'Because you count yourself to be but an ordinary thread in the tunic.' What follows then? You ought to think how you can be like other men, just as one thread does not wish to have something special to distinguish it from the rest: but I want to be the purple, that touch of brilliance which gives distinction and beauty to the rest. Why then do you say to me, 'Make yourself like unto the many?' If I do that, I shall no longer be the purple.—Epictetus

Tara had first come into prominence seven years ago when she had shocked everyone by suddenly kissing a leading Bollywood actress when she was an extra in her song. She'd been twenty-two at the time; a final-year mass communication student. It became the most watched YouTube video during his college days. It had been funny really. She'd just lunged at the poor woman. But there had been something about her then, even in that embarrassing, opportunistic move—something in her smile when she had pulled away.

She'd disappeared after that and had resurfaced just as suddenly when she was hired as a news presenter by the channel. She did not have the fake beauty spot now, and she seemed to be able to get stories nobody else could. People said it was because she slept around, but Navkar knew people would say that anyway.

By the time Navkar had collected the equipment, there was no space left in the TV vans for him, but that was expected. Thankfully, he had left his bike at the office yesterday. The roads were jammed even at eleven in the morning, the air suffocating. Navkar wondered once again how there were always so many cars, even in the middle of the day. Weren't these people supposed to be at office or college or something?

Within minutes his shirt was clinging to his back like an ex you couldn't get rid of. It was only on the sea link that he could pick up some speed and feel the sweat dry slightly. The sky had started to turn grey. It would rain soon. Just a week more, then everything would change.

The symposium was being held at the Rustom Grand Residency, the Rustom Group's flagship hotel located at the heart of a sprawling complex, which had an enormous arch at the entrance that opened into a wide promenade lined with iron columns. The hotel itself looked like the Colosseum if it were boxed up into a square. A series of open-air galleries ringed by pillars led up to it. Navkar had never liked the place. Its architecture was too strong and forceful for him. The hotel was dwarfed, however, by the group's headquarters—the gigantic One World Tower that loomed behind it. You had to crane your neck to take in its enormity. It had been the tallest structure in India when it was built. It was still the most daunting. Structured like a flattened obelisk, with its facade of polished black granite and darkened glass, it stood as a dark behemoth brooding over the city. At its very top, invisible to all but helicopters, lay Vishnu Rustomjee's famous garden. The media had nicknamed it Babylon, after the ancient hanging gardens.

The auditorium was packed with media people by now. The monumental dome covering the room echoed with a hundred sound-checks and a somewhat muted sound of impatient swearing. Tara had ensured that their channel had pride of place right at the front, just below the stage. Navkar hurried forward and started setting up the equipment as the handpicked audience trickled through in ones and twos and the odd threes.

The curtain rose about an hour later and the room became a cathedral of light. The emcee was a television actor who'd made his name playing the *damaad* in a popular saas-bahu drama. He was much shorter in real life, but his smile was as toothy as his show promised.

The first person to be called up on the stage was the chief guest, Chief Minister Rajender Chauhan. Flashlights started going off furiously from the photographers section, as if to prove their existence. A spotlight appeared, stalking the man as he made his way to the stage. Short and rotund, as a politician should be, he was clad in a black safari with a shock of white hair on his head. He walked slowly, carrying the weight of age, hands clasped in greeting, shoulders slightly stooped. His voice was robust though, booming over the microphone.

'I am thankful to my dear friend, Vishnu Rustomjee Mistry for hosting this important forum,' he opened, 'It comes at a significant time. As we know, this city, as well as our country, is going through a difficult phase. Prices are rising. Our neighbours are getting more hostile. There are problems with law and order. The common man on the street is anxious, disillusioned.'

Navkar cringed at the clichés. He considered himself the common man on the street and he was neither anxious nor had he ever had any illusions. He could see, for example, that this was going to be a long and boring afternoon. The only solace would be to see Vishnu Rustomjee Mistry in person. His mother had sent Navkar a text message asking for an autograph as soon as she had heard he would be covering the event. Just last week, Mistry had been polled as the most popular man in India, far above any superstar or leader. Navkar couldn't help but be curious.

The same curiosity made him glance at Tara. She was sitting five seats away, tapping away on her phone, looking carelessly stunning, as is the habit of beautiful women.

'I believe,' Chauhan continued, 'that we, as a nation, a society, can only battle these challenges if we stand together. The government cannot do it alone. We must encourage and involve the private sector to engage in solving the problems of society. We must discuss our challenges and create solutions together,' and with this he concluded, 'I fervently hope that this forum goes a long way in making that happen.'

He waved a few times before leaving. The spotlight followed him nervously. Navkar felt relieved. It had been a short speech for a minister.

A roar went up from the crowd suddenly. Vishnu Rustomjee Mistry had stepped on stage. Unlike the emcee, he seemed taller in real life. The room was now buzzing with anticipation.

He waited for the crowd to become quiet. His face was serious. He started slowly, his voice grave. 'This past decade, as the world stagnated and reeled under recession, India has grown. We know that well. All of us here have profited from this growth...'

That was true, Navkar thought. The guests present probably sweated money.

Vishnu's voice had gone heavier. 'All of us also know though,' he said solemnly, 'that we, as a society, have also faltered; our women cannot walk secure on our cities' streets, our kids cannot play in the streets like we used to. Sometimes it feels like we live in a war-torn country, or a jungle. We're always afraid.'

Navkar was surprised. He had expected a corporate speech—hurrahs for the Rustom Group and their great initiatives, pictures of poor children with shy yet hopeful smiles, followed by pictures of windmills. Mistry's grim tone was unexpected.

The crowd was sensing it too, their excitement beginning to abate. Vishnu was walking around the stage now, each step deliberate, measured.

'We will not reach our promises of prosperity if things remain unchanged. There is a sickness here, a sickness rotting our society, festering and growing every day. I don't know what to call it. There are no good words to describe it, but it is an evil.'

The words sank in slowly. The whole room had gone quiet now. Navkar found himself sitting up. The spotlight shone down harshly on the stage, the shadows on Vishnu Rustomjee Mistry making his film-star face look gaunt for a moment. He let out a long breath.

'It is an evil that has entered deep into our society: It tells the politician he can steal public funds. That he can hire goons, get people killed. It tells the government officer that he can harass someone for a bribe. It tells the businessman that he doesn't have to obey rules. It tells the man on the street that he can steal, bully, kill to get his way. Everyone, top to bottom—it tells everyone that might is right. We are becoming...no...we *have* become, a completely criminalized society.'

Vishnu stood at the centre of the stage, his eyes scanning the crowd. 'Might is right. The corrosive, self-destructive idea that the law doesn't work. That the state cannot protect us, and worse, it cannot stop us!'

The silence was palpable; Navkar could almost hear the silence in the auditorium, the uncertain, nervous drawing in of individual breaths. They'd all felt what he was saying, he knew that.

'But there is a way to fight back,' Vishnu said suddenly, jolting his audience with his abruptness. 'Today, the Rustom Group wants to announce their support for the Justice Renewal Bill, currently before the state government. This bill will increase the scale of our judiciary tenfold. It will clear the way for private institutions to come into the picture—to train and meet this demand for lawyers and judges. It will increase policing capacity threefold by bringing together private agencies and the police. It will create special laws and regulations for private security agencies to augment government security.'

There was a rising murmur in the crowd, reflecting its surprise, and then a wave of questions. Everyone knew Vishnu Rustomjee Mistry's long-standing activism for judicial reform, but it was clear that this was something more.

It better be, Navkar found himself thinking. No political party was interested in that bill. It had been around forever and it had never got passed.

Vishnu raised his hands and called the audience to silence. He smoothed his hair back as flashlights went off throughout the auditorium.

'And I want everyone to know that my commitment is real and not just words.' His hands rose as every eyeball in the audience followed it. 'The Rustom Group has acquired Eagle-Guard Security Services, one of the leading security agencies in the country. I now promise that I will provide security guards for every local train and every bus in Mumbai from next week. Thirteen thousand personnel will be provided, free of cost. There has been rampant crime in the trains these last five years—it threatens the very life of this city. That will stop.'

He smiled and spread his arms. 'This is my gift to the city that has given my family everything.'

~

The taste of tobacco diluted the stench of humidity and politics. Navkar took a long, deep drag, leaning against the wall outside. The feeding frenzy of the reporters had started inside. Navkar figured he wouldn't gain much from it. When there were a hundred reporters fighting for every crumb, he wouldn't find anything that would actually help his career.

Besides, his career wasn't all that important.

Navkar couldn't help but wonder if Vishnu's activism would change anything; if his railway guards would change anything. He couldn't help but wonder what would've happened if such security had existed eleven years back, on 14 May. Would it have changed anything then?

He took another deep drag. The sun was at its zenith, casting small intense shadows. He noticed a large tree by the side wall. An old man in a dhoti sat underneath, smoking a beedi. Curious, Navkar walked towards the shade. He wondered who the man was, how he had got into the hotel compound. The man's eyes turned to him, unseeing in the noon sun. Rings of smoke rose from his cracked lips.

Before Navkar could reach him, he became aware of a commotion by the side gate. He shaded his eyes for a better look. It was a middle-aged woman, her posture bent from hard labour, wearing a simple sari. She seemed to be arguing with the hotel guards to let her in, beating at them with her weak fists. Her face was contorted with grief. He could hear her broken voice rise and heave. He changed his direction and walked towards them.

'He took everything from me, he took everything!' she wailed, clutching at her unkempt hair. Her body was frozen in a half-crouch as she pleaded with the guards. 'I've lost everything!'

Suddenly she lunged at the gate again and one of the guards reached for his baton, but before he could swing it, Navkar gripped his arm.

'Relax, relax!' Navkar said hurriedly, as the man turned glaring. 'She's just an old woman,' he said soothingly. He turned to the woman before the guard could respond, helping her up. 'Why are you creating a scene here? There are important people inside.'

She didn't respond. 'He took everything from me,' she repeated again and again, clutching at his shirt. He noticed there was a streak of red on her palms.

'What happened?' he asked. 'Who took everything from you?'

She wasn't listening. Her eyes flicked here and there, at the guards, at the hotel, the tower, the gate. Her whole body was trembling.

'Listen,' he said, soothingly. 'I'm trying to help you. Don't create a scene here or they'll hand you over to the police. Alright? Where do you stay?'

That seemed to get through. She focused on his face. Her lips opened and closed but with no sound.

'Where do you stay?' he repeated. 'What's your name?'

'M-m,' she stuttered. He gripped her wrists firmly as if to give her some reassurance and she finally said, 'Mohammed Ali Road…the b-basti there.'

'What's your name?' Navkar repeated.

'Kamla,' the name came in a whisper. 'Kamla.'

He pressed his business card to her hand and she clasped it tightly, as if it were a lifeline. Her eyes had a certain kind of wildness about them and her body wracked with sobs as she repeated, 'Kamla…'

'I'll take you home,' Navkar offered.

'No,' she suddenly screamed, 'No, no, no…' She pushed him and backed away.

'It's alright. Don't worry,' Navkar started saying but she had already started running, her fear obvious.

'You know her?' the guard asked.

Navkar shook his head, watching her go. 'The street makes them crazy,' he said.

The wind picked up as he walked back to the building. Pieces of discarded newspapers skittered through the yard. The shadow of the tower now fell across, as if a colossal hand had stamped out the sun.

Suddenly he noticed Tara Verma standing on the landing, talking on her phone. She looked anxious. She saw him and started waving. He turned backwards to see if he was mistaken, but there was no one there. She was calling out to him. Now she was coming down the landing, her movements hurried. Navkar loped forward, as casually as possible. He wondered how she smelt.

Her face was agitated, her lips parting, pursing as she spoke. He couldn't help remember the countless times he'd seen her video. And now here she was. He noticed that her eyes were chocolate brown, large and limpid in their vulnerability, though her eyebrows rose in sharp, straight lines. It created a paradox. Maybe that was her secret.

She snapped her fingers. It brought him back to what she was saying, 'Are you listening?'

'Y-yes, yes of course,' he stammered.

'You work for Channel 10, right?'

He nodded.

'Do you have a car?' she asked.

'Yes…well, no…' he said uncertainly. 'I brought my bike.'

She glanced back at the building, as if making up her mind. When she turned back to him, she was frowning in concentration. 'Alright, listen to me. I just got a call from my contact in the CM's office. Apparently, he received a threat a few days. Through a letter. Do you understand?'

Navkar shook his head, confused.

'My contact is saying that it is the most unbelievable thing he's ever seen! So we have to go there now! We have no time! We have to get there before anybody else does! I can't even wait for the crew here to wrap up.'

'You want me to take you on my bike?' Navkar said slowly, unsure what was happening.

She reached out and caught him by his shoulders in a surprisingly strong grip. 'Listen to me. You have to get me there in time. I promise you, this will be the biggest story of your entire life!'

THREE

Eagles wheeled overhead as they passed the masjid, circling for scraps of meat. The third call of the day rent the air, blasted from a megaphone atop the minaret. The sound fragmented, with the flapping of wings drowning out the human voice for a few moments.

He sped as much as he dared, cutting in front of cars, sliding across the road and slipping into corners. He felt her cling to him, her slender frame draped along his back and her strong, claw-like fingers anchored on his shoulders.

'Faster,' she hissed, and he obeyed.

They entered Parel within half an hour, taking the new flyover that knifed through the centre of Mumbai. The squalor of crude tarpaulin and asbestos hutments, and dingy apartments with prison-like windows, was broken by giant columns which seemed to have erupted from the earth. Towers shooting up from the body of the city like stalagmites.

They had all been made in the last fifteen years—hundreds of them—clearing out all the broken-down mills. Now they lay on both sides of the road, near and far, pillars holding up the sky in a land of giants and gods.

Tara asked him to take a left off the flyover and into a narrow side street busy with children and shaded by trees and the shadow of a hulking tower.

'The municipal library,' she said, pointing to a rickety two-storey building, with a half-broken tiled roof and the feel of a cemetery. It was dwarfed by the neem tree in its courtyard.

'You wait here,' she ordered, and he couldn't manage to object.

It was dark inside, a dank, cold darkness that hadn't seen the glow of real activity for many, many years. The stone floor echoed with each step of her heeled sandals. A strange rotting smell filled the building. Tara guessed that it was either the books or the wooden shelves bent under them. She glanced up at the stray beams of sunlight that fell through. The rains would puncture right through this ceiling.

The man was waiting at the reading tables at the back. There were two other people in the room, huddled in a corner, both probably in their eighties, wearing white dhotis and kurtas that had seen better days, their bony fingers rustling through equally faded newspapers.

The man's name was Chamak Ram Pandey and he worked in the cafeteria of the Mantralaya. He stank of tobacco, paan and sweat, a smoky-sweet overpowering mix. He was clad in his uniform of khaki shirt and pant of rough spun hew and the government peon cap—the bastard child of the Nehru cap.

He looked up when she approached. He had a handsome face, with high cheekbones and a neatly kept moustache. He often spoke about his family; he was from a line of purohits back in his ancestral village.

'It'll be a bad monsoon,' he said, folding the newspaper he was reading, as she sat opposite him. 'Kerala and Tamil Nadu are facing floods. The nuclear plant is in danger.'

She undid her hair and a wave of it fell forward on her face. She knew that went well with her kajal. 'I don't care about what's already in the news, Chamak Ram. What do you have for me?'

He moved his tongue in his mouth, as if to suggest that something was stuck in his teeth. When he sat up, the creak of his chair echoed through the room. 'Is it true, madam, that you're with Vishnu Rustomjee Mistry now?'

She regarded him coldly. She'd been to Chamak Ram's house to meet him once. His wife had had half her face swollen up with the sickly purple colour that a bruise takes on after a few days. She'd tried to cover it with her sari draped over her face.

'I'm here to take information, Chamak Ram, not give it,' she said grimly. She took out the chequebook she had carried in her bag.

He eyed the poised pen and the cheque with no apparent hurry. 'Madam, I really admire how fast you move,' he said. 'You're going to become a very important lady, a very rich lady.'

'You're lucky you met me then.' She let the pen trace out his name, slowly. 'What does the letter say?'

He grinned, his face transforming into something slightly unpleasant. He took out his mobile from his pocket; an old model, scratched and worn. He tapped it gently, but his eyes never left her face.

'Why are you still interested in all this?' he asked. 'Now that you're with Mistry Sahib? He has enough money to buy half this city.'

She frowned and sat back, forcing herself to relax. 'I think,' she said slowly, 'we actually do it for the same reason, you and I.'

'I'm a small man, madam. I do it for the money.'

'No, you don't, Chamak Ram. You'll never stop. And one day, the minister will find out, and then you will be killed.'

Chamak Ram gave her an unpleasant look. 'Put six zeroes this time, madam. You won't regret it.'

She wrote out their usual three, and followed it with three more. She would have to convince the company to pay this. If she couldn't she would have to forget her plans to buy a flat. She tore out the cheque, signed her name and waited.

'I want to see it first.'

He brought up the picture on his mobile. It was a hastily taken photo of a document. She looked at it for a minute or so and passed him the cheque.

He shook his head.

'We'll exchange mobiles, madam,' he said with a smile. 'And we won't delete our pictures.'

Tara nearly snorted with laughter. She wondered if he'd thought she would protest. Probably not!

She transferred her address book to her sim card, deleted her messages, removed the sim and tossed the phone to him. He winced at the action but managed to catch the phone. He'd already removed his sim.

'Buy your wife something nice so she's happy with you,' Tara said coldly, as she walked away from him and out of the building.

There was a triumphant look on her face as she met Navkar. She held up the phone in victory, and let him see her acquisition.

'It's unimaginable,' she said, quietly.

Navkar peered at the screen. He blinked a few times and read it again. It was a simple letter, printed in a neat font. It detailed a series of transactions through which the CM's party had gained money. Most of them were clearly illegal. They were laid out carefully in a list, and the total came to forty-three-and-a-half crore. Below was a note:

You had previously been warned to not exceed forty crore in funding before the forthcoming municipal elections. Despite clear rules and penalties your party now has an excess of three-and-a-half crores. As mentioned earlier, you will be fined an equal amount that will be removed from your party within the next two weeks. There will be further loss that will not be so easy to quantify. It will involve blood. The responsibility for that loss lies on your incapability to lead your party in a disciplined and cognizant manner.

It was signed, *The Guardian of the People.*

'What does it mean?' Navkar asked. 'Who wrote this?'

Tara shrugged, 'We'll ask that on television. But I can tell you this. Something very big is happening. Let's go.'

Navkar revved up his bike and said, 'It'll take us an hour to get back. We should call someone at the office and tell them so they can broadcast this as breaking news immediately.'

She quirked a brow incredulously, wondering if she'd heard him wrong. Could he actually have suggested that she give away her story?

'How long have you been a reporter?'

'Three years.'

She gave him a look of disdain, 'And still a rookie?'

FOUR

Nobody was happy.

The letter had been taken right to the top, to the owners of the channel, and the main news presenters. Navkar had never had the opportunity to talk to any of them before. He stood silently by the door of the conference room, knowing that if they noticed him they'd ask him to get out.

Malhotra, the promoter of the channel, a wiry man with a slight paunch and oily hair, leant back and crossed his legs on the table. He wore baggy white Bermudas and had a haunted expression.

'You're going to get us screwed, do you know that?' he asked, his expression dour.

Tara smiled with a tilt of her head. He was probably her only friend here, Navkar thought, listening in on the conversation. Everyone said she'd slept with him. Most of the other presenters would knife her between the ribs if they could get away with it.

'I'll take it as a compliment,' she said.

He grunted and shook his head. 'It's not.'

There was silence in the room. Three of the other four men, Malhotra's secretary and two newscasters, seemed to be concentrating on avoiding each other's eyes.

The fourth was David Agarwal, who was seventy and had stopped having reservations many decades ago. It was the main reason his talk show was still popular.

'I think it's good work,' he said bluntly, adjusting his thick glasses as he peered at the projection of the mobile photo on the screen. He turned to Tara, his face covered in age spots and some skin disease, hidden under his beard and moustache. 'There's something of value inside those tight clothes after all.'

Tara's eyes flashed. 'Took you a while to recognize it,' she said, lightly. 'But then you are quite old.'

He laughed and shook a finger at her. Then he pointed at the screen. 'That's some great information the girl has got,' he said, addressing Malhotra, 'It's the best ratwork I've seen in a decade,' he declared. That was his term for investigative journalism. It was the highest praise he ever gave.

It jolted the others.

Chatterjee, one of the co-founders of the channel and its biggest anchor, reacted immediately.

'It may be great information, but what does it mean?' he said. 'What story can we run on this?' He stood up and walked to the screen. His belt curved in a graceful arch beneath his ample belly as he stretched to reach the writing. 'Look at this. The Guardian of the People!'

'Must be a communist,' muttered Pathak, Malhotra's secretary.

'This is not the time for jokes,' Malhotra growled, sitting up. 'Look at the damn thing! Look at it! You think this is a joke?'

'What if it is?' the other newscaster, Prateek Sharma, said quietly. He was a good-looking, sensible man, even talented, but people said he was too soft-spoken to make it really big. 'How do we know it's real?' he asked.

'Yeah,' Chatterjee agreed. 'It looks pretty fake to me. Reads like a prank.'

'That's bullshit,' Tara said hotly. 'It reads like a blackmail note. There's nothing mysterious about it. And my source is solid. We've used him before.'

'The railway scam?' Malhotra asked.

'Yeah,' Tara confirmed. She moved to the screen. 'Look, it's clearly blackmail. He's giving information that he knows could get these guys to sweat. Then he's hinting that he wants three crore. What's the problem?'

'My problem,' Malhotra barked, 'is that he's giving too much information. Look at this bloody list. It's half-a-page long. Do you know how much trouble this will cause?'

'It's not the first scam we've exposed, Rakesh,' Tara said calmly.

Malhotra grimaced at her use of his first name and then ran his hand through his hair, 'I need some whisky.' He looked around and spotted Navkar. 'You, what's your name?'

Navkar was leaning against the doorway. He straightened. 'Sudhir. Sudhir Navkar.'

'Should he be here?' Malhotra asked Tara.

'He helped me get the photo. He's already seen it.'

'Screw it!' Malhotra grunted. 'It's not going to be a secret for long anyway.' He tossed a key at Navkar. 'You know my room…bottom shelf of the big cabinet on the right, as you enter. You will also find glasses. And don't touch anything else. I will know if you have,' he glared.

Navkar returned within five minutes with a bottle of single malt and two crystal glasses. Malhotra poured himself one drink and one for Chatterjee. He dismissed Navkar without a glance. Navkar took that to mean that he could stay.

'The difference…' Malhotra said, taking a long swig of the drink and swirling it in his mouth, 'is that usually the scam is about some politician. Then we can all get together and burn him.' He stood looking at the others, and then gestured at the screen. 'This is against the entire party. That's tough. The fish is too big.'

'And each of those transactions will have a counter-party,' Chatterjee added.

'Exactly,' Malhotra nodded. 'And they'll all be powerful. It'll kill us.'

He slammed his glass down. David was stroking his beard thoughtfully.

Navkar could see Tara's body rise and fall with each breath she took in that chilly room. The air seemed heavy. He knew he had to say it now. He wouldn't get the chance again.

'I've been wondering…' he started, and stopped as everyone turned to him. He stood up a bit straighter, 'I've been wondering, if it was indeed blackmail, why is he just asking for three crore?'

They were staring at him. Not talking, just staring, like vultures waiting for his corpse to stop moving.

Although he was nervous, Navkar decided to continue, 'It's not a lot of money these days,' he said with a shrug.

Malhotra sighed. 'Why are you still here? Who are you, man?'

'Sudhir Navkar,' he repeated.

'No, no,' Malhotra waved his hands. 'I meant who the hell

are you to talk here now? Everyone wants to be a journalist these days!'

'Sir, I am a journalist,' Navkar replied calmly.

'You won't be much longer if you don't get out of my sight. Out…now. Out!' Malhotra shouted.

Navkar thought to argue his point, but gave in. He knew what these people were like.

Malhotra slumped on the table as the door closed.

Chatterjee was already talking. 'We can only reveal parts of it, perhaps? Just say that someone is blackmailing the CM?'

Tara had her hands on her hips now. Gritting her teeth she said, 'We can't let this go, Rakesh. This is our job. We can't ignore a story like this.'

'Don't give me that preachy shit!' Malhotra exploded. 'You just want to get famous! You'll bring some half-baked sensational bullshit from some random junkheap to get your bloody moment in the sun!'

There were a few seconds of surprised silence, a moment of dissection. Tara's voice was ragged when she finally spoke. 'Alright, then, screw the story. I'll pass it on to my friends. Maybe some other channel will have the balls to pick it up.'

Malhotra stopped her by the time she had swung the door open. His fingers were massaging the back of his neck; as if he wanted to release the knot of tension that was threatening to break his neck.

'Go ahead,' he said, looking exhausted. 'Go ahead and run it. Give it the whole evening. Start with a bulletin, then the story, then discussions. All that jazz!'

'I'll present the bulletin,' Chatterjee began decisively, but stopped at the look Tara gave him. 'Alright, I'll moderate the discussion.'

Tara left. Malhotra shook his head and laughed, and began pouring himself another drink, 'She's such a bitch.'

An hour later the cameras rolled, the lights came on, and the country celebrated the birth of another scandal.

FIVE

Chauhan could feel the bile rise in his throat with every moment he looked at the news being broadcast on every channel now. This was the worst thing that could've happened! They knew. Everyone knew.

He peeked out of the window wondering how many hands had been oiled for this.

It was dark and gloomy outside. The clouds hung low, weighed down by smog and ash. He felt sick—old, tired and sick.

He let out a weary sigh, 'Do you have a cigarette?'

'Sir, I don't think you should…' his servant started.

His secretary was eager to impress, however, and held out one in his hand before the servant could even finish. Chauhan hadn't smoked in ten years. He took a long, slow drag. The embers glowed, flickering playfully through the tobacco, a beautiful auburn roast. The warm smell rushed into his throat and lungs, filling every hole in his heart. It still felt as good as ever. He reclined a bit and puffed out a fine trail of smoke, and let the minutes pass as slowly as he could.

Suddenly, all the phones in the room started ringing, almost simultaneously. The shrill cacophony startled him, breaking the tense mood. He instructed his servant and

Chamak Ram to turn off his mobiles and unplug the landline. But it was too late! He could hear a noise outside now.

The media was here—like a pack of hunting wolves—at his door.

He peeked through the blinds. The crowd was larger than he had expected. Voyeurs had come to see the discomfort of the new caged beast. Chauhan understood that denials wouldn't be enough.

'Get me Shinde on the line,' he instructed, his voice grave and dry.

He knew it was pointless. The police commissioner was good with excuses.

'Do you have anything on him yet?' Chauhan shouted angrily into the phone, more so to relieve his stress than to expect answers. 'It's almost been a month!'

'It's not so easy. We are doing our best,' came Shinde's serene baritone.

Chauhan wondered whether he was even trying.

'So you have nothing?' Chauhan asked roughly. 'Is that really the best you can do? What is he? A ghost? Are you even making an effort, Shinde? This man is a blackmailer! He is breaking the law!'

'If I too could break it, then I could perhaps catch him,' came the brisk reply.

Chauhan snorted. Shinde probably liked the idea of being a vigilante more than a cop. He had been lobbying for more police freedom since the day he took charge. He had even used this incident as an excuse. More freedom, then he would investigate this case properly. Chauhan shook his head in resignation. This wasn't Chhatisgarh. Shinde's methods would be too costly politically. He cut the phone line abruptly and turned to his aide.

'I want the other phone,' he snarled. He didn't want this tracked back. He had no choice. The conversation would be short. The man would want a deal. It would still be better than giving in to Shinde.

The phone rang three times, as always.

'Chauhan? I just saw the news. It isn't looking good.'

'I need your help, Vishnu,' Chauhan said with a sigh. 'I need this diverted.'

'You know what I want, in return.'

'I will try.'

'Try, Mantriji?'

'Okay, I'll get it done,' Chauhan hissed. He heard a click; the call was disconnected without another word.

The crowd outside was growing with every passing minute. Sunlight was breaking through as morning spread. There was nothing to do now. The sheep had to put on wolf's clothing. It was time.

He fixed a smile on his face and walked to the main door. His hands clenched for a moment and then he turned the knob.

The door opened and he was greeted with flashes of a hundred cameras.

SIX

The tube light was going grey at the edges, as if there was mould growing within. In this dull white illumination, the yellow of the walls looked vomit-sick, like the inside of a government hospital. Navkar often wondered why they always seemed to choose that colour.

He fiddled with his food unenthusiastically. What was it? Pumpkin? Lauki? It all tasted the same in these watery curries his mother made. She'd stopped cooking properly many years back, when maids first became unaffordable. Perhaps it had never been her cooking in the first place. Perhaps his childhood memories of his mother's cooking had always belonged to the bai.

The television blared in front. His mother was staring at it, though he knew she wasn't watching. She had no interest in the news. But she didn't object to it, while he was having dinner, only because he worked with the channel.

'Do you remember Anisha, ma?' he asked suddenly.

'The girl from your class?' his mother asked, frowning. 'Who was killed?'

'Yeah.'

'What about her?'

Navkar shrugged. 'I got reminded of her recently.'

'The media made so much hulla over her,' his father interjected. 'Nowadays the media shouts too much. They're always shouting about something or the other. There's no dignity left.'

It was true, of course. Navkar tried to finish his food so he could leave.

'They'll just pick anything up, and make a big deal of it,' his father continued. 'Can't even trust what they say. They're like a pack of crows.'

'This one is real,' Navkar said quietly.

He could hear Tara's voice on TV now, her slightly shrill, strong voice, with clipped, confident sentences. They'd shifted back to the newsroom. He watched her; dark hair framing her face, facing the camera with unwavering eyes.

Navkar silently rose from the table and went downstairs for a smoke. The evening felt stifling, it's wet, clammy hands almost choking the air from his lungs. There were a few other youths lounging by the low fence, tendrils of smoke rising from their silhouettes. He wondered if their reasons were the same as his.

He looked at his watch. The newscast would end in another half hour. They'd finally cornered Chauhan this morning. He'd had no real defense to the hundreds of barbed questions. Navkar had almost felt bad for the guy. He wondered what would the minister do now?

Navkar took a deep drag of smoke and felt it clean the suffocation from his arteries and nerves. He could imagine the wood-panelled walls in the Mantralaya; an urgent meeting, desperate tension, the blare of horns from the cavalcades of the powerful.

It was a different world. He'd almost seen it today. Almost!

He went and bought himself a chocolate bar and munched on it thoughtfully. His phone started ringing.

It was a woman's voice. It sounded like she was sobbing. 'Saab, saab, it's Kamla. Do you remember?'

He stopped walking, startled. 'Kamla? From the hotel?'

'Yes, saab,…are you really a reporter? I…I don't know what to do! I don't know who can help me…' she spoke through gasps.

Navkar stood silent for a few confused seconds. 'Calm down Kamla, I'll come meet you,' he said finally.

SEVEN

Sun and sweat! Like one of those beach ads for Westerners, but without the laughter.

Mumbai lay sullen and grim, festering in the heat, stench rising from the train tracks and slums and fly-crowned heaps of rubbish. Stray dogs lay across roads like they had a death wish, their thirsty tongues lolling out sideways. The pavements in front of him were occupied by the homeless, groaning in anger and heat. Office-going men loosened their ties, cursing their jobs and families and wives.

It was the first time Navkar had been to this part of the city. Today was not the right day for the introduction, though the basti here wouldn't be a treat on the most pleasant of winter mornings. The narrow dirt lanes were splattered with muddy puddles, gutter water mixing with flattened earth and stray dung and urine, squelching under his sorry leather shoes. His shirt was soaked transparent.

This felt like a terrible idea with every step.

He stumbled along the patchwork of small lanes, wide enough for just one cow to pass, so when he happened to find one lounging on a path, he had to find another route. Tarpaulin and asbestos shacks crowded in on both sides, lined by bright red, lime, purple Scooties and black Pulsars.

Satellite dishes snuck out though crude roofs. Many had air-conditioning units sticking out of the tin walls. There were a few shanties made of brick; two to three storeys, squashed and moulded together as if built with plasticene.

People were squatting in the doorways of the cramped houses or in the muddy, filthy lanes, chatting idly amidst piles of plastic-topped garbage, their faces mirroring the disgust he felt. Their fidgety eyes followed him. He was quite clearly an outsider, quite clearly dispossessed of their pain and odour. Some of the hutments sold cold drinks, and he stopped at one to ask for directions.

The place where Kamla had said she would meet him was at the centre of the basti, in a clearing where a large boxy building stood awkwardly, away from the drainage and density of the basti.

It was supposed to be an apartment building—the ill-begotten child of one of those government projects to reclaim slum land by shifting its dwellers to vertical homes. Promises were made, construction started, but people changed their mind once the demolishers arrived or once they'd sold the rights to their flats. Then nobody could push the project through, no matter how strong their hand; the votes per square kilometre are high in slums. As long as they lived in shit, they could stand up to anyone!

The construction on this building had stopped many years back. All that stood now was a hulking mass of concrete and dirty windows.

Navkar checked his watch, it was two already. He took a seat on a bench in what was perhaps meant to be a garden around the complex. A large puddle of water lay in front, leakage from the rain-water collection tank of the building. There was no one around. It was a complete contrast to the hustle-bustle of the slum, an island of silence. The wind whistled through the carcass of the construction as the concrete rotted away. Navkar noticed a decrepit stall across the street which said: 'Raju's Coffee Palace'. Navkar was surprised to find a stall selling coffee in these surroundings. He couldn't make out if there was anybody in the tiny shop. Glasses were stacked neatly on the small counter beside a simmering kettle. He decided to try calling out to whoever was behind the counter. After a few minutes, something finally rustled. A lanky boy woke up and ambled over to Navkar, scowling theatrically.

'What do you have?' Navkar asked him.

'Coffee,' he said pointing to the name of the shop.

'Nothing else?'

The look that the boy gave him made Navkar change his mind about asking further questions; after all, he was in unfamiliar territory and the boy did not look happy on being woken up from his beauty sleep.

'Uh-uhm...I'll have a cup.'

The boy walked away sullenly and returned with a stained glass filled with a grimy brown liquid. Navkar looked at it suspiciously. He took a sip, immediately spitting it out.

'What did you put in this thing?'

'Your mother's love!' the boy snarled and disappeared into the cramped little stall again.

Navkar threw the coffee into the large puddle in front and checked his watch again. Kamla was late. Indian standard time! It was normal to be late.

But something told him that wasn't the case. She wasn't late. She wasn't coming. He could feel it. This was all just a waste of time. Just a momentary whim of his, trying to be a hero.

He felt his sweat could fill the glass if he waited too long. Maybe he shouldn't have come. He still didn't know what he was doing here, what he was waiting for. How would he be able to help her?

He concentrated on the puddle in front to calm down. He turned to the watch again. It was 2.23 p.m. Something was wrong. He knew it.

He sat quietly wondering what he should do now, when a crow cawed in fear.

Navkar sat up, startled.

Suddenly, a deafening scream shattered the silence, and the puddle in front of him exploded with a loud splash as something fell into it. It took Navkar a couple of seconds to register that it was a body. His glass fell on the ground, rolling towards the lifeless form. Blood had splattered everywhere from the shattered corpse now occupying the puddle.

He could feel the blood and mud and water splashed on him soaking into his shirt and jeans. He stared at the body, his mind too dumbstruck for it to sink in.

Navkar tried to stand up and felt his legs give away, slipping into the puddle, and he fell over slowly, his knees sinking into the brown-red squelch. He felt a whiteness at the edges of his vision. Her face was turned towards him, jaws shattered, the splinter of the bone jutting out of her cheek. The impact had crushed her skull, pushing her brain out of the cracks. Her left eye hung out, dangling on a length of gristle. He felt his stomach heave, his heart give a painful squeeze. Her arms and legs were twisted out of their joints, splayed out as if to embrace him.

Vomit spewed out of him, some falling on her before he turned his face. He stared at the whirls and ripples in the puddle as his disgorge blended in. He got up slowly, heaving once more, his hands gripping his knees to keep him steady. He took a few uncertain steps back, and felt his back touch the concrete of the building. He had to breathe now. He had to breathe. Navkar stared at the body, and breathed deeply; in, out. One at a time! In and out…

The lanky boy from the stall had come running. He was screaming now; a high-pitched adolescent scream. But Navkar could hardly hear it; his senses had become numb. He could just make out the gaping mouth, the boggled eyes of the boy as he looked around him frantically. Navkar felt his senses return as he could feel the coldness of the concrete against his palms as he just stood and breathed deeply.

Others were arriving now. They came in twos and threes and fours, from all the lanes surrounding the chawl, like ants driven out of their hill. They swarmed the emptiness around the building, leaving a large space in the middle—a space just for the body…and him.

Some of them were shouting questions while some were just shrieking in horror.

Navkar felt his breathing return to normal. He felt his heart slow down. But the whiteness was invading his vision, crowding out everything else. His fingers scrambled for his mobile in his jeans pocket. He took it out and pressed the call button. His eyes were going white. He scanned through his recent calls. His mother. His father. Tara. The grocer. His boss. His friend.

He called Tara.

'There's been a murder…in the basti behind Mohammed Ali Road…Yes, I saw it. Yes. The dead body is in front of me now.'

EIGHT

Forty-six years old, female, mole on right shoulder. Broken ribs and collarbone. Displaced Hip. Dislocated right shoulder. Shattered left ankle. Dead. Cause of death: Thrown off the Mahapura building. Location: Mohammad Ali Marg, Bhindi Bazaar.

And there she lay, face down in the miserable brown puddle. Her face broken, her hand clutching a picture of the man she was married to for thirty years.

The lean, scraggly havaldar with the discoloured uniform stuffed his small notebook in his pocket as one of his associates, a hefty bug-eyed brute, shoved Navkar into the back of the police jeep. Navkar was still in shock and his body was seized by a strange kind of fatigue. The jeep drove away as another came by to take charge of the disfigured corpse of the woman, and Navkar finally lost consciousness.

It was evening by the time Navkar awakened. He found himself sprawled on a grimy, cold stone floor. The hard surface had left his neck stiff and his body aching. A shrill whistle from a tea kettle broke through the drone of a lulling fan. His groggy eyes could make out the outlines of four men sitting under a flickering tube light, cards in their hand. They were all wearing the same clothes. Uniforms...police uniforms. And he realized that he was in a cell.

It all came back to him suddenly—the deafening screech, the loud splash, the eyes... And then so many eyes accusing him. A jeep, the thin man and this bug-eyed brute. The police had come soon after the murder. He didn't remember if he had called them. He only remembered that he'd tried to explain, but he couldn't. How does one explain death? They didn't listen, they smirked. And they arrested him, since he wasn't supposed to be there. He didn't want to be there, he didn't want to hear her scream. He shuddered at the thought, grimacing against the dark musty walls of the cell, which reeked of urine.

'Hero, finally decided to get up?' One of the men in uniform stood on the other side of the bars, the steam from his tea cup fogging his crooked glasses.

'I want water,' croaked Navkar.

'Do you have anything to tell us first?' said another officer, peering over his cards.

Being a reporter, Navkar was aware the cops knew that he had nothing but they had orders from above to follow this protocol, since he had been found at the scene of crime. He was just the easiest suspect.

'I didn't know the woman,' grunted Navkar.

There was no point. They weren't listening to him. The card game was far more interesting.

'Can I make a phone call at least?' he asked. 'Please, sahib? I'm sure my friend can clear this up.'

'Unless your friend wants to give us a donation, you're going to be here until you can tell us a nice story,' declared the bug-eyed policemen, snorting in laughter.

'Please, just one phone call?'

'Two aces. My round!' bellowed the lanky officer, throwing up his arms. 'Chal, hand over all your money.'

Navkar sat back, looking up at the ceiling. They were pigs, the police. He'd known that for a long time. For eleven years. The paint at the top of the cell had been eroded by years of poor waterproofing and general neglect. Dense cobwebs swirled around each other in drunken patterns. Navkar wanted this to be over. He wondered if he had managed to call Tara before the police had come. He couldn't remember now. It was all a blur. He felt a sudden anger course through him.

He got to his feet again with a grunt, 'Let me make a phone call. It's my right!' he yelled, 'I'm a journalist! I know Tara Verma!'

'Then introduce her to us,' winked the officer cheekily, 'I haven't met a nice girl in a while.'

'I don't like nice women, they make me feel guilty,' offered another officer, 'Two of diamonds!'

'I'm not joking,' Navkar said, his parched throat causing his voice to crack. 'I work in Channel 10, and they'll come asking questions!'

One of the officers slapped his cards on the table and turned, 'Arre, let him out na. He is ruining the mood. I can't play when I'm distracted.' The others looked a bit startled at their compatriot.

'It's already been three hours,' Navkar pressed, 'You're wasting your time by keeping me here. I'm a reporter!'

'Shut up!' the officer yelled suddenly, 'Just shut up!' He turned to the constable. 'Check if Salim bhai wants to ask him something.' He pointed a finger at Navkar in warning, 'And you, sit down before I break your legs.'

Navkar sat down. He knew what they were like. There was nothing else to do. He closed his eyes to keep the reality of his circumstances at bay. He wondered what would happen now. What would his parents do when he didn't turn up? They were too old to handle things like this. It was hard to imagine what indignities they would face at a police station.

His last thoughts as he dozed off were…Who was Salim bhai? Was he a senior officer?

Navkar woke up with a start. His left cheek was stinging. He'd been slapped. That's what had woken him.

He blinked in the dim light. A lanky man was standing over him, wearing shades even inside this dark room. Ray Ban, Navkar noticed groggily. Expensive. The man's hair was spiked with gel and he was wearing a purple satin shirt; the top three buttons open.

'Me, Salim,' the man said casually, his hand catching Navkar's collar.

Navkar could make out the face clearly now; tanned skin and paan-stained teeth. The man's eyes were boring into him. They had a deep menace in them, the look of men who have seen people die. Navkar wondered if he had that look now as well, somewhere gouged deep inside his eyes. He felt nauseous again.

'So this is the chhokra!' Salim bhai said, standing up to stretch. Navkar could see the policemen standing in reverence behind him.

'What's his report?' Salim asked the officer.

'Suspected for the murder in Mohammad Ali chawl. Sudhir Navkar. Says he is a journalist.'

'I am a journalist!' Navkar hissed. 'In Channel 10.'

Salim bhai was unimpressed. He spat out a perfectly straight stream of paan juice at the wall opposite and shuffled towards Navkar, leaning in till his breath hung over him.

'Achha, listen closely boss,' Salim said. His hand slipped to his back and slid out a gun from his waistband with a flourish, 'What is this?'

Navkar's eyes widened.

Salim brought the gun up to his face, 'What is this, Navkar sahib?' Salim repeated quietly.

Navkar's felt his jaws move, but no words came out. He realized he was trembling.

He saw Salim shake his head in amusement. 'You're like this already? I haven't even done anything yet.' Salim was laughing now. 'Listen, Navkar sahib, you look like a seedha guy, so let's keep it simple. Tell me truthfully if you know anything about Kamla bai. What were you doing there?'

'I didn't know her,' Navkar said.

Salim gripped his face and looked into his eyes. 'Then what were you doing there?'

'She asked me for help,' Navkar said. 'She was making a scene outside...outside the Rustom hotel. The guards were going to throw her out so I had given her my card. She called me asking for help.'

'Help for what?' Salim said.

'I don't know! She was like a madwoman...'

Salim's grip tightened. 'You came all this way to talk to a madwoman?'

Suddenly, there was a commotion outside. A policeman rushed in, 'Sir, sir, I can't stop her. She has a camera.'

Salim bhai immediately tucked his revolver in, straightening out his shirt.

Navkar looked up, and for a while he couldn't believe his eyes. It was Tara. Here in the police station. There was a cameraman trailing her.

'Who's the officer in charge here?' she shouted. 'Pinto, focus here please,' she instructed the cameraman, pointing at the inspector, 'Sir, are you the senior officer here?'

The men in uniform seemed confused. The inspector took his time answering. 'Madamji, any problem?'

'Why have you arrested my man without any charges? This is illegal.'

'Madamji, it's no problem. We have just brought him for some questions, that's all.' He waved at the constable, 'Bring some *chai* for madam. Come, madam, let's sit and talk.'

Tara glared at him. 'I want this man freed immediately,' she stated authoritatively.

'Madamji, we have not finished our questioning,' the officer said, a bit stiffly.

'Pinto, hand me the mike.' With this, Tara pointed the large Channel 10 mike at the officer, 'Roll camera. What's your name?' She glanced at his tag, 'Gaurav Kaul. Inspector Kaul, please tell us why you are questioning a news reporter who was at the bottom of the building at the very moment when the victim fell?'

'Listen, madam…' the officer started.

'Do you have a warrant, Inspector Kaul?' Tara interrupted, 'Have you let Sudhir Navkar speak to his lawyer?'

'Madamji, this is not right!'

'Can you tell our viewers, Inspector Kaul, if you know how many constitutional clauses you have broken today? Please show our viewers your knowledge of the law.'

The officer had taken a step back now. He waved to the constable frantically, 'T-take the camera!'

Tara laughed. 'This is 2020, Inspector Kaul. Video is sent live to our satellite. There's no tape inside the camera any more!' She gestured Pinto to offer the camera. 'You can check. Now, go get a warrant and if you do, then please bring Sudhir in for questioning in the proper way.'

Within minutes the numbing handcuffs came off. Navkar could feel his wrists again. Tara signalled him to hurry towards her. He mouthed a silent thank you.

'Sorry, Madamji,' the officer offered sheepishly as they hastened out of the big blue doors into the gloomy evening.

Navkar took a deep long breath of that smog-filled, stench-laden air as if it was a flower field in an empty valley. A breeze rustled through. His shoulders rose and fell with his breath.

'That guy,' he said slowly, 'in the satin shirt. He was a bhai.'

Tara frowned and glanced back at the police station. 'Who? I didn't see him.'

'He was there. He slunk back when you arrived.'

'What was he doing there?'

'He was asking me questions,' Navkar said, frowning. He turned to look at her. Her face looked oddly tender in the evening light. 'I think I was in big trouble there.'

'You have to tell me what happened,' she said.

He let out a ragged laugh. 'I didn't think you'd come. I was in real trouble.'

She smiled. He felt her hand patting him, and he nearly flinched at the touch. Her smile flickered and she looked him in the eye and said, 'Someday, if I am in real trouble, then you can repay me.'

Navkar's mother was cooking dinner when he came back. She beamed at him when she noticed his return, but her face immediately contorted in disgust.

'You're so dirty!' she shrieked. 'Where were you? What did you do?'

He stared at her, and then down at his clothes. She was right. He was filthy.

She hurried to him, her nose wrinkling. 'Gutter! You smell like the gutter! What happened?'

Her bindi was out of place, her hair matted over her forehead with sweat. She always looked so tired after her day's work, so exhausted by the heat and the effort. He wondered how old she was. He could never really remember her age well.

'What are you making for dinner?' he asked.

She was picking at his sleeves with a grimace. 'Hmm? Parval.'

Her parval curry tasted like dishwater. But after the ordeal of the day, he laughed.

'I am very hungry. Don't work so hard, okay?' he said and went to take a bath, leaving her standing.

He slept early that day, without telling his parents about the murder and the lock-up, even the basti. He slept like a dead man, an exhausted and dreamless sleep.

The next morning he couldn't bear to go to work. Kamla's distorted face kept flashing before his eyes. He remembered her twisted, crushed body; broken like a toy carelessly thrown away… And then her severed eye; the memory causing him to stumble out of bed and into the bathroom before the rising vomit spewed out.

He stood there in the doorway, heaving, breathing harshly, listening to the chirping of the morning birds.

When he washed up and looked at the wall clock, it was 7.15. His clothes from yesterday were bunched in the corner of the wash area, mud-stained, crusted.

He ran away from the house, down the stairs, away from

the building. He kept walking, out through the neighbourhood, feeling the sun parch his soul, feeling the overripe smell of Mumbai.

He found himself crossing the dusty maidan where he used to play as a kid, right next to his school. He could still remember it. He could still remember falling, rolling, fighting in this dust. He tried to picture what they'd looked like, what his friends had been like as children. Where had they all gone? Was he the only one left here still?

He found his feet turning towards the school. The maidan started to get greener. The school had a gardener, though its play area was small. He reached the cement-grey boundary wall and green-painted metal gate. An old guard dozed on a red stool next to it. It took Navkar a while to recognize him. Girish bhaiya. He was still here. But he looked so old now, his hair a shock of white, his face unshaven and speckled with white bristles. Navkar wondered how someone could age so fast. Eleven years wasn't that much time, was it?

Navkar leaned over and shook him gently. The old man woke with a start and peered up at him.

'Girish bhaiya,' Navkar said. 'Do you remember me? Sudhir Navkar. I studied in this school.'

Girish blinked, confused. There had been so many kids in the school. How could he remember. He nodded and smiled uncertainly. He didn't want to appear rude.

'I wanted to…see the memorial, bhaiya,' Navkar said. 'Anisha's memorial.'

The old man nodded. He'd never been a very good guard. Navkar stepped into the compound and stared.

The school looked so much smaller than he remembered it to be. Just a squat little building in brick with a small patch of grass around it. Where were the endless corridors of his memory? The green expanse?

Navkar could hear the faint sounds of instruction float to him. Classes were going on. There were no children outside. At the other end of the building, against the boundary wall, there was the small space made of grey stone. It was in the shape of a house in a child's drawing, two rectangular walls, and a triangular roof. Inside was a small inscription.

Navkar made his way to it and crouched in front. He couldn't really remember her face any more. He knew that, even though he pretended otherwise to himself. All he could really remember was the picture they'd put in the newspaper clipping.

Anisha Sharma, aged 15, found raped and murdered outside Andheri station. 14 May 2006.

He hadn't really known her. He hadn't been in love with her. She was a sweet girl, quite pretty, but quiet, so she didn't have many admirers. Perhaps he'd been one. He didn't even remember any more. It was difficult to remember those things correctly. Her death overwhelmed his memory.

He remembered how he would imagine her face, her deadened face, after he'd heard the news. He couldn't help it. It would make him vomit and drive away his sleep, but he couldn't help it. He'd never seen it, of course. That horror was only for her family.

Now finally, he had seen death.

With his jeans covered in dust and the wind raking his hair, he knelt there and let himself weep.

NINE

The sea was kind this morning. Its soft, cool breeze, almost like the touch of a lover, swept through the city, through its avenues and homes and shops and cars and people. It rustled through Tara's curtains, and skittered into her room, ruffling her hair and tinkling the little bells she hung from her ceiling in a neat row.

She woke in a slow, long, languid stretch. She rolled over and buried her face in her pillow for a few more minutes. It was a Sunday, she had a day off and the coolness of the breeze on her shoulders and the comfort of the smooth linen of the pillow were joy.

When she finally sat up, eyes blinking, a grin spread across her face. It was a rock-star story. For the last three days, all the headlines had been hers.

She hopped out of bed and rubbed her feet on the cold floor. Her mother was still asleep, snoring in a gentle melody, like a motorcycle's lullaby.

Tara made her way to the kitchen and started boiling water. She ground some ginger and put it into the water with the sugar. As she added the tea leaves and milk, its fragrance rose in hot vapours, mixing with the smell of the sea. The earth-brown beauty of the tea spread in languid swirls till it soaked through the entire liquid. She ran it through a sieve, pouring the tea into two cups. She had shouted too much at her mother recently. It was time to make amends.

Their window was patterned with a wooden jharokha, causing the sunlight to fall in dimples on the bed. Tara woke her mother with a soft shake of the shoulders and the scent of hot tea.

'Good morning,' she said with a smile.

Her mother sat up slowly, grimacing with the pain of her arthritis as she uncurled herself from sleep.

'Move slowly,' Tara said. 'I put adrak in the tea today.'

Her mother beamed. She loved ginger tea. She took a deep draught and let out a sigh. 'It makes me feel young again,' she said with a laugh.

'You are young. You're the same age as Salman Khan. And you're both single.'

Her mother chuckled. 'What about your Salman? Is he coming today?'

'Yeah. He'll be here around 10.30 a.m.'

Her mother looked alarmed and tried to get up, nearly spilling the tea.

'What are you doing?' Tara asked, surprised.

'He'll be here this early! I've to get ready!'

Tara pressed her back onto the bed. 'You don't have to do anything.'

'I have to get ready!' her mother repeated. 'Did the maid clean the house yesterday? We have to clean the house!'

'Look, it'll be alright!' Tara said, a little annoyed. 'I'm not bringing him here to impress him.'

Her mother became quiet. 'What are you bringing him here for?' she asked, looking at Tara intently.

Tara shrugged and got up. 'Have your tea, mummy. It'll get cold. And you relax. Don't get another heart attack.'

A pile of washed clothes was waiting to be ironed on the living room couch. Tara pushed them into the wardrobe and looked around the room. It was neatly kept despite all odds. The furnishings were a mix of old, simple pieces and the luxuries she'd bought over the last few years—a home theatre system, a massage chair, a recently renovated modular kitchen. She laughed to herself at the thought of showing them off to Vishnu Mistry. Look at this chair, isn't it great? It costs as much as your tie.

She heard the sweet ting-tong of their calling bell precisely on time. Vishnu was standing at the bottom of the three small steps that led to their door.

He was clothed in a faded chequered shirt, dark brown, three-quarters and silly-looking shoes. His face was half-covered by aviators and a baseball cap pulled down.

'Normal-people clothes,' he said, noticing her amusement, 'I got them specially.'

'Impressive,' she smiled, leaning on the doorway. 'And no bodyguards either.'

He spread his muscular arms and tilted his head, 'Do I look like I need them?'

He slipped his hand behind and retrieved a Beretta. 'Besides, I'm carrying my gun.'

She frowned, 'So you actually never leave your house without it.'

He nodded. When she remained quiet, he smiled. 'I'm a committed sportsman.'

She shook her head and gestured him in. 'Come in. My mom is waiting to meet you.'

Vishnu followed her into the cool shade of the house. 'Should I say namaste or touch her feet or what?'

'Just don't give her your famous smile. She has a heart condition.'

She found her mother decked at her wedding best, hurrying out of the bedroom, breathless; hobbling painfully.

'Hello, Mrs Verma,' Vishnu said, and Tara's mother spluttered something unintelligible in reply. 'I've heard a lot about you,' he tried again, but stopped when he saw her face pall.

Tara rolled her eyes and went to her mother and rubbed her shoulders. 'Mummy, why don't you make him some *chai* and pakoras. Vishnu doesn't get to eat home-cooked food often.'

Her mother seemed relieved at the idea and went into the kitchen, after a few backward glances at Vishnu.

Tara sighed, 'She's always afraid that I've been complaining about her. She feels guilty.'

Vishnu took off his aviators, and she could see his troubled eyes. He walked to the wall beside her and stared at the framed pictures. He began to trace the glass frame of one showing a young man in a crew cut with a fierce look.

'So this is your dad,' he said quietly.

'Quite a looker, huh?'

Vishnu's eyes flickered across the frames. 'You have his eyes,' he murmured. Then he turned to her.

Tara raised her eyebrows. 'His mad eyes? Thanks.'

He looked thoughtful. 'Was he actually mad? You keep telling me that, but what does that mean?'

Tara sighed and fell back on the massage chair. She glanced at the kitchen to see if her mother had any chance of returning to the sitting room soon.

'He wasn't really mad. But there was something slightly off about him. He shook sometimes. And he walked funny. He was physically, I don't know…a bit strange. Just your opposite, I guess.'

Vishnu leant back against the wall, watching her. 'Not on all counts.' When she felt silent he asked, 'That's all? Most of the members of my board of directors are madder than that.'

She seemed to cringe and drew up her knees to slide her arms around them. 'Well, I don't think there was anything so mad that he couldn't have controlled it. I don't know.' She shrugged, her hair ruffling in a sudden gust of wind. 'Maybe I just don't want to forgive him.'

He looked at the photos again. 'You've kept so many photos.' His eyes rested on one where the man was younger, receiving a degree.

'A statistician. He was good at math,' she said and paused to tie up her hair roughly. 'He was good at a lot of things. His brain was like…like a surgeon's knife. He couldn't get distracted, even if he wanted to.'

There was a clatter from the kitchen and Tara jumped to her feet, hurrying to help. 'You stay,' she told Vishnu, when he made to follow.

He heard her voice from the kitchen, 'Come, mummy, come. It's ok. Come.'

They returned to the living room. He could see her mother refusing her support to walk. She was trying to hide her limp. Tara brought the tray with three boiling cups of tea, first to him, then to her mother, and then she perched on the armrest of the couch with the third. Her mother beamed at him.

'This is my second cup,' she said. 'Tara made one for me in the morning, with ginger, because I love ginger tea.' She glanced at Tara and looked back at him. 'She's a good girl that way.'

He could see Tara nearly spurt out her tea in a laugh. He didn't feel like laughing. He took a slow sip, his eyes focused on the cup. 'It's very good,' he said solemnly.

Her mother brightened at the words. 'Then you should stay for lunch, beta. I'll make something nice for you! I'll go make it right away!'

'No, mom, you're not going to hassle yourself,' Tara said sternly. 'I'm going to take him out and show him the neighbourhood. Then he can go back to his hotel for lunch.'

'Beta, it's not a problem,' her mother hissed to her and then lowering her voice in the hope that he couldn't hear her said, 'I'll make something quickly. He should have our homemade food. He'll like it.'

'No,' said Tara firmly and her mother didn't say anything.

Vishnu kept quiet. They finished their tea and Tara got up immediately.

'It was great meeting you, Mrs Verma,' he said weakly.

Tara took his hand in hers and bid goodbye to her mother. Vishnu followed her out. When he looked back, he could see her mother's eyes on him, shining bright within the gloom of the house.

Tara took him out into the lane and they walked down a tree-shaded, ochre-tinted path. She didn't speak. The path opened to a small park where a few boys were playing gully cricket.

'This is where we used to play when we were kids,' she said, her voice unemotional.

They found a cement bench under the swishing leaves of a large mango tree and sat there, holding hands in silence.

'She gets worried,' Tara said, after a while. 'She thinks I'm crossing the marriageable age.'

'I figured,' Vishnu said simply.

Tara glanced at him. She drew her legs up to her chest again; the posture seemed to give her some kind of comfort. She knew what he wanted to talk about. 'See, we were like furniture for him,' she said finally, 'Just things kept in the house. He had no interest in us.'

Vishnu looked at her silently.

'He wasn't violent. He just had no interest in us. In fact, he didn't even like us. He hated people; hated everyone. Everyone was stupid and there was no meaning to anything.'

'He didn't find anyone smart enough?' Vishnu asked.

'I don't think he tried,' she said bitterly.

Vishnu wondered if he should hug her. That's what one usually did to comfort another. But something about her crouched, curled body made him hold back.

'How old were you?' he asked quietly.

She shrugged. 'Twelve.'

Vishnu leant back, looking up at the tree. There were brilliant bursts of sunlight as the leaves moved, hiding and revealing and hiding the sky. Shadow patterns covered their hair and shoulders. He heard the shout of jubilation as a wicket fell. The sea breeze ruffled through his curls, and he took off his cap.

'How did he do it?' he asked quietly.

'He slit his wrists,' Tara's voice was bland. 'There was a lot of blood.' She unwound her limbs, sat up and looked at him, her eyes large, a challenge held in them. 'It was good in a way,' she said slowly, 'I looked after my mother and she looked after me. We could live.'

'You loved him.'

'No,' she said, trying a smile. 'No I didn't. But I wish I could.'

The boys were arguing now and play had broken up. Two of them were wrestling on the ground in happy anger. Dust got thrown up, radiant swirls in the sunlight.

'Come,' she said, getting up and holding out her hand. 'We'll have coconut water. My treat.'

The man's stall was below a large gulmohar at the corner. He was sleeping, and a few stray flowers, fragments of brilliant orange, shorn by the wind, lay covering him. There was beauty in his old, leathery skin, the folds of cloth atop his head, his peaceful slumber.

Tara tucked a fifty-rupee note beneath a coconut, and with a few deft swings hacked holes into two. The man didn't wake up at the sound.

They sat beneath the shade of the gulmohar tree. Vishnu stared at her as she sucked on her straw noisily. 'Why did you want to tell me all this?'

She frowned, looking at him over the coconut. 'I shouldn't have? Have your coconut.'

Vishnu obeyed, his face thoughtful. 'It's not making you more marriageable,' he said finally. 'Why're you telling me?'

She met his eyes, raising her head slowly. She shook her head and smiled. 'We both know that was never going to happen.'

Vishnu didn't reply. She shuffled closer to him, and rested her head on his shoulders. 'You can't have a normal life, Vishnu,' she said gently. 'It's too late for that.'

The warmth of her cheek felt peaceful against him. He could feel the gentleness of her breath. Flowers tumbled over them and around them, dancing in the breeze.

'And you?' he asked.

She smiled. 'It's probably too late for me too. We're broken people.'

He put his arm around her. They sat there in silence amidst the soft whispers of the wind through the narrow lanes of the neighbourhood. Tara looked at him. The sun shone on him through the trees, giving him a golden ethereal look. She could feel his breath, slow and deep, peaceful. He turned to her and kissed her cheek gently, his lips tender and delicate. He cupped her face with his palm and regarded her. She could see something was troubling him. She liked looking into his eyes. They were the only part of him that had a trace of vulnerability. He placed his other hand on her face as well.

'I want you to change the story,' he said finally. 'Chauhan has to pass the bill. His government can't fall.'

TEN

Navkar and Tara often bumped into each other in the office canteen after the incident at the police station. She was always cheerful.

Today, however, Navkar noticed that she looked wan, her expression pinched and her eyes unfocused. It was strange, since she had had some time off now. The headlines had shifted to the love life of the Indian cricket captain. The Chauhan story was now being carried only in debates and talk shows. Today they'd got a professor of law and history, with some reputation as an intellectual, for a long interview. Navkar could see him on the TV in the canteen.

'You see,' the man was saying in a drawling voice, 'It's easy to condemn. All politicians are corrupt—that's always the reaction of the public. And if it's the English-speaking public like your audience, they'll probably add that they are luchhe-lafanges, because they look like villagers. But tell me this, what can they do? Try to understand their problem. Money wins elections. Everywhere in the world money wins elections—more so in a poor country. So what can they do? Even if they are actually committed to the nation's progress, they have to win the election first. They have to raise the funds somehow.'

Chatterjee was outraged. 'Are you saying this is right?' he exploded.

The professor laughed. 'What is right and what is wrong?' he said. 'I'm talking about causality. The system of democracy creates a genuine need among political parties for illegal fund-raising. In academic circles we call it the democracy tax.'

Navkar didn't listen to the rest. He spent most of his day lounging around the office, doing nothing much. He still couldn't get Kamla's face out of his mind; the smashed, broken face of the woman kept flashing in front of his eyes. He also remembered her desperate wails at the symposium, the panic in her voice on the phone, and then her broken body in the puddle. Why did she die?

He lit a cigarette on the landing outside and stared at his reflection in the window. There were people who knew why she was killed, he reminded himself. There were people who killed her. She didn't just slip off the twenty-fourth floor of an abandoned building. There was a reason.

If only he had found out more from her that day at the symposium.

The walk home from the station seemed longer that evening, with shadows pooling low on the streets and a sultry mist throwing haloes of streetlight. The sun had fallen and the darkness was quiet, broken only by the dancing of insects and the wind.

Navkar noticed a tall, lanky man stretched out on the landing of his apartment, listening to music on his phone, his form lit by the flickering bulb that hung at the entrance. He looked up when he saw Navkar approach and a grin spread across his face.

'I was afraid I was parked in front of the wrong house,' he said.

Navkar stood there and stared at him, at the face he'd seen just a few days ago. The same spiked hair and fake Ray-Bans, those menace-filled eyes and paan-speckled lips. He blinked a few times in disbelief before he spoke. 'Why are you here?'

Salim bhai shrugged. 'I want to talk to you, boss.'

'Why?' Navkar said, and he heard more anger in his voice than he'd expected.

Salim bhai grinned at him, 'Haven't you heard? Curiosity gets you killed.'

Navkar remembered the man's breath rolling over him. mixing with the stink of the lock-up. He remembered the cold metal touch of the gun.

Salim stood up and casually put an arm around his shoulder, 'Come, boss. We'll have paan.'

Navkar felt the bony arm tighten around his neck slightly till he gave up resisting and began to walk.

'Smart,' Salim smirked, his breath reeking of gutka.

There was a famous paanwala in the next street; a small, illegal shack at the crossroad, under an old intricate streetlamp. The shack had now been divided into two due to a fallout of the brothers who'd inherited the property. They sat side by side, separated by a plywood wall—both in identical lotus positions in their one square foot of space, screaming obscenities at any customer who went to the other.

Salim made him buy the most expensive paan they had and then made him amble some distance away. Finally, he gestured Navkar to sit on the pavement next to him. The wind had risen now; it wailed through the lane. It took Salim three attempts to light his beedi.

'Two more days, maximum,' Salim said. 'Then it will rain.'

Navkar glanced at him. He was sitting right on top of a paan stain. 'Who are you?'

'Questions again,' Salim snorted, 'Ok, I'll tell you boss. Because we're friends now, aren't we?' Salim grinned and made himself comfortable. He looked up briefly at the ring of mosquitoes swirling above him like a crown. He tried to chase them away with his hand but then gave up.

'If only you could shoot mosquitoes,' Salim sighed. His jaws worked thoughtfully on the paan. 'I'm like a detective,' he said suddenly, with a flourish.

Navkar stared at the dried out frame of the man. 'A detective?'

'Yes,' said Salim smiling. 'Yes, you see, in the underworld, there is a code. There are rules. You can even say there is justice. If somebody does something wrong, there is some betrayal…well, you don't want to kill your friends. You have to be sure. It's hard to make friends in our business.'

At the mention of the word *underworld*, Navkar looked around him cautiously.

In the street opposite, an old man, selling vada pav pushed his rickety cart. Small children were playing on the street outside their home.

'You're saying you investigate for the gangs?' Navkar said slowly. 'Like a detective would?'

Salim blew out a few rings of smoke and laughed. 'It wasn't my plan. I wanted to be a thief, like my uncle. Or a poet, like his mistress. She was very nice, very talented.'

Salim glanced at Navkar. 'In those days, the police didn't come into our place. Even if there was one death in the Muslim neighbourhoods, there would be riots. So, my uncle used to steal; something small, anything really. And if the police came after him, he would go up to one of the terraces, in the neighbourhood, with a megaphone and threaten to jump off if they got closer. He did this trick for ten years. By the end, he used to drink *chai* with the officers on the roofs.'

He patted the empty place next to him. 'Come here. Sit closer. I don't want to speak too loudly.'

'You're sitting on a paan stain,' Navkar pointed out.

'Saale, come here!' Salim barked and Navkar obeyed.

'What does he do now?' Navkar asked. 'Your uncle?'

Salim shrugged. 'One day, after the 1993 blasts, when he was again running after a theft, a new officer followed him. My uncle probably just wanted a chance to have *chai* and talk with the new guy. He was shot in the head.'

Salim was looking straight ahead, his voice gentler than before, 'That's when I joined the gang. I wanted the policeman dead.'

He turned to Navkar, his teeth gleaming in the darkness of the night, 'The first job I did was to prove that he'd made the gang's accountant an informer. The man was the boss's brother-in-law. Corrupting the family was stepping over the line, even for a policewallah. So I had my justice.'

Navkar took a drag from his Marlboro. 'Why are you telling me all this?' he asked finally. 'Why are you here?'

Salim shrugged casually, 'To give you a nice story. You work for that lady, Tara Verma?'

'I work with her.'

Salim looked around the street carefully. His voice dropped to a whisper. 'I need protection. I need new papers, a new name. I need to get out of this city.'

This took Navkar by surprise. He'd expected Salim to ask about Kamla again. A gust of wind rolled through the street and he had to protect his cigarette from dying out. Everything felt so unreal. He glanced at the man sitting next to him. A gangster carrying a gun, who had been asking him questions about a strange woman's murder in a police station only two days back and now asking for his help.

Navkar rubbed his temple. He could feel his head throbbing now. What was happening?

'You want to get out of the gang?' Navkar said slowly, trying to clear the swirl of thoughts in his head.

Salim had been smacking his head gently against the cement wall behind him; eyes closed, deep in thought. His eyes snapped open. There was fear in them.

'The gangs are dying,' Salim's voice sounded grave. 'There is something very big happening.'

He sat up suddenly and gripped Navkar's shoulder. 'Listen to me. Just two weeks back, one of our boys, Munna, turned on Mohammad bhai; the man who had married his mother thrice and brought him up for thirteen years. He is just a boy. When they caught him, he said he had been paid by a babu; someone with an umbrella. Did you read about that in the paper? Mohammed bhai was in the auto union.'

Navkar remembered his local-train acquaintance Chawla's words and his grimy finger pointing out the story in the newspaper.

There was silence in the neighbourhood now; a strange silence torn only by the howling of the wind. Salim was talking again.

'The week before that Aslam killed Sameer bhai, saying he had been promised a Mercedes. He said he was paid by an accountant in a pinstriped shirt. Aslam, this *bewakoof,* who wouldn't even have known what a Mercedes was till last month!'

'What work did he do? This Sameer bhai?'

'Something in the line of construction.' Salim's eyes were white discs now, reflecting his horror. Navkar could now smell the fear emanating from him and felt his grip tighten on his shoulders.

'Do you understand what is happening? Our business, it works on trust. It works on stability. You are paid by your boss, your bhai, and he takes care of you. You are like family.'

'And...that has changed?'

'The gangs haven't seen this much money since the blasts,' Salim whispered. 'We've never known so many betrayals. We don't know where the money is coming from. Our boys, the fools, they run off saying they have work, and we don't know who they're working for. But they *are* doing something. They *are* working for somebody. And then, here and there, once in a while, almost callously, there is death.'

'Like with Kamla?'

Salim nodded and let his shoulder go. 'She...and her husband.' Salim's body seemed to deflate, sink in upon itself. He looked exhausted.

Navkar couldn't stop himself. He had so many questions. He remembered her lifeless face. 'Did you speak to her?' he asked.

Salim held up his hands, 'She had gone mad with grief; just kept wailing and couldn't get out a damn sentence straight. She just clutched her husband's clothes and pictures and screeched! And then she kept saying strange things—how her husband was trying to do good for the first time in his life, how they would have been rich, how he was going to get them out of the basti. She was so irritating. I almost felt like killing her myself.'

He fell quiet suddenly. And then breathing deep, as if to gather himself, he sat up straight, 'Listen boss, here's the deal. I'll get you the whole story about the gangs, everything that's been happening, the whole funda; all of it. But you get me out of here. Talk to your madam. Get me out of this city. I already know too much.'

Navkar got up slowly. The world seemed to have lost its familiarity. He rubbed his temples again, and found his skin heated. He couldn't help remember Chawla now, and the flower show. It seemed like a lifetime ago.

Then the face returned again; the jawbone jutting out of her cheek, the dangling eye. Navkar could feel the breeze sink into his flesh, cut into him, like it had on the motorbike with Tara Verma's arms holding him tight.

She had come to get him out of trouble. He'd been so flattered.

'I'll talk to Tara,' Navkar said, his voice sounding faraway to him. 'I'll talk to her and let you know.'

Salim looked up at him, took a deep breath and stood up. 'Don't tell anyone else. Don't tell anyone you don't have to.'

Navkar almost smiled at the incongruity of the whole thing. 'How about the police?' he grunted.

Salim started laughing; a ragged, hysterical laugh. He clutched his stomach as he bent over with laughter.

Navkar could hear his laughter echoing as he got up and walked away.

~

It was 11.00 p.m. when Malhotra got a call from Vishnu Mistry.

'Hello, sir,' Malhotra said, nervous, though he'd been expecting the call.

'Tara told you I would call?' Mistry said without preamble.
'Yes, sir.'

'Don't call me sir,' Mistry said laughing. 'I'm half your age. Did Tara tell you what I want?'

Malhotra paused, deciding on the right words. 'Not quite.'

'I want you to pay more attention to the fact that the chief minister of your state is being threatened. That is a serious matter.'

'Yes, sir, we know that.'

'It's a shame.'

'It is, sir,' Malhotra said soberly, 'But so is the list of money laundering and black-money transactions that precede it.'

There was no response at the other end for a few minutes. Vishnu's voice had an edge when it returned. 'Mr Malhotra, the situation is grim. As someone who is deeply committed to improving the security situation in the country, I am concerned that the public understand what is happening. I want to help the media educate them.'

Malhotra ran his hand through his hair. He had wondered if it would come to this. 'We would welcome any partnership, sir, definitely.'

'You are also the owner of the channel?'

'Yes, sir. I started it ten years ago and we've done well, by the grace of God.'

'Then Mr Malhotra, listen to me. I am sure that Chauhan is a good man. He is going to benefit generations of our citizens. We now know that he has been threatened, perhaps blackmailed. I would like to ensure his well-being and stop the gross police incompetence that's letting the current situation happen.'

Malhotra ran his tongue over his dry lips. He'd been reading up. The net worth of the Rustom Group, till he had last checked two hours ago, was fifty-six billion dollars.

'What do you propose?' he asked.

ELEVEN

The palm trees outside the Channel 10 office clashed violently against each other, like gladiators in a battle, because of the strong winds. Navkar kept to the sides of the road hoping for some shelter as he walked from the station to the office. The blustery weather had left the streets empty of its vendors and stalls, a little ghost town in the middle of Mumbai. He tried to protect himself with his umbrella but a strong gust of wind destroyed it, leaving a sorry capsized mess. Posters and flyers flew about searching for a home, mixing with the lost leaves of a dozen trees. A lean jacaranda tree, which had stood firm by his office window for so many years, was now using the electricity pole as a crutch. Navkar hurried inside as the entrance door slammed shut behind him.

The office was full of bad hair days. Half the women and most of the men were patting or stroking their hair. Navkar almost felt like laughing. It all seemed so trivial.

He knew what he must do. He walked over to Tara's cubicle and peered in. She had her feet up on the table and was talking on the phone. He stood for a moment, feeling stupid, and just as he was about to turn away she noticed him and smiled.

'What's up?' she asked, removing the phone from her ears.

'Breakfast?' he asked.

Her eyebrows rose for a moment and then she signalled that he wait for a minute as she finished the call. She got her sunglasses and perched them on her hair and rose. 'Upstairs?'

They took the stairs to the rooftop canteen. The place was mostly empty. The wind bellowed through the streets. It was strange weather. The smell of monsoon flowers had been in the air a few days now but the skies had remained silent. But now the clouds were getting restless.

He pulled a chair for her and asked her what she wanted.

'Coffee,' she said simply, leaning back in the chair, her hair flying across her face.

He managed to get her coffee and a plate of pakoras for himself without dropping either. He took the seat opposite and found her studying him.

'How are you feeling now?' she asked.

'Much better,' he said. 'I really owe you one.'

She frowned. 'Is that what you wanted to say?'

'Wanted to say?' He was taken aback.

'That's why you asked me to come up here, right?'

He hesitated, and looked up at her. She was watching him, but she didn't seem impatient. Her words brought back the image that had been haunting him; a mangled face covered by a mass of hair and blood. He winced. The images changed. He could now see the fear-filled eyes of a man; Salim's eyes.

He nibbled on the pakora he'd brought, wondering how to put it. The wind blew in a sudden gust, snatching the paper plate, now free of its burden, even as he tried to catch it. It flew away, rolling over the ground, trailing mint sauce and ketchup.

She laughed. 'That happens to me all the time.'

He glanced up at her, surprised. That wasn't what he'd expected to hear. She was not someone who was known to laugh at clumsiness. He found her looking at him intently, thoughtfully.

'That man came to see me,' Navkar found himself saying, 'The mafia guy.'

Tara sat up. 'He did? What did he want? Is he threatening you?'

'No, no. He-he's a gang member,' Navkar said. 'Apparently that murdered woman's husband was one too. He said there has been a lot of trouble in the gangs, lot of disappearances, murders.'

Tara's eyebrows rose. She leant forward. 'And he knows why?'

Navkar shook his head. 'No, but he says he'll tell me what he knows.'

'And what does he want in return?' Tara asked, frowning.

The wind howled in Navkar's ears, as if screaming for mercy. 'He wants protection,' Navkar said and paused for a while before continuing. 'He wants to get out of the gang. He saw you, at the station, and thought that since I worked with you, I could arrange it for him.'

She looked surprised at first and then gradually grew thoughtful. Her eyes seemed to focus far away; she seemed to be looking through him. The wind seemed to drive into Navkar's bones as he waited. He noticed that her pupils caught the light and brown turned to opal.

'You know,' Tara said, 'When I did my first big story, the big sting at the coal ministry, my mom went crazy. She didn't understand why I did something like that. Something that put my life at risk. More so, because I'd never been like that. I'd always wanted to be an actress.'

Navkar remembered the video. She's been a dancer, a wannabe actress. 'Why did you do it?' he asked.

Tara glanced around, saw that no one was there and put her feet up on the table. 'I realized I would never be taken seriously if I wasn't…' she paused, 'incredible.' She shrugged. 'And I realized that actresses aren't heroines. They're just play-acting.'

Navkar stared at her. 'Did you actually get threats when you were investigating the coal scam?'

'Twice,' she nodded. 'I met some ministers after the first time. The second time I got a threat I had names to drop.'

Navkar stared at her. 'That's so cool,' he found himself saying. She was running her hands through her hair, tying it back. The delicate angles of her face seemed stronger when exposed, harder in the brightness of the day.

Tara gave a dry smile, 'Yeah, that's what I'd thought too. I'd thought I would become this big heroine, and everyone would worship the ground I walked on.'

'That's what has happened, hasn't it?'

'I suppose,' Tara said, thoughtfully. 'Perhaps it's just that being worshipped is not the same as being liked.'

She finished her coffee and glanced at him. 'What about you? What made you become a reporter?'

'A girl,' Navkar said, before he could stop himself.

She was taken aback by that. 'A girl? I didn't take you to be a romantic! You became a reporter to impress her?'

'No, no,' Navkar said hurriedly. 'Not impress.' He paused. 'She…you could say she…she made me realize justice is important. The fight for justice is important.'

Tara looked at him. He waited for her next question but it never came. 'I never thought of us as fighting for justice,' she mused. 'But I suppose you're right.' She sat up. 'You've not had a story of your own yet, have you?'

'Of course I have,' Navkar said, feeling some defensiveness creep into his voice. 'I've covered a few events and some police cases too. Some important criminal cases.'

'What happened to them finally?' Tara asked.

'Nothing. No one got caught.'

'You've not had a big story; something that would shake up the country.'

'No,' Navkar said. 'No, of course I haven't.'

Tara threw her scrunched-up cup at the dustbin and missed by a mile. She turned to him. 'See, nobody reads about criminal cases; there are so many. But an exposé on the underworld, with a real insider's perspective…that could be a start of something big.'

Navkar frowned. 'Maybe it'll help me find out who killed Kamla too.'

Tara gave him a quizzical look and asked, 'That's important to you?'

'Shouldn't it be?' Navkar replied. 'I saw someone get murdered. Shouldn't that be important? And the police never catch anyone. It's like no one even cares any more.'

'That's true.'

'People should! We should care when something like this happens.'

Tara reached out and patted his arm. 'Tell your informant what you need to. I'll talk to David and Malhotra.'

They made their way down to the office. As they parted ways near her cubicle, she turned to him, 'What were you saying the other day? About the letter not being blackmail?'

Navkar was taken aback at the sudden question, 'No, it

was nothing. Just that three crore is a very small amount for that much information. That's all. It was just a thought.'

'It's a good thought,' she said frowning, as the glass door of her cubicle closed.

TWELVE

It was 6.20 in the morning when the monsoon arrived. The night before had been unnerving, eerily calm. There had barely been a gust of wind, barely a rustle of leaves. The hissing, whistling wind of the past few days had vanished. Weather forecasters had told people to stay indoors. The few fishermen still surviving on Mumbai's edges had tied up their boats, and shifted their families to pavements deeper in the city. Schools had been put on alert.

But Vishnu had not gone indoors. He had been awake all night, waiting up in his high lonely tower, with its silhouette darker than the night sky. He had been waiting in his garden, beneath his tree, as the ranks of the storm had advanced. He had seen the sun, a small orange disc, flung far in the horizon, blotted out by the incoming storm. He had stood at the edge of his tower and seen the city spread beneath him. His city and that of his father's and that of the monsoon's. It was sunrise, but around him it looked like the end of the world.

He had watched as the lightning drew pathways from sky to earth, crackling into building and road, illuminating land, man, concrete, stone and metal as far as the horizon. Vishnu wondered if his tower would be hit by a bolt, if he would survive it. It would be a fitting judgement on his hubris, and the hubris of his people.

He took his watch out and waited. At 6.42, the clouds finally shed their weight and the first drops of rain hit the city. Vishnu looked up as it happened, savouring the moment, savouring his privilege. The first raindrops over Mumbai fell on his face and mouth and lips.

That was what his abode meant to him. The first taste of monsoon, the first fragrance of wet earth, in the greatest and worst city in the whole world.

It would all change, of course. As everything must.

~

Navkar sat by the sea. He was drenched by the rain. Waves crashed in front of him with increasing fury. He knew he must move soon. But he would give it a few more minutes. This was one of his favourite spots.

He had first come here on a school outing. Anisha had been there. She'd been huddled with her group of girls, sharing a packet of mumfuli. He remembered how the wind had ruffled her hair, overpowering the meagre defenses of her hair band.

He rose reluctantly, crossed the near-empty road and ducked under the tarpaulin of a chai stall. It didn't keep away the rain, but it provided enough cover to take out his phone. He asked for a hot cup and called Salim.

'I spoke to Tara,' he said when Salim picked up. 'We're getting it arranged.'

'Really?' Salim sounded suspicious. 'If you're lying to me…'

'Then we're both dead, right?' Navkar interrupted brusquely.

There was a moment's silence. 'So what can I do for you?' Salim said finally.

'I want the inside story of the gangs in the last five years; everything that you know.'

'Where will I be taken to?' Salim asked. 'Which country?'

Navkar hadn't thought of that. 'Thailand?' he tried. 'Thailand?'

'Is that a problem?'

'No, no, I love Thailand!' Salim said enthusiastically. 'I'll give you a call. Then we can meet.'

~

The sun returned only in the afternoon. It had rained for eight hours at a stretch. Sunlight sparkled on droplets everywhere, as if the world had been sprinkled with diamonds.

Salim knocked softly on the rotting door of the hut, mentally renouncing the smell of dung from the cowshed behind the house. He was just in time. The door opened and an old lady peeked out. She didn't seem pleased to see him.

'Go away,' she said feebly. 'You shouldn't come here like this.'

'Maaji, I thought I'd help put up the clothes for drying,' Salim said enthusiastically, his leg sliding into the doorway. 'The sun is out.'

'Go away,' the lady repeated, but her daughter's voice interrupted her.

'I'll get the clothes, ma,' the girl said.

'No, no, you stay inside,' her mother protested, but her daughter, Layla, was already at the door with a pile of wet clothes in her arms.

She was a young girl, not more than seventeen and quite petite. 'Let's go,' she told Salim curtly, and he saw that her eyes caught the sun.

The clothesline was laid out at the back. The place had that sickly sweet, fetid smell of cattle. Two buffaloes belonging to the family stood in the shed, wearing the same dull expression Salim always found on them. Layla's father had been a milkman and an informer; the first still brought the family a sizable income and the second had got him killed.

'She's right,' Layla said, as they started setting up the dripping clothes on the line. 'You shouldn't come here any more. Khurram bhai doesn't like it.'

Salim felt a trickle of cold water run down his arm. 'Khurram bhai had asked me to protect your family,' he said simply.

Layla didn't look at him. 'You weren't very successful,' she said quietly. They both knew what she meant.

'Khurram bhai's protection…' Salim said stiffly. 'His right to take it away.'

'That's what will happen to you too,' Layla said flatly. 'He doesn't like you any more. He doesn't like the fact that you are probing.'

'Have you heard anything?'

Now she glanced at him, her eyes flashing, 'Muni was here yesterday. He brought a big crate. It had some weapons in it. They didn't let me see though.'

'Weapons?' Salim asked. 'Did it have guns?'

'Sounded like metal, from the way it clattered. They were discussing some operation that is going to happen. And they were also making plans for some guests who would be coming and where they would stay.'

'Wait,' Salim interrupted. 'What operation?'

'I don't know,' Layla said. 'Muni didn't want to talk in front of me, because I know you. He's wary of you—because you're the investigator.'

'But I'm the investigator for Khurram bhai and Muni is in our gang!'

'Muni was asking him how your investigation was going. Khurram bhai spat on the ground saying you were good for nothing. He said they should get a new investigator. You're too weak.'

Salim didn't reply. His arms carried on the calming motions of the work at hand, picking up the wet clothes, hanging them and putting the clothes peg on them.

The sun was warm on his back. He felt her hand on his shoulder.

'Are you actually leaving?' she asked.

He shrugged. 'There's nothing left for me here.'

She turned him so that now he was facing her. Water from the clothes dripped on his sandals. 'What will I do?' she asked.

He looked away. What could he say? 'You'll have a good life,' he managed finally. 'Khurram bhai will take care of you.'

He paused and then added, 'Just don't die.'

~

The money was too small to be blackmail. That's what Navkar had said. Tara could now see that he wasn't the only one.

She had spent the last few hours searching the net for people's reactions on the Internet, and she was shocked at the number of people who believed the letter to be from an actual vigilante. There were already twenty to thirty groups dedicated to the Guardian of the People. There were dozens of fan pages. There were even conspiracy theories floating around as to who it could be. Some said it was an ex-RAW agent, some speculated that it was a policeman who had got sacked by the minister. One man from Chattisgarh even felt it was Commissioner Shinde himself.

Most of the stories and posts were amateurish. They reeked of simplistic, wishful thinking. They were far too poorly punctuated. But Tara could see that there was something real underneath. A real and desperate need! People wanted a guardian to do what they couldn't; punish the criminals and the corrupt and save innocent people since no one had the time and strength left to save themselves. Since the only ones with time to change anything were the scoundrels—the ones who cheated, who stole. The ones who didn't have to work for their time.

The politicians, the goondas, the shortcut men.

What was it Navkar had said? Something about justice?

THIRTEEN

The narrow road in front of Chauhan's bungalow was choked with traffic even in this mad, lashing rain, on a day where no sane man would set his foot outside. Where were they all going?

Chauhan shook his head, standing by his window as it got buffeted by whips and chains of water. It struck him once again how little he knew the people of his capital. He had grown up in a small town off the road to Nagpur. There was one road that bisected the town, an offshoot of the highway. There were crops sold on the shops on both sides of that road. Crops, and toys from the plastic factories. It never rained like this there, and by the gods if it ever did, people would have the good sense to huddle inside their brick houses and pray for their lives.

'Have you got the Pajero?' Chauhan asked the driver with a sigh. 'I'm not going out into that madness in anything else.'

The driver said he had. He looked unreasonably happy. His eyes danced with light and rain.

'Were you born here?' he asked the driver dourly.

The man shook his head enthusiastically and replied, 'My grandparents made their home in the shanties near the Hanging Garden. We have always been drivers in this city.'

'I can't stand this...this torture,' Chauhan grunted, gesturing outside. 'It'll go on for months now. Everything will be a mess.'

'This is when Mumbai is alive, sahib,' the driver said, smiling.

Chauhan made a sound of disgust. He had begun to accept that it was his bad time, when the stars were aligned against him. Everything was going wrong. Ever since that first damn letter. If someone would only find out who sent it...he would make sure the man's limbs and tongue were separated from his body and found swimming in a gutter.

He beckoned his servant to bring two umbrellas and got him to hold both above him as he made his way from the door to the car. The servant got drenched head to toe, and Chauhan felt some small satisfaction, some sense of revenge on fate.

The road outside was already flooded, and each vehicle sent up splashes of muddy water, so that the world was decorated by an explosion of liquid fireworks. The pavement dwellers had vanished, driven or washed away. Skyscrapers loomed silent and sullen, blurred by the wash of the shower.

Within minutes, all the windows of the Pajero were rivers, and the world outside, ghostly and shifting. Lights blinked from other cars, dim and pooled and vague. Chauhan held his rudraksha clenched in his fist and chanted whatever verses he knew. Those hadn't helped him over the last few months, but he still tried because he really didn't want to die in a car crash. Not in the middle of his term. Not when he stil didn't know who was threatening him.

As the radio blared to life he realized with a jolt that now his too was one of the cars out on the road in this mad weather.

They were soon caught in the web of lanes of South Mumbai, some with cobbled surfaces, some rising and falling, most lined by gnarled trees and narrow footpaths. The old trees with knotted roots had seen many monsoons, but some of the new ones that the municipality had planted a few years back had fallen. One of them had crashed into an electricity pole, which had careened to one side, with its snapped lines sunk in the gathering water. Chauhan wondered if someone had died from it. People died so easily in this country.

Chauhan shook his head, retreating into his thoughts. He knew in his heart that the letter was a prank. Some do-gooder, some social activist. Maybe even some policeman; they hated him nowadays.

Why did the media have to blow everything up?

But what really gnawed at him, and everyone in the party, was how the damn prankster knew so much about their dealings. It couldn't be Tiwari. He'd been their accountant for too long. But someone in his office had let it out.

He would have to talk to Tiwari today. There would have to be a shaking up.

On one of the roads, a municipality truck had braved the elements to set up a pump. Water had risen to knee level in this neighbourhood. Chauhan could see utensils floating out of a small asbestos-covered shack in one of the bastis, followed by a laughing child doing the backstroke. In fact, in all the bastis they had passed on their way, youths were out in the narrow, overflowing streets that snaked between the low buildings, laughing and dancing and pushing each other into the water. There were even some girls, their clothes sticking to their bodies as they got drenched in the downpour. God knows what would happen to them in the frenzy of the monsoon mob. Chauhan shook his head in disgust at their callousness. It was all those damn movies they made here. Everyone seemed to live in a world of their own, even inside hutments that didn't cross four feet by four.

It took an hour for them to reach the expressway that led out of Mumbai, cutting through the endless, ever-expanding spread of the metropolis. It would be three hours more to Karad, where the party was having a rally. The town was one of their strongholds; most campaigns were launched there. In light of the recent scandals, this rally was meant to show their strength to the public.

Chauhan's posture began to slump as the soothing pace and evenness of the expressway lulled him to sleep. He seemed to only get sleep in cars nowadays. The rain washed the world outside the car but in the silent warmth inside, he dreamed of guava trees and sun-soft mornings in the schoolyard of his childhood. There were no reporters there, no ministers and opposition, no threatening mysterious letters. Only a bat and ball, a horde of classmates wanting to play and the red blush the guavas took when they first realized their ripeness.

They reached Karad by noon and found that the monsoon had advanced ahead of them. The town and its muddy, half-baked main road was smashed by the storm. It wore the look of a war. The town's inhabitants cowered in their respective doorways, the shops were closed, shutters drawn. Stray pieces of debris lined the road; a broken pot, some bricks, an abandoned bicycle.

Party workers who had the responsibility of organizing the rally looked broken-hearted and were huddled beneath umbrellas, sporting drenched scowling looks.

'Who will come now, sir?' Tiwari, the accountant, and one of the chief organizers of all activities of the party, told him as he stepped out of the car. 'We will get maximum a hundred to attend. People will not come even if we paid them a thousand an hour.'

Chauhan felt the thorns of the rain sink into his face, cold and merciless. He puffed up his chest and pulled in his generous stomach to present a brave front.

'We'll make do. We're not going to cancel it now.'

Tiwari nodded and tottered off, his white pants splotched with mud. Chauhan looked around the field. A stage had been set up, covered in canvas and featuring a dais and a mike. The cover was now buffeted by the wind, straining to tear away. There was a solitary neem tree guarding the field, its unmistakable scent brought out by the rain, its emerald leaves aflutter. Chauhan took refuge under it, waiting as, one by one, a few stragglers were brought to the field. Soon the place lay dotted with red and yellow saris, white kurtas and umbrellas of all colours that were imported from China.

Once the field was about a quarter full, the audience carefully spread to give the impression of a dignified turnout for the cameras, Chauhan was called on stage. Tiwari stood beside him and the MLA for this district next to Tiwari. Chauhan tapped the mike to test it, and looking at the benign faces of his listeners and felt a strange sense of shame wash over him. There was no one here. Only party workers and a few locals they could bully out of their houses. No one was there to really support him; no one really cared about his presence.

It continued to rain heavily as he spoke. The sound system still worked, his voice booming across the field. Chauhan felt the emptiness in his chest grow with each word. He felt his throat dry up, as this meaningless, pathetic display continued. His eyes blinked in the rain. In the distance, at the back of the crowd, some of the audience members were standing up. Were they going to leave? In the middle of his speech? He looked up at the sky. Was the rain that bad?

But then he realized they weren't leaving; they were coming towards the stage. No. They were running. They were running towards the stage.

Suddenly he heard shouts of alarm. He stopped speaking and looked around. People were confused, shouting. Chauhan realized suddenly that the people running towards him had weapons. He could see the curve of a sword, axes and sticks, as the men let out a cry and sprinted towards the stage.

One of the organizers tried to get in their way, shouting at them. There was the swing of an arm in response, and a terrible, bone-crunching sound, as a wooden mallet crashed into the man's face and his head twisted backwards.

There was pandemonium now. Chauhan felt a hand tugging at him, but he stood frozen to the spot, unable to move, to tear his eyes away. He heard Tiwari's voice in his ears, but he didn't know what was said.

Party workers surrounded the dais to stop the attackers, but they were too few in number. Too few had come in this rain and none of them had weapons. Chauhan saw a man take an axe in his stomach, and a long, stream of blood spurt out with the axe head.

Tiwari was pulling him now. He turned to look at him and saw widened, fear-white eyes.

'We have to go!' Tiwari was screaming.

Chauhan felt himself agree, felt himself talk. Then

suddenly one of them jumped onto the stage. A large man, with the eyes of someone who's done this before, with a curved sword in his hand. With one motion, he gripped Tiwari's head and drew his sword across the jugular. Chauhan felt a splash of hot liquid. His eyes started burning. He was blinking, cursing. All he could see was blurred in red. He felt the strength of the man's arm grip him, and he felt his legs give way. It was the end. This is how it would all end.

But he didn't feel the cold harshness of the metal's edge. There was a voice by his ear. He realized there was a phone pressed to his ear. He struggled to understand the voice coming from the other end. It was a cold, mechanical voice, almost inhuman.

'Mr Chauhan, you can consider the penalty that was earlier mentioned now imposed,' the voice said. 'When you reach home you should check the financial statements of your party.'

'What?' Chauhan asked, confused. 'What?'

The voice repeated the message. There was no change in the tone. The message came again. It was a recorded message. The grip on his neck was easing. The man was pulling away. In a mad moment of fury, he grabbed the man, hitting, scratching, crying in fear and anger. He felt a sudden blow on his stomach, followed by a blinding pain. He fell to the ground. His body was burning in pain. He lay there, at the mercy of the rain, curled up in pain and fear.

He didn't know how long it lasted, how many minutes he lay there. When they brought him about, the field was empty. There were splotches of red here and there, rain water dyed with blood. Someone was wiping his face, cleaning the blood from it. He could see Tiwari lying dead on the ground. He could smell the coppery taste of blood.

'Who were they?' he screamed. 'Who were they?'

Nobody answered. Nobody knew. Seven of their people had been killed. None of the attackers had been caught. There was no sign of them now. Some of the locals said they'd come in vans.

Chauhan scrambled in his pocket and took out his phone. His hands were shaking. He called up the party secretary and asked him to check the main bank accounts of the party.

Half an hour later, when the Pajero was on its way back to Mumbai, the secretary called back. Their Swiss bank account had been depleted by around eight lakh seventy-five thousand Swiss francs. It was about seven crore in rupees. The records said Tiwari had withdrawn it. He had the authority.

Three and a half, and three and a half as penalty.

FOURTEEN

'Once again, we'll show you the footage of the chief minister's car pulling into the hospital followed by an ambulance, which has the body of Shashank Tiwari, an important member of the ruling party. We have learnt that he was killed with a sword. The doctors at the hospital have pronounced him dead on arrival and said that in all probability, he died almost immediately after he was struck.

The chief minister has not suffered any serious injury, but as can be seen here, his clothes are stained by Shashank Tiwari's blood, since the two were standing together when the incident happened. All in all, seven party members have been killed. None of the assailants have been caught. The police are investigating, but have so far failed to give any real response.

This is truly one of the worst incidents of violence we have seen in recent years. The entire nation is shocked at the audacity of such ruthless violence against a serving chief minister. The question on everyone's lips is, who, or which group, could have organized such an attack? Is this the beginning of political warfare, the likes of which our democracy has never seen? Or could it be that the attack is linked to the blackmail that Channel 10 first uncovered a few weeks ago? Stay tuned as our analysis continues on *Insight* on Channel 10, with Prateek Sharma.'

'Alright, cut!' said the cameraman, and Chatterjee stared at the camera for five seconds more before disconnecting the microphone from his ear.

'Is Prateek ready?' he asked.

'Almost,' said a spot boy. 'He'll be ready in two.'

Chatterjee nodded and hurried offstage. A bustle of activity took over to prepare the newsroom for the next show. Chatterjee found David waiting outside for him.

'Let's go,' the old man said. 'Malhotra wants to discuss the angle we're going to take.'

Chatterjee sighed. 'It's going to be a long day.'

Tara and Malhotra were already arguing by the time they got to the conference room.

'I'm just saying that it matches exactly!' Tara said heatedly. 'It's too much of a coincidence!'

'What matches exactly?' Chatterjee asked.

Malhotra had a pained expression. 'Tara and the coffee boy have been discussing story angles.'

'I-I'm not a coffee boy. I'm actually a reporter here,' Navkar said coldly, stirring from the corner where he stood with a tray of coffee cups.

'Junior reporter, coffee boy, all the same, kid,' David said.

'Well, he has a point here,' Tara put in. 'The letter said there will be a *penalty*, some kind of bloodletting, and it's happened.'

David frowned.

Chatterjee was not convinced, 'You really think a blackmailer could go to the extent of arranging an assault like this? There were at least ten attackers.'

'With swords!' Malhotra added in disgust. 'With goddamned swords.'

'It's some political thing,' Chatterjee muttered. 'They do that, they use swords and tridents and so on. It helps with their voters. All these riots, this danga *fasaad*, they're all for votes in the end.'

Tara rounded on him, 'You don't think the attack is connected to the letter?'

'It could be,' Chatterjee shrugged. 'I said so in the news. We can take the story there if we want.'

'Navkar was saying that maybe we were wrong and it wasn't a blackmailer. More like an activist or a disgruntled citizen,' Tara said, rushing through the words.

David and Chatterjee exchanged glances and the former looked confused.

'Who,' he asked slowly, 'is this Navkar?'

'It's me,' Navkar said with a sigh, raising his hand.

'Ah!' David said. 'Sorry, sorry. My apologies!' He grinned. 'Clearly we should know who you are, since you've impressed our super heroine.'

'So much that she's gone off her rockers,' Malhotra grunted.

David tilted his head and asked quietly, 'Why do you say that?'

'What? You agree with her vigilante story?' Malhotra glared at him. 'Does it appeal to your romantic nature?'

David looked around the room over the rim of his spectacles. His voice was grave. 'I think it is quite clear that some people, whoever they are and for whatever reason, are threatening the chief minister and the ruling party, and they have the ability to carry out their threats. It is not merely some outpouring of violence, some riot. A threat was made, and it was carried out.'

The room fell silent as the words sank in. The coldness of the declaration cut closer than the news or the footage of splattered blood. David's face was grim, his bushy stare lost in thought. 'We are upon bad times,' he said quietly.

Suddenly, the door swung open and Ambi, one of the young reporters rushed in. 'Sir, News India is running the next segment. The angle is "How did the chief minister's security fail?"'

Malhotra switched on the channel in the conference room TV. A party spokesman was explaining how they never expected such a thing, so they hadn't beefed up security. When the host asked whether they hadn't taken the letter seriously, the party spokesman looked tense.

'We have said many times over that the letter is a hoax, made by other parties to tarnish our image,' he said stiffly.

The reporter turned to the camera, 'Stay tuned. After the break we have Vishnu Mistry coming to the studio. We have heard that he has asked the CM to turn down the Z-class security that centre has offered and pledged to bring in Blackwater commandos to guard the chief minister. We'll talk to him in just a few minutes, after this break.'

'Blackwater commandos?' Malhotra mused.

'The ones in Iraq,' Chatterjee said. 'They cost a fortune.'

'Your lover boy is afraid of losing his trump card,' Malhotra smirked at Tara.

'The so-called vigilante could even be the police,' Chatterjee said, thoughtfully. 'They hate Chauhan nowadays. Maybe that's why your Vishnu is getting him private bodyguards.'

'Listen,' Malhotra said, leaning forward. 'We have to decide fast. I want the analysis slot right after Sharma's show. So tell me, what will it be?'

'Why don't we focus on the mystery itself?' Tara said. 'Why don't we just keep the focus on the question—*Who is behind the letter and the attack?*'

'Because we don't know who it is,' Chatterjee grunted.

'But why don't we try and find out!' Tara said, springing out of her seat. 'Why don't we run the story on finding out who is behind it?'

'What nonsense, Tara. We're a news channel, not bloody detectives!' Malhotra snapped.

Tara quieted at that. Chatterjee was about to speak when Navkar interrupted him.

'If there is indeed a vigilante involved, most likely he would've sent a threat to other parties too,' he said.

Everybody turned towards him. Chatterjee looked irritated. Malhotra seemed angry. 'Why is he talking again?' he said in exasperation.

'He has something important to say,' David said sharply. 'Listen to the boy.'

'Good god!' Malhotra exclaimed. 'Now we all have to listen to the coffee boy!'

David ignored him and turned to Navkar, saying, 'Go on. What do you mean?'

Tara could see Navkar's Adam's apple bobbing in sudden nervousness. He wasn't someone who liked an audience.

'Go on Sudy,' she urged.

'W-well,' Navkar started, surprised at the sudden nickname, 'Well, if it's someone, some group against corruption, he might have sent the threats to all parties. If other parties have received threats, it probably means there is some sort of a vigilante. How can there be a feud against more than one party at the same time?'

'That's perfect!' David cried out, slapping his hand against the table. 'That's it. That's what we should find out.'

'How will we do that?' Chatterjee asked. 'We don't have informers in every party. Besides, this will be top secret.'

David was smirking. He looked at the others in the room. 'What would the letter writer do now that he has shown his power? He will call again.'

Tara stared at him, and he grinned.

'We can pretend to be the Guardian!' she said, understanding. 'We can pretend we're giving a...a follow-up call.'

David glanced at the others. 'Then we see their reaction.' He stroked his beard thoughtfully. 'I think this is the first time I've been aroused in twenty years.'

Tara caught Navkar outside the conference room once the meeting was over. 'You did good! Very good!' she beamed. 'Wait, I'll introduce you to David.'

Navkar waited as she ducked back inside and dragged David Agarwal out. The old man was beaming. 'Our ratworker has found herself an assistant, eh?'

'He's not my assistant, David,' Tara said. 'He's working on a very important story himself.'

'We seem to be surrounded by important stories these days,' David grunted. 'It's making me very uneasy.'

'Navkar is working on an exposé of the underworld,' Tara continued. 'He has an informer who wants to get protection from the gangs.'

David frowned, 'Does Malhotra know?'

Tara shook her head, her voice dropping, 'I was wondering if you could…'

'If I could help tell him?' David asked and then laughed, 'You have some nerve.' He glanced at Navkar, 'It's dangerous. Your story. You know that, right?'

'Yeah I do,' Navkar said.

'Why are you doing it?' David asked, peering at him.

Navkar frowned. He tried to find the words. 'Someone died,' he said finally. 'I was involved.'

David regarded him carefully and finally said, 'I'll help, but you have to tell me whatever you learn.'

He seemed thoughtful.

'An upheaval in the gangs and chaos and violence in political circles,' he sighed, 'I have a feeling this is all connected somehow.'

FIFTEEN

The rain had let up by the afternoon. The city looked pure again, exhausted but glowing, a blushing bride woken to a new world.

Navkar sat on the bottom steps of the entrance to his apartment, looking at the people passing by. Everyone looked so busy. So borne down with the weight of routine, their hopes leased out to time, collateral for their children's dreams. That's how his own parents had been throughout their entire working life.

Navkar lit his first cigarette of the day, his morning love, and gazed out at the street, feeling a strange calm wash over him.

Yesterday's events turned in his head; the shocking attack on the chief minister, Malhotra and David and their new plan. Navkar had never even spoken to any of them till a few weeks back. Yesterday they had actually listened to him.

He remembered David's words. 'Your story will be dangerous.'

Navkar's phone buzzed to attention. He took a long puff of the cigarette before picking it. It was Salim, as expected.

'Bakrawadi Station. In an hour. Don't be late, I won't wait,' he said, sounding hollow and haunted.

Navkar felt a rush of adrenaline. He had set up the meeting last night when he got back from office, and he'd been waiting since then.

The station was extremely crowded despite it being the middle of the day. Trains from the small towns arrived at regular intervals with hordes of starry-eyed men drawn to the lure of a life in Mumbai. Navkar finally noticed Salim snaking in through the crowd. There was a packet in his hand.

'I thought you wouldn't come, hero,' Salim said lightly and handed him the packet. 'Change and then we'll talk.'

'Change?' Navkar asked. 'What is it?'

Salim grinned. 'There are toilets on the right. Go and change into these clothes or I can't take you with me.'

Once in the dirty, stinking toilet, Navkar looked at the clothes properly. They looked straight out of Salim's closet. Tight blue vest, gaudy sunglasses and a pink shirt. Navkar took a picture on his cell phone.

'Walk,' Salim said sharply when Navkar returned. He rushed through the crowd, Navkar barely managing to follow him. Out through the side gate, and down a narrow street. Salim was walking fast, Navkar could barely keep up.

'Was it really necessary to wear all this?' Navkar shouted out to him when they got to a clear street.

'There's been a lot of activity. Just follow,' Salim barked back without turning.

And so Navkar followed.

They walked a long time through the festering, humid afternoon, down long streets that got increasingly narrow and odorous. After a while, Navkar was covered in sweat, his shiny shirt plastered on his back.

'Where are we going?' he panted.

'Fakruddin basti.'

'But that's near Anand Vilas Station!' Navkar exploded, incensed. 'You could've just told me to come there!'

'Then you might not be sweating,' Salim said grimly. 'The clothes aren't enough for you to blend in.'

It took ten more minutes to reach the basti, a slow long crawl for Navkar. He was panting by the time but even in his exhaustion he could see that there was something strange about this place. The same maze of confused lanes winded about but there were no people strolling through. Only shadows. Navkar could feel eyes following him from every shack, hidden by barricades of wood or plaster. A living breathing ghost town in the middle of the most crowded city on earth. The place smelled rank and rotten. Navkar noticed that some of the kholis had locks on their door. He knew enough to know that this was uncommon in these sort of bastis.

'This place was caught in the middle when the gang war broke out last month', Salim hissed, gesturing to Navkar to hurry. 'We shouldn't stay here. The police clamped down last night. Gang members are scrambling around trying to hide their stuff. Everybody is scared. Nobody wants to talk to outsiders. If they find out you're a reporter…'

Navkar's skin shrivelled up immediately. This wasn't good. He cursed Salim under his breath but rushed behind him.

'Now you see why I need protection?' Salim said.

'Unfortunately,' Navkar said. He looked around warily. Death…that's what the place reeked of. Suddenly, he wasn't sure if he would get out of this place safely.

He should turn back, he knew that. Was this worth

risking his life? Nobody even wanted to read about gangs nowadays. He could go back to his usual stories, making up the innards of news channels, the four o'clock spots. He could keep doing that and live happily.

Salim turned the corner in front of him. Navkar found himself following. They made their way into the courtyard of an old house. It was a dilapidated place with a lemon tree and a rusted hand pump giving each other company.

'Khurram bhai gave this house to me as a reward for solving a case,' Salim said, a trace of pride in his voice. He placed his hand on the pump. 'Help me here.'

The hand pump budged slightly as they both pulled at it. Underneath was a metal box with small carvings on it. Salim thrust it under his shirt before Navkar could say anything and carried it inside.

The house had a musty smell to it, as all old houses do, and small slits for windows. Salim removed some documents and photographs from the box and handed them to Navkar.

'Here are the cases from the past month alone. Twenty-four dead; almost one each day.'

'Is there any pattern to them? People don't care how many died,' Navkar responded, immediately realizing his thoughtlessness as he noticed Salim flinch.

'Uh, I mean is there anything that stands out which I can use?' he fumbled.

'That's the problem They've mostly been random—contactors, chhokras, transporters—small guys. It's a problem for us because if you don't know why people are dying, it increases suspicion. Breaks trust. And for us, trust is important—it's everything!' Salim answered solemnly.

'When did these murders start?' Navkar asked.

'Some say two months back, some say three. But, I think it's four actually. Since March.'

'Why do you think it started then?' Navkar pressed.

'See March is end of the financial year for you people, so the gangs are usually busy collecting their money for the year. Nobody wants to start a fight then because if you are fighting, it disrupts collections. Every day you lose a few weeks' worth. There are never any murders in March,' Salim looked intently at Navkar.

'This year, there were six. Five match the profile; all gang members.'

'What about the sixth?'

'That was a strange one. Buddha Lal. He had been a small-time thief back in the eighties, nothing much. Just a few cases here and there and then he retired very early. Used to run the candy shop in his basti. Everyone loved him. Turned up dead one day. We never found the killer or any reason for his murder.'

'Could've been just a normal murder. Were there any other murders of people outside the gang?'

'That's the only one, as far as I know. But it's not even that. It was the way he was murdered which shocked us all,' Salim explained, his eyes wide. 'He had been shot very carefully to make him suffer longer, in the stomach, in his palm, everywhere. His toenails and fingernails had been ripped off. The poor old man! Nothing like the other murders.'

'So all the murders in, say, the past month have been active small-time guys?' Navkar asked, trying to piece together something.

'Not really. This month actually, there have been far less of these random murders than normal. Most of the murders have been due to the rift between Khurram bhai and Naushadji.'

He explained further, 'This was because Kayla bhabi said Naushadji raped her. See, she was Khurram bhai's girl. Naushadji said she'd come with him willingly. We told him to let it go because Naushadji was his uncle but Khurram bhai wanted revenge. It started from there—ten dead already. Bhai himself killed Naushadji and a few days later, he slit bhabi's throat as well. For losing his honour,' Salim explained patiently.

Navkar sat back with a frown. He didn't understand this world. He didn't really want to. The rain had begun again, leaking here and there through the thatched roof. The gentle pitter-patter felt soothing; it helped him keep calm. Perhaps he was just grasping for something familiar.

He told himself that since he was here, he had to find out more. He asked Salim, 'Does Kayla have a family? I want to talk to them.'

'I know them well,' Salim said quietly.

Kayla's family lived at the edge of the basti. It was an awkward squat house, smaller than the shed for the buffaloes. Navkar could smell the dried dung cakes burning, the smell masking the stench from the shed.

Salim turned to him, 'Khurram bhai might be there, so be careful.'

Navkar was taken aback, 'Why? What would he be doing here now?'

'The mother is trying to give him the other daughter, so that the family gets protection,' Salim explained. 'Don't say a word if he is there. If he finds out, I don't think he'll let me go.'

'But I thought he liked you. He gave you a house,' Navkar said, confused.

'That was a long time ago,' Salim responded ambiguously, 'Before everything else.'

The interior of the house was sparsely furnished, except a few shiny new items like a TV and a computer. Navkar guessed that these had been presents to Kayla from Khurram bhai. The younger daughter, Layla, sat quietly on a straw mat tracing the length of the floor. The mother was not too pleased to see Salim but warmed up when Navkar began to talk to her. His questions seemed to be an opportunity for her to vent and reminisce about the old days. She just wanted to talk, she didn't want to say anything. Navkar understood that. What else could she do? He looked at the girl who was looking down intently, trying to avoid their gaze. She was still a teenager, sixteen, perhaps, seventeen at the most.

A loud pounding on the door broke Navkar's thoughts. He turned to Salim, who had gone white with fear.

'Khurram saab? I'm coming,' the lady called out as Navkar's ears pricked up.

Salim hissed at him, his eyes wide, 'Shit! Shit! We shouldn't have come.'

Navkar didn't know what to do. He looked around nervously and caught the young daughter looking straight at him. Her eyes were cold, unblinking and had no emotions.

'Bhai jaan, what a surprise!' Salim said jumping to his feet with a wide fake smile, furiously tapping at Navkar's shoulder to do the same.

Navkar rose as the girl rushed to touch Khurram bhai's feet. He was an intimidating figure, with a gun tucked openly at his belt. His eyes grew menacingly large as soon as he saw Navkar.

Before Navkar could greet him, he was swept off his feet and pinned against the wall.

'Who is he? Why is he here?' Khurram growled as Navkar struggled to breathe against his large frame. The women shrieked as Salim tried to explain.

'He is a new chhokra, bhai. I was in the area so I thought I'll check on Maasiji,' he pleaded.

'Where is he from? Why are you bringing new guys here, Salim?' Khurram roared as he tightened his grip around Navkar's collar.

'Na-Nagpur. I'm sorry bhai, I was just showing him around.'

Khurram loosened his grip and brought his face close to Navkar, who by now was shaking like a leaf. Khurram was smiling now, smirking at his fear.

'Have you ever shot a gun, chhotu?' He thrust his gun into Navkar's shaking hands.

'Can you shoot this man if I ask you to?' he snarled, pointing at Salim.

Navkar stood unmoving. The women were clutching each other.

Khurram rounded on Salim. 'What use is he, huh? He's a weakling. You're a weakling too, Salim,' Khurram barked shoving Salim to the ground. 'You just talk big, but you're useless…and weak. Pathetic! You can't check up on Layla and Meera bai any more, Salim. You aren't strong enough to take care of anybody.'

Meera bai tried to stop the situation getting worse and pleaded with Khurram bhai to calm down. He ignored her, but then Layla fell to his feet crying. He stopped himself as Salim retreated to the corner.

'She doesn't like to see you angry,' Meera bai said.

'I'm leaving,' Khurram said gruffly.

Layla looked up at him and said softly, 'You came for lunch. You should have lunch before you leave.'

Lunch was sombre. Khurram hadn't let Salim or Navkar leave. Meera bai had prepared a feast. Navkar suspected the meal would have taken a month's savings. Salim and he ate silently, their heads not looking up from their respective plates. Layla was feeding Khurram bhai with her dainty fingers as Meera bai looked at them with a smile. The TV was rumbling in the background.

'How's your investigation going?' Khurram bhai asked Salim after a while. 'Any progress? Do you even do any work nowadays?'

Navkar glanced at Salim and saw his jaws tighten at the question. He sat up straighter with, 'I'm looking into Kamla bai's death. That could give some leads.'

'That madwoman?' Khurram snorted. 'You're even more useless than I'd thought. You should just leave your investigation. I can see it's not going to succeed.'

Navkar noticed Salim bite back what he was going to say. Was that a look between Layla and him?

'There's a lot going on that I don't understand,' Salim admitted.

Khurram grunted and tore at a leg of chicken with his mouth. Katrina danced on TV. 'Is there anything you understand?' Khurram asked with his mouth full.

'There's money coming in from the Middle East,' Salim said quietly. 'I found that out last week.'

Khurram lowered the chicken leg and stared at him. 'Money coming in? For whom?'

'I don't know,' Salim replied, a bit nervously. 'The hawalas I met last week said money has come in this month.'

Khurram glared at him and threw the chicken leg at his face. 'You're a piece of shit!' he roared. 'That's all you know? You don't even know who the money has gone to?'

Salim balked. 'I-I'm meeting another guy this week,' he stammered. 'A hawala who gets in money from Dubai. M-maybe he'll know more!'

Khurram bhai became quiet, though he was still glowering. He glanced at Navkar. The gun at his belt glinted dangerously in the afternoon light.

'You've served me faithfully for a long time, Salim,' Khurram bhai said finally.

'Y-yes, bhai,' Salim said, 'I have.'

'So I won't throw you out yet. I'll give your investigation another chance.'

'Thank you, Khurram bhai!' Salim said, leaving his food and almost grovelling at Khurram's feet.

'Get up! Get up!' Khurram said. He patted Salim's cheek, looking him in the eye. 'I know this businessman. He specializes in laundering Gulf money.'

'W-who?' Salim asked.

'I'll introduce you to him,' and then glancing at Navkar, said, 'Take this chhokra too. Give him some experience.'

SIXTEEN

Moonlight flooded the room on top of the tower, the soft silver sprinkling the space, and Vishnu's skin. His powerful chest rose and fell in a sweet, gentle rhythm.

It felt good to see him like this, when he was at peace.

Tara's fingers traced his splayed arm, feeling the denseness of his flesh. She had been awake for almost an hour now. In another six hours it would be morning and Channel 10 would begin the calls. It always felt unnerving, dealing with politicians. Even after so many years she could feel her body tense at the thought, her mind abuzz with fear. But why fear? What could they do to her? She was Tara Verma. She was famous. She was Vishnu Mistry's lover.

She looked at his curled-up figure. He slept like a child, on his side, as if aching for something to hug. But whenever she tried to sleep in his embrace, he excused himself. He said he didn't get sleep if somebody was too close. A child waiting for an embrace, but unable to accept one.

She wondered where he kept his gun when he was at home. Would he protect her if she actually got into trouble? Would he protect her even if it created problems for him? She'd changed the Chauhan story for him once, but what could she do now? Could she let this go? The biggest and most exciting story of her career?

Yet, if she didn't, it would hurt his plans. It might disrupt them altogether. Years of hard work that had got the judicial reform bill this far. The bill that no one thought could ever work. If she probed further and uncovered something that made Chauhan's government topple, all his work would go to waste.

Tara's fingers ran over his, intertwining them. Her eyes fell on faint white lines on the insides of his wrist, below the palm. She paused, frowning, and sat up for a better look. Suddenly she felt his grip tighten painfully, crushing her small hand. His eyes had snapped open.

She pulled her hand away. 'That hurt.'

'I'm sorry,' he said flatly, his eyes unblinking.

The moonlight fell over his face, painting him in inhuman hues, silver-grey skin and gemstone eyes, like a spirit of the dead and departed.

'You had cut yourself, more than once,' she said softly. 'I never noticed before.'

He didn't answer. She looked at him. 'You never told me.'

'It was a long time ago.' He sat up slowly.

'When?'

He smiled. 'When I was sixteen, seventeen. Long ago.'

She took his arm in her hands and held it up to the light. Her thumb caressed the scar tissue, so faint now, but still there, as it would always be.

'How did you stop?' she asked.

He let out a laugh that wasn't a laugh at all. 'I started exercising.'

His frame was accentuated by moonshadow, its strength and lines in sharp relief. 'A different way to feel pain,' she said.

'A way where pain made me stronger and not weaker.'

She let his hand drop and stood up and walked to the window, feeling the coolness of the glass under the touch of her fingers.

It was raining outside. A light drizzle, silver strings of moonlight in the dark sky. The city spread out below like a million fireflies in the night. Golden threads of lamp-lit empty roads and pinpricks of light flickering in houses and hutments. The next morning, from six onwards, there would be cars on the roads, maids in the houses, children going to school. How did it work? How did this firefly city live when it should die?

'You can't see stars in Mumbai,' Vishnu said, from the bed, 'unless you look down at the ground from a height.'

She turned and leaned back against the glass, feeling the cold tingle against her skin. He had his legs drawn up, his hands around them.

'You love this city, don't you?'

He shrugged. 'It's mine.'

'Why is this bill so important to you? There are so many bigger problems here.' Her hand ran along the surface of the glass. 'There are millions living in slums, their children growing in gutters. The whole city stinks. It stinks like shit.' She looked at him. 'Don't you see that?'

Vishnu frowned and leant back, his arms taut as they got stretched. He watched her, silhouetted in silver light against the dark night.

'Everything begins from law and order,' he said slowly. 'All civilization, the foundation of society, the peace and prosperity of our lives, it all rests on order.'

She looked straight at him. 'You just can't get over what happened to you.'

'No,' he said, sharply. 'That's not it. That was a crime. But law and order goes far deeper than preventing crime. It defines our life.' He got up and walked to the window, looking out. 'Do you know why there are slums in Mumbai?'

She thought about that. 'Because the poor come to the city in millions and the city can't give them enough. That's what everyone says.'

He shook his head. 'Slums do not exist because there are poor people. Slums exist when people who can earn a living cannot afford a place to stay.' He turned to her. 'Many decades ago, when this problem was still young, there were proposals to shift the development of the city to its eastern coast, and then to the mainland. All that was required was rezoning, a few large bridges, a few new train lines and moving the government offices to the new areas. In the mainland there would then be space for the millions coming in. The city could grow like Delhi grows now, spreading out over the land.'

She felt the words sink in. 'It never happened.'

'They couldn't implement the zoning. Bribes were given. Many people owned land in the island, including politicians and businessmen. They didn't want the offices relocated. The value of their land would then go down. They, in turn, corrupted the system. The pattern of development never got changed. They never even got till the coast to build the bridges.'

'It was built later.'

He shrugged. 'It was meaningless by then. There are a hundred proposals on how to clean up the city even today, even proposals that will give slum dwellers concrete homes, but they cannot be implemented. Anyone who would lose out can pay to maintain the status quo, even if it affects millions.'

She sighed and put her arms around him, sinking her face into his chest. His heart beat powerfully, his pulse beating through her body.

'You think this bill can stop all that?' she said, looking up at him, holding him tight. 'All this corruption, this evil, can be stopped by just reforming the courts and the police?'

He cupped her chin in his large hand. 'We have to try. If we cannot enforce the laws, this city has no hope.'

'Laws,' Tara rolled the word in her mouth.

Her eyes imagined the attack that had happened just two days back. The blood-splattered field, the menace in the letter. 'What do you think it was? The letter to Chauhan that we did the story on?'

Vishnu shrugged, 'Blackmail, some madman, some politician, the police...I don't care. It's all a gutter and to clean it up, first the rats in the gutter must pass a law that will change the cleaners.'

'How will that ever happen, Vishnu?' she said softly. 'It's impossible.'

'It can happen,' he said firmly. 'It can happen if Chauhan remains.' He gripped her shoulders and his eyes glittered madly, beautifully. 'I am this close, Tara. I have him.'

'The attack must have scared you. He could've been killed.'

His grip slackened. He took a deep breath and straightened up. 'I've given him my own security guards now. Nobody will touch him now.'

'And if the government falls?'

He stared at her, suddenly understanding. 'You have a new story...'

KARM

'It is not against Chauhan,' she said, and she could hear the plea in her voice. 'It's not about him, really.'

He said nothing but walked away from her.

Tara felt her heart ache with emptiness. She closed her eyes and saw gardens and happiness and children with mad, beautiful eyes and fates she did not deserve and would never have.

'I think if everything was different we could have loved each other,' she said quietly.

Vishnu did not reply. He left her standing there, and made his way to his garden.

SEVENTEEN

Everyone agreed that David Agarwal was the best man for the job. He had the voice for it, and he could pull off anything as long as it involved being grumpy.

The calls were conducted in a soundproof conference room. The idea would never work unless it was kept a secret. There were only six people who knew, and except for Chatterjee who had a show on and Navkar who was too junior, they were all gathered around the glass table. Tara, Malhotra, David and Sharma. There was an electric thrill in the air, a feeling of adventure. Even Sharma was smiling and Malhotra had a stupid grin plastered on his face. Only Tara was grim, the memory of Vishnu's silence heavy on her mind.

They had got the number they would be calling from scrambled by some telecom guys, so the people they called wouldn't be able to trace it back. It was surprisingly easy. They started the recording and made the first call.

It was to Kirloskar, the head of the right-wing party; a middle-aged, angry man whose father had been the founder of the party in the state. He was known for his temper, his love for Batman comics and his admiration for Kareena Kapoor. He had blocked thirty bills last year, but his party had never won an election under him. People said he owned half the factory land around Thane, so he didn't care.

He picked up the phone almost immediately. 'Hello,' his voice came through, surprisingly soft. 'Who is this?'

'Have you been following our instructions?' David asked, cool as ice, as if he'd been making threatening calls for decades. 'I hope you understand we're perfectly serious.'

'What?' the man sounded confused. 'Who is this?'

David's eyes flickered over the others. 'You saw what happened to Chauhan, didn't you? He didn't follow our instructions. He thought he couldn't be touched.'

This was it. This was the moment. There was silence at the other end. Tara could feel the cold grip of expectation crush the room.

After what seemed an eternity, the voice spoke, 'We don't want any trouble.'

Malhotra sat up, and Sharma had to hold back to stop him from making any sound. They all looked at David, leaning forward, tense. The old man grinned.

'Then why didn't you follow what we said?' The others stared at him. David shrugged and continued, 'Why did you collect so much money?'

The man's voice dropped to a whisper, 'It's the boys; the workers. They're difficult to control. They don't listen. They're young.'

Nobody knew what to say. Malhotra had a look of amazement on his face. Sharma was shaking his head in disbelief. David was frowning.

'We had said...' David paused, thinking, 'We had said forty crore was the limit. How much do you have now?'

They all waited for Kirloskar to contradict the statement, to become suspicious and demand to know who they really were. There was nothing...just a humble, quiet reply.

'I don't know. I don't want any trouble. If you want, I'll check up.'

Malhotra couldn't hold himself back any longer. His hair looked even more henna-red then usual. He ended the call and let out a howl of excitement.

'It's true! Damn it, it's all true! The whole bloody thing is true!' He was shrieking now, laughing. He jumped on David, hugging him wildly. 'Goddamn it! You're a bloody genius, you bastard!'

David's hawk eyes rested on Tara, 'You should thank her... And that boy.' He smirked. 'But first, two more calls.'

The second man they called was Nagarajan, the head of the communist-backed unions. They never won much in the municipal elections, but they were always there. The man himself was seventy-four but a stolid campaigner. He hadn't missed an election for fifty-two years.

His voice was practically shaking, 'How could we have crossed it?' he roared when asked the question. 'We haven't raised that much money in thirty years!'

The third man was Anand Kumar, the head of the backward caste party, a breakaway from Chauhan's party. He swore before every election that he would never support Chauhan's government. He had supported them thrice out of the last four.

'My answer is the same even now,' he said calmly. 'Do your worst. We'll see.'

There was a sense of the unreal after the third call was over. Malhotra was sprawled back in his seat, grinning. Sharma looked beatific, as if he'd discovered the secret of the universe. David was frowning thoughtfully, perhaps even grimly.

'How did you know it was the same threat, the same forty-crore number?' Tara asked him.

David blinked a few times and responded, 'It was a hunch. It's…it's the most logical thing to do.'

'Logical?' Tara looked confused.

David steepled his fingers, the tips scratching his beard. 'This man, this group, whoever it is, they're trying to do what the election commissions of many countries have proposed.' He looked over the rim of his spectacles, his hawk eyes glittering. 'He's trying to set a ceiling on election funds and removing the need for corruption.'

'Like auction ceilings in sports,' Sharma put in.

David jabbed a finger in his direction, 'Exactly!' He looked at Tara and Malhotra. 'You see, elections are like IPL auctions, money helps you win games. But you see, no matter how much you spend, only one team can win. Then there is pressure on the other teams to match your spending, or beat it in the next round. But still in the end, only one team wins, even with the increased spending. So it becomes a spiralling cost. Every team has to pay more and more to achieve the same result.'

'It ruins the game…' Sharma added, 'It drives everyone to bankruptcy eventually.'

David nodded. 'Which is why in some of the sports leagues, they put a ceiling on the amount that can be used to buy a team.'

The thought sunk in slowly, like a heavy, cold fog.

'And you're saying election commissions have tried this?' Tara asked eventually.

'They've proposed it,' Sharma said, 'It generally doesn't get passed.'

'Wouldn't make a damned difference even if it did,' Malhotra said harshly. 'Majority of political funding is black anyway. Laws can't put a ceiling on what is illegal to begin with.'

'You're right,' David said grimly. 'The only thing that can put a ceiling is coercion, a penalty of blood, like the letter said.'

'But then,' Tara asked thoughtfully, 'if this Guardian can actually coerce the political parties, why would they allow any black money at all?'

'You can't cut off all funding. It would put the parties in an impossible position. They would have to resist, they wouldn't have a choice.' David's face was dark now. 'We are dealing with some very practical people.'

~

'Why're you doing this?' Salim asked thoughtfully, as they left the chawl, 'For that reporter girl? Tara Verma?'

Navkar didn't look at him nor did he reply. They walked back towards the station. The air was humid and the road, slick with rain. Navkar could hear stray dogs fighting.

'C'mon, hero,' Salim prodded. 'Tell me! It's for her, right?'

'No,' Navkar shrugged. 'Not for her.'

'Then? You must have some girl right? Some old flame?'

Navkar almost laughed at that. 'Old flame? I suppose, in a way.' He kicked a stray pebble and glanced at Salim, 'What about you? You have a girl?'

Salim shook his head. 'Law of nature,' he said bitterly, 'Small men cannot have love. That's why you should be a big man.'

Navkar could hear the roar of the sea in the distance,

beyond the clamour of the station, the sudden crashing of waves. 'Why is money coming in, Salim?' he asked suddenly, 'What do you think? What's happening?'

Salim grew thoughtful, scratched his head. 'I don't know…' he said, stopping in his tracks. 'But it's something big. I can feel that. It's something so big that it's beyond my imagination. That's why I can't figure it out.'

EIGHTEEN

The alarm rang in shrill hellish titters, jolting Tara out of her uneasy sleep. She sat up with a start, disoriented, her hand clutching the sheet. She looked around slowly; the curtains and almirah and the row of bells swam into view. She was not in the tower. She was home.

She hurried to the kitchen and quickly made two cups of tea, glancing at the clock a few times while the kettle boiled. They would launch the vigilante story today. She could feel the tremors in her stomach, the fluttering of her heartbeat. It felt like being a teenager in love. The anxiety…and the rush. Tara almost laughed as she filled the cups. Her mother was already awake, sitting propped up by pillows by the time she brought the tea. She wore a calm expression and sat very still.

'How's the tea?' Tara asked casually, glancing at the clock. She had half an hour more. She felt her insides tighten.

'It's wonderful, beti. You go get dressed. You have an important story today, right?'

Tara looked at her, surprised. 'How did you know?'

'You're jittery,' her mother said smiling, 'I haven't seen you this jittery in a long time.'

She laughed adding, 'It's a crazy story. It's absolutely unbelievable.' She reached forward and affectionately pinched her mother's cheek. 'Big things are happening in this country, ma. Big things!'

Her mother didn't smile back though. Nor did she ask any more about the story. Her eyes held sadness as she reached out to touch Tara's hair.

'You look so pretty when you laugh,' she said. 'You're such a beautiful girl. I used to be so afraid, because your father was…you know…'

'Ugly?' Tara looked away. 'Ugly and crazy…what a great combination!'

'Tara!' Her mother's tone was sharp. 'He couldn't help what he was. There's no point being unkind.' Her hand cupped Tara's face. 'What is important is that you turned out so good, so beautiful. That's what I'm grateful for.'

Tara's eyebrows rose and she laughed wryly. 'Ma, I'm not good. I'm a madwoman. Running around with her head on fire.'

'You're like a princess,' her mother continued, 'You deserve to be one.'

Tara didn't want to look at her. She knew where this was going.

'You've fought with him?' her mother asked finally.

Tara groaned and got up and said brusquely, 'I have to get ready.'

'Tara, beti, listen,' her mother called out, 'Why don't you take it seriously? It's important, isn't it? To be settled and have a family, have someone to support you…'

'Like papa supported you?' Tara shot back, and immediately regretted it.

Her mother seemed unfazed though. There was a determined set to her face. 'Not everyone ends up like that, beti. It is rare. I-I was very unlucky.'

Her eyes were growing moist now and she was fighting to keep her voice steady.

'He seems like a good man. You'd be happy. You'd be a princess. You deserve it! You deserve to be happy!'

Tara sighed and came back to keep her mother's teacup aside and hug her tightly, 'I am happy. Don't worry so much. And I'll marry someone. Men fall for me all the time.'

'You'll never find anyone like him!'

'Someone who'll make me a princess?' Her voice was grim as she got up. 'I don't want to be a princess, ma,' she said as she left to change. 'I want to be a heroine.'

She was ready in twenty-five minutes, but her driver came late. She had to start working on the phone as they got stuck in the traffic. Outside her tinted windows, the squalor of the city writhed awake to another day's agony. Small children traipsed through sullied streets and dirty puddles, their hair and faces unkempt, to beg for scraps. Young men with angry eyes began their chores, their jobs collecting trash or digging ditches. Old ladies left for the train station for their job as housemaids or ayahs.

What would they say if they knew there was actually a vigilante? A self-appointed guardian of the people?

Some people would see the faces of these unknown, obscure, miserable souls and guess that they wouldn't care. They wouldn't have anything to say about a vigilante. Tara knew that wasn't true. She knew they had ears and eyes and minds. They read the news, they watched TV. They changed channels. In her business, they knew these things. They tracked them. She knew there was anger in this city.

Outside, the clouds let loose once again, and what had been a boon only days ago was now a bane; destroying shanties, filling up roads and choking traffic. The vile scent of humanity packed together to live on streets rose with the rain, ripening even while it got cleaned.

With a gust of the air conditioning, Tara suddenly realized that if she lost Vishnu she would lose the tower too and would never escape these crowded roads. She told the driver to hurry, though she knew he couldn't.

Tara couldn't shake that feeling of loss and longing as she marched into the office. There was a curious silence on the floor, a hushed formality she didn't expect on a big day like today. Usually, their office was a chaos of activity. She suddenly realized that there were armed men stationed around the floor, their presence so incongruous that it'd taken her several minutes to become aware of their presence. They stood at attention, wearing helmets with military-grade machine guns.

Ambi rushed towards her.

'He's here,' she hissed, squeezing Tara's arm. 'He's in the conference room with Malhotra. Sir has asked you to go there immediately.'

Tara frowned, looking around, 'He?' she asked.

Ambi didn't elaborate. She just raised her eyebrows. Tara walked into the conference room and saw the reason for her silence.

There he sat, upright, his large frame overwhelming the chair, his hair shimmering, his eyes unblinking. Like a god.

Malhotra got up as she arrived. 'There you are!' he exclaimed, with a mixture of anxiety and relief. 'We've been talking about you.'

Her eyes met Vishnu's as she took a seat. His face wore that stillness he sometimes had, an almost inhuman calm, as if he was carved from rock. Only his eyes showed a sign of life, though they too were cold, like glittering diamonds.

'What were you talking about?' she asked.

'I was telling him,' Malhotra said, with a stuttering laugh, 'how obstinate and troublesome you are.'

Tara smiled politely. 'And what were you telling him?' she asked Vishnu.

Vishnu didn't answer immediately. She could hear the faint hum of the air conditioner and the anxious, uneven rhythm of Malhotra's breathing.

'I said you are…' Vishnu's voice was hesitant, soft. 'You are amazing. I've known it since the first moment I met you. You are amazing.'

She heard herself taking in a deep breath.

'Why are you here?' she asked, a strange anger filling her. 'What do you want?'

'You know what I want.'

'The story has nothing to do with Chauhan!' she said, her voice rising despite her effort.

'I don't care about Chauhan.' He leant forward and said, 'I care about the one chance that we have to save the fabric of our society.'

'How will this story affect that?' she asked irritably. 'This vigilante is threatening all the political parties, not just Chauhan's. How does this story hurt him?'

Vishnu's calm demeanour finally cracked. His voice became louder, his eyes sparkling with anger. 'This story is about someone trying to stop corruption by unearthing illegal deals. Can you imagine what the public's reaction will be if you play up the corruption angle? It will make the government look absolutely criminal. It will make them look pathetic. It will destroy them!'

Tara grit her teeth, her mind felt numb. She stared at him. 'Maybe they should be destroyed.'

Vishnu held her gaze. She could see him calming himself, gaining control over his emotions. 'You destroy one ruler and another takes his place,' he said quietly. 'We need to strengthen the rules of the game itself…' he paused, 'No minister will ever want that. But I've got this one hooked. I need him alive and kicking.'

She didn't know how to answer that. He believed what he was saying. She had seen it on his face and in his eyes many times. Vishnu had the eyes of a crusader. She knew he would jump headlong into fire and brimstone for his bill. He had worked on it for years.

Tara could sense Malhotra's eyes on her. She felt a flush rising up her neck to her face. She knew that Malhotra didn't believe in anything. There was nothing beneath that henna-dyed hair but greed.

'This is the biggest story we've seen in our careers, Rajesh,' she said turning to him. 'This is the best we've done. How can we let it go? What's the point in turning up every day in this stupid office and wearing this stupid make-up if we let stories like this go?'

Malhotra didn't answer.

'This will be the most incredible story on air for years to come,' Tara pressed. 'We'll be the biggest name in news, Rajesh.'

Malhotra was frowning now. That had got him thinking, the greedy bastard that he was. She could see his little eyeballs concentrating as his greasy mind turned.

Vishnu's voice cut the silence like a sword, 'Fifty crore. I'll sign the cheque right now, in front of you. To your personal account.'

Tara could see Malhotra's eyes widening, the slow, amazed turn of his head. She could feel the weight of power smash into her, suffocate her.

'You can't do that!' she cried out, even as Malhotra stood up in slow bewilderment. 'You can't do that!' Her palms slammed on the table, and jolts of pain shot through her. She stood up, shaking with fury and blind rage.

Before she knew it, there were others in the room; armed guards with their guns, their stance menacing. They looked at Vishnu for orders. He shook his head. One by one, they withdrew and shut the door behind them softly.

'I'll take the story elsewhere,' she found herself saying. 'I'll get David to come with me. Any channel will take us. We'll have it out by tomorrow.' Her hands were clenched and she spitted fury with every word. 'We'll give it out for free! We'll put it on the net! It's not difficult.'

'Yeah?' Malhotra growled, rounding on her. 'Go do it! We'll see what you can do! You're fired. You understand? Go! Do your worst! Who do you think you are?'

Tara shook her head. Her head felt like it was about to burst.

She felt like laughing. 'You think I won't? Don't you see, that'll just make it better for me. That'll really make me a star!'

Malhotra's mouth wouldn't close. He was staring like a gutted pig. He wanted to scream out, she knew that. He wanted to abuse her and her lineage and threaten to wipe them out. That's what men always did. She could see the uncertainty in his eyes as Vishnu patted his shoulder.

'She's got you,' Vishnu said calmly. 'She's got us both.'

Malhotra blinked, confused. He looked from Vishnu to

Tara. 'You don't care?' he asked her, 'You really don't care? It's fifty crore! Look, I'll give you half the money! I'll give it to you!'

They were both laughing now, Vishnu and her, laughing at the thought of Malhotra paying her off with that money. Didn't he know? Didn't he know what she was losing? Her sides hurt, her whole body shook from the incredulity of it all. She could feel tears spill out her eyes, and she didn't know whether they were born of laughter or sorrow. The room was spinning, and then Vishnu came and hugged her tight.

'You're ruining everything for me,' he said as he held her. 'You know that?'

'I know, I know! I'm sorry, I'm so sorry!' she whispered, her voice hoarse. 'I have to do this. I'm sorry. I have to do this, or nothing will mean anything.'

Vishnu pulled away, sober now, though his eyes were still warm and they wouldn't let her go. 'Maybe someday after all this, things will be different,' he said gently.

She could feel herself emptying away, melting into an ache that went deep into flesh and bone, that would never fade. 'I hope so,' she said, her voice small, like a child's. 'I really hope so.'

'Sorry for the inconvenience,' Vishnu said to Malhotra with a shrug. 'Be nice.'

Within the next hour, the story was launched, the bulletin about a strange vigilante who was doing what no one had ever thought possible.

Tara blinked more than she should have when presenting it. She had to steel herself, fight with every word, fight to not break down. She froze her face into excitement, she willed her tears dry. She smiled.

Someone had struck fear into the rotten, maggot-eaten hearts of the rulers of this country. Someone had made puppets of them. Someone had killed to do so.

It had to be told.

NINETEEN

The meeting with Khurram's businessman contact was scheduled at five in the morning. Navkar had left a note for his parents so they wouldn't be worried. He looked up at the red night sky and sighed. He didn't want to go back to the basti again, to those ghostly eerie streets, especially not at this hour. Salim had been grumbling continuously. Navkar wondered if he was scared too. He rummaged through his pockets for a cigarette and realized that he didn't have one. He needed one now. His thoughts were broken by Salim frantically beckoning him to stop walking.

'This is the place, the old municipality building. It looks different in the night.'

It was a brooding socialist-era construction, stoic and menacing in the darkness. Salim approached it tentatively, wondering if it would collapse the minute he touched it.

'I don't like abandoned buildings,' he muttered.

Navkar didn't know anybody who did. This wasn't going to be a good morning. He needed nicotine.

'Do you have a beedi?' he asked Salim. Anything would do.

Salim turned around surprised, 'Really? I thought your type don't smoke beedis.'

'My type isn't out at five in the morning sneaking into a deserted old building,' Navkar said dryly.

Early mornings were also colder since the monsoon had started.

Salim laughed as he surrendered his packet of beedis. They were small, delicate and tasted heavenly.

The door gave a loud creak as they entered the building. Rats squeaked about, unhappy at the intrusion. There was another door on the right, opening out into a larger room. It looked like it had been the office canteen. Tall windows framed the length of the building, the glasses dirt-caked and cracked and in some cases, missing. A cold monsoon morning wind gushed in through the cracks and shards and whistled through the long room.

Salim walked about the room aimlessly, fingertips tracing the half-rusted, long metal tables and broken chairs. Navkar sat at the edge of a table and felt his uneasiness deepen. The cold crept up his spine, slithered into his brain and gripped his heart.

Navkar's thoughts wandered once more to the look on Khurram's face as he'd gripped his throat. Navkar could see it clearly right now. The eyes—bloated with alcohol, with cruelty, with what? What had he seen there? There was stress, undoubtedly. The man had been stressed. There had been exhaustion in his eyes. There had been suspicion. Fear perhaps? Why? What was he afraid of?

Salim was looking at his watch. It was 5.30 already. Navkar noticed the end of the beedi light up like a firefly.

There was a soft sound outside, a light crunch of grass underfoot, too quiet to be from a normal gait.

'Duck!' Salim shouted immediately, throwing his beedi aside.

Navkar felt his own body react instinctively to the word, almost as if he had been expecting it all along. He threw himself down. He could see the end of the beedi cartwheel in the air, a ring of quiet fire, before it hit the ground. At that moment the world exploded in sound and heat as machine guns were let loose from outside.

There was no time to think, to feel—just a terrible, overpowering panic as Navkar curled up on the ground, head touching his knees, and closed his ears to block the mind-numbing noise. Above him, glass crashed and metal sparked on metal as the bullets hit the tables and chairs surrounding them. He could see that Salim had overturned a metal table behind himself. He slid over now, dragging it like a shield behind him even as bullets ricocheted against it.

The noise stopped and Navkar heard Salim's voice shrill over the din of the silence. He couldn't make out the words. Plaster was crumbling from the ceiling. Salim was pointing upwards.

'They can't control the recoil,' Navkar finally understood him saying, 'They aren't used to machine guns.'

'M-machine guns,' Navkar repeated, 'Wh-what's happening?'

Salim didn't answer. His eyes were glinting wildly, his face shiny with fear. He took out the crude pistol tucked in his belt and fired it in the direction of the assailants. Navkar felt as if the sound slapped him in the face. Salim fired again, then lay back on the ground.

'They will probably be cautious now,' Salim said. 'They'll try to cut off the exits and storm us. Unless of course, we move.'

Navkar's eyes darted around rapidly. The words sank in

slowly, cold and dreadful. They would encircle them and then kill them carefully. That's what Salim meant. There were people out there with machine guns, waiting to kill them. Even if they tried to run to the exit, the guns would fire.

'Will they be able to hit us if we run fast and carry the table as a shield?' Navkar asked desperately. '

Salim glanced at the entrance. It was at the opposite end of the hall, more than fifty feet away.

He shook his head. 'Impossible.'

Looking around, he noticed a cement staircase that hugged their end of the wall, just about a feet away, leading to the upper storeys.

'This way,' Salim pointed, 'You have to match my speed.'

Salim crouched, ready to run.

Navkar reached out and gripped his arm, 'Ever been in one? A gun fight?'

Salim frowned and said, 'Never with machine guns.'

With one quick motion, he raised the snout of his pistol above the table and shot at the windows near the entrance. Immediately, machine-gun fire sprayed that area. Salim picked up the table, kicked Navkar, indicating that he move urgently, and they ran.

Navkar could feel his brain throbbing, drumming against his skull as if it wanted to burst out. He couldn't breathe. His legs were moving as fast as they could. His eyes were focused on the stair, the first, the second… He didn't turn, didn't think, he knew he just had to run, run till the bend in the staircase. The sound of gunfire grew, echoing through the dilapidated building, which seemed to tremble. Were the shooters closing in on them?

He suddenly felt Salim's hand grab his collar and push him, and they both fell forward on the landing as bullets crashed into the table and the cement banister.

They scrambled up the stairs on all fours, hiding behind the banister. The guns had stopped. They rounded onto the first floor and locked themselves inside a room. Salim was laughing.

'Can't even find good killers in this country,' he said, laughing hysterically. 'The government should have better training schools!'

Navkar stared at him, sinking to his knees, leaning back, breath coming in gasps. 'What happens now?'

'They'll come into the building and climb upstairs, shoot the door down and kill us.' Salim looked at him thoughtfully. 'Maybe I should just shoot you and leave you to them. That'll slow them down.'

Navkar's eyes widened.

Salim grinned. 'Alright, let's go upstairs. You keep behind me, since they can only shoot us from behind.' He cocked his gun and said, 'I'm not joking.'

They stumbled out into the expanse of the terrace as the first blush of dawn appeared as a red line on the horizon. The pale coldness of the morning lay calm and still. Navkar could hear his heart thump so loudly that it seemed to drum through the silence of the world.

'Who are they? What's happening?' Navkar asked.

'I don't know,' Salim said. He had made his way to the side of the terrace and was now running along the edge. Suddenly Navkar heard him shoot and give a whoop of joy. He then sprinted back.

'I got one of them in the leg as he was entering. I think

there are two guys.' He motioned Navkar to rise. 'We have to run before the other guy comes up.'

'C-can't we just wait for him, if there's only one?'

'I have only two bullets left. If you want, I'll give you the gun, and you can wait for him,' Salim responded sarcastically.

'I'll run with you.'

'Behind me, not with me.'

Salim ran to the eastern side of the terrace where a tall, dirty-leafed tree grew near the building.

'Follow me,' Salim said and taking a few steps back, ran and jumped, his hands grabbing hold of a branch, his body slamming into the tree, but then holding on. He dropped to another branch and scrambled down.

Navkar took a deep breath; staring in disbelief. He was two floors up from the ground. He tried to judge the distance to the tree. Just a few feet. But he would have to jump and catch hold of the branch. What if he couldn't? What if he slipped? When was the last time he'd climbed a tree?

Suddenly, gunfire rent the air, and Navkar whipped around in alarm as bullets crashed through the door. He felt fear punch his heart. There was nothing to do but run. Run or die. He made himself take one step, then another, then another, towards the door of the terrace. Just as the door began to open, he turned and ran towards the edge. He ran, two steps…three…and he lunged. He felt the tree trunk crash against him, impossibly hard. Pain shot through him as his fingers struggled to hold on and failed, and he was falling and gunfire was shredding the tree above him.

He felt a branch slam into his back, tumbled over and crashed onto the ground, face down. He felt his ribs take the impact of the fall; they hurt so badly that he was sure that some were broken, the pain so piercing he just knew his lungs had been punctured.

He then felt hands pulling him up and as the world blurred in front of his eyes, he ran, ran into the narrow slush-and trash-covered lanes of the basti that started right beside the municipal building. He felt an unbearable stench flood his senses and saw dark, empty eyes staring at him from doorways and windows. There was a large queue in front of the public toilet and Salim fired a shot in the air, causing them to break out into a panic.

Navkar felt the world solidify now. He stopped for a second, amid the swirl of the panicking crowd. Salim's face appeared before his, and he felt hands gripping his shoulders and shaking him. 'Let's go!' Salim was saying. 'I only have one bullet left. Let's go!'

The streets had become a mass of people, all trying to avoid them, pressing up against walls and doors as if trying to sink into the cement or asbestos as they passed. Asbestos, thought Navkar suddenly; that's what Mumbai actually was. A city of asbestos and tarpaulin.

He could hear sounds from behind them, shouts and cries. Someone was telling people to move. There were sounds of running feet. The man with the gun was still chasing them. All Navkar knew was that he had to keep running, keep putting one foot in front of the other. He could feel each step with a jolt of pain up his heel and legs, and his lungs seemed to burst with each second. But he had to keep running. The man was coming for them, and the moment he saw them, the machine gun would go off. He wouldn't care if there was collateral damage.

Faint words reached his ears. He shook his head, confused

with exhaustion. 'Wallet,' Salim was saying. 'Give me your wallet!'

Navkar fumbled into the pocket of his jeans and took out the faded fake Gucci that he carried. Salim stopped for a minute and Navkar sank to his haunches watching him. He could see that Salim was tired too. He was struggling to stay on his feet.

Salim took out all the money Navkar was carrying, about two thousand, held it out and approached a thin youth with dark, liquid eyes who hadn't run when he saw them.

'I'll give you ten thousand, if we live,' Salim said, between desperate breaths. 'Tell the man we went left.'

'Why should I believe you?' the youth asked.

Salim smiled, 'Allah will never forgive me if I don't repay you.'

The youth took the money. | 143 |

'Make him go left,' Salim repeated, as they staggered down the right-hand street and slipped under the tarpaulin of a shed that was unoccupied at this hour of the morning.

The sun had risen above the horizon now. The tarpaulin roof glowed bright blue, like a dream of sapphire. Glorious golden sunlight flooded through the streets and the dust-dyed windows of the shack. Navkar tried to move his calves to get his blood flowing, but Salim held him firmly, gesturing him to stay still. They both lay there, not moving, not breathing for what felt like ages. Navkar could hear his heart beating, it was too loud. He hummed an old Kishore Kumar melody in his head to calm down. *Main hoon jhum jhum jhum jhum Jhumroo.* The street outside echoed with the sound of footsteps and he felt Salim suck in his breath. The feet shuffled past, too casual to be the shooter. Navkar felt his breath return slowly. The minutes ticked by, endlessly. No one disturbed them. The man was gone, chasing shadows in the sunlight. Navkar could feel every heartbeat of his, every jolt of pain in his body, more vividly than he ever had. He looked at his hands and imagined the rush of blood coursing through his veins, the stretch and pull of his muscles, the widening of his lungs.

'So that's what a gun sounds like,' he heard himself say. 'I'd always wondered.'

'This is what you reporters dream of, eh?' Salim said, sitting next to him. 'Adventures like this…'

Navkar felt a strange sensation rise in his throat and it rose and rose and spilled out as a laugh. 'No,' he shook his head, laughing, 'No, not really.'

'I thought that's why you middle-class types took this job? To brighten up your ghisa-hua lives.'

Navkar couldn't remember, at that point, why he'd taken the job, or if it'd ever been a choice. He couldn't remember anything really, nothing before the last hour. He peeped out from the tarpaulin cover and then looked at Salim.

'We are safe now, right?'

Salim nodded, 'Yeah, I think he would've given up by now. The sun is out. I think we're safe.'

Salim scratched his stubble thoughtfully. The strange machines and tools in the shack looked awkward in the golden glow of the morning and together with the swirling motes of dust, created a surreal atmosphere.

'Khurram bhai tried to kill me,' he mused aloud.

TWENTY

Chauhan hurried through the dank corridors of the Mantralaya towards a small wood-panelled room nestled deep in the heart of the building, where the all-party meetings usually took place.

There was a guard outside with a trimmed moustache sporting a baton and a machine gun. He checked all entrants for any cameras or microphones they might be carrying. The room itself was similarly checked every day. Whatever else the parties might have learnt, over the last year they had learnt this lesson. How else did this vigilante know so much?

Kirloskar and Anand Kumar were already there. Nagarajan was late as always, true to his communist roots, and had to be called thrice before he finally arrived.

They were each served watery, lukewarm tea.

'Was it the phone call?' Nagarajan asked after he took his seat, sipping his tea and scowling with distaste. 'That was the sting?'

The others stared at him. 'You haven't seen the news programme yet?' Chauhan asked.

Nagarajan shrugged. 'I don't have a TV in my office.'

'After all, in Lenin's time nobody did!' Chauhan commented dryly. He swivelled in his chair, 'Those sons of bitches screwed us, Nagarajan. Well, they screwed you. I was already screwed.'

'We should teach them a lesson,' Kirloskar said sombrely, adjusting his glasses. 'A sting operation here and there against some minister is one thing. But to do this to all of us is a bad precedent.'

'You have the foot soldiers, you do it,' Anand Kumar said, acidly, glaring at Kirloskar. They had never shared a good rapport.

'Don't play coy,' Kirloskar snapped. 'We all have the soldiers. All of us here. We can smash that damn channel and teach them how to respect people. Break some limbs. That old man. He was the one who called. And the bitch who thinks she's some big shot.'

Suddenly the door swung open and Nagarajan jumped. The others stared at the six-foot frame of the newest entrant. It was a secret meeting; they weren't expecting anyone else.

'Vishnu?' Chauhan stood up confused, and asked, 'What are you doing here?'

The man's face was grim and his eyes cold when he answered, 'I've come to see you, Chauhanji. Your peons told me you were here.'

'But nobody is allowed in here!' Nagarajan growled. 'Get him out of here, Chauhan! What are you doing?'

'I-I-I…' Chauhan stammered. 'Listen Vishnu, I'll be with you in a few minutes. Just wait in my office. I'll tell Deshpande to get you some tea or coffee.'

Vishnu was looking past him, his eyes focused on Kirloskar. 'I think now I must stay.'

He nearly shouldered past Chauhan and took a seat opposite Kirloskar, 'I had come to talk to you about the vigilante story, anyway. Perhaps I can help here.'

'I don't think you can,' Chauhan said, his voice reflecting panic.

'Why don't you try me out? Tell me,' Vishnu said quietly, meaningfully, 'What were you talking about?'

Kirloskar stared at him for a few moments. Vishnu held his gaze almost casually, but there was no mistaking the challenge. Kirloskar knew the meaning of his words. He'd read Page 3. He knew about Vishnu's relationships. He leant forward and, with an edge in his voice, said, 'We were saying we are going to break the bones of that bitch and the old man. Can you help us in that?'

Vishnu smiled. 'Of course I can help you...' he said pleasantly. 'I even have a gun.' He brought out the Beretta he usually slung in his belt and deposited it on the table, its barrel facing Kirloskar.

Vishnu could hear their shock; the sudden widening of their eyes, the sharp intake of breath. It made his smile even friendlier.

'How did you get a gun in?' Kumar asked in disbelief.

Vishnu shrugged and responded casually, 'I never leave my gun behind. Chauhanji knows that.'

They all stared at Chauhan.

'How could you allow this?' Kumar demanded.

'Your minister keeps a Kalashnikov in his office!' Chauhan snapped.

Kirloskar had stopped listening to them. His eyes didn't leave Vishnu as he stood up. He readjusted his glasses and his voice was dangerously soft when he asked, 'Are you trying to threaten me?'

'Nobody hurts her. It's as simple as that. Channel 10 is just doing its job,' Vishnu said, looking up. 'If the government and the police did the same, you wouldn't be in this situation. I want you to concentrate on a way out, not on trivialities.'

'Now you're ordering me?' Kirloskar's almost roared, 'You think you can order me? I'll cut off your tongue and feed it to you, you son of a dog! Who do you think you are? I'll tear you apart!'

Vishnu didn't answer. His fingers strayed to the gun and he flipped it from hand to hand. He leant back in the chair and waited. There was soon silence in the room.

'You know, Chauhanji and I started on much the same note,' said Vishnu finally.

Vishnu's eyes swept around the room and then came back to Kirloskar. 'Look, I think all of you harbour the same misconception when you first meet me. You see, the reason people like you can usually threaten people like me is because you generally don't mind resorting to violence. You're used to it. You've understood that it's a part of life. And generally, people like me have not.' Vishnu smiled, almost wistfully. 'But you see…I have. I understood that when I was eleven. Do you know what I'm talking about?'

Nobody answered, but they all knew. Everyone in the country knew his story.

'You see how that changes things?' Vishnu asked evenly. 'Because I have more money than all of you put together, and to be perfectly frank, probably more brains as well. So whatever you can do, I can do better.'

He regarded the gun carefully before adding, 'I can also shoot better than anybody you have ever met, including anybody you could possibly hire.'

Kirloskar looked frozen; his eyes stayed on the gun. It was apparent that he didn't know how to react to this.

Chauhan came and patted him on the shoulder and made him sit down.

'What do you want, Mistryji?' Kumar asked cautiously.

Vishnu turned towards him. 'Let's just say that if nothing is done about this vigilante, and about this story, we all lose. I'm here to help.'

Chauhan cleared his throat and then got back to the head of the table. 'We have made some progress.'

He took out his cell phone, and showed everybody a picture, adding, 'One of the local guys took this. This is the man who killed Tiwari.'

It was a blurred, grainy picture of a tall, bulky man getting into a van. The quality of the photo was so bad his features could barely be made out.

'This is nothing,' Kumar said, tossing the phone back.

'The aam aadmi needs better cell phones,' Nagarajan's tone was sombre as he took out a notepad and carefully jotted the line down.

Kirloskar handed the phone to Vishnu and turned to Chauhan, 'Send me the picture. I'll spread it among my boys.'

'I'll send it to all of you,' Chauhan said. 'But we have been searching already. It seemed like he knew what he was doing, so we thought we would ask around for professional killers fitting this description.'

'No luck?' Kirloskar asked.

Chauhan shook his head. 'Everyone has gone underground. Nobody's talking.'

He glanced at Mistry and asked, 'Have you had any luck?'

'I have no connections among those people, Chauhanji,' Vishnu said dryly before adding, 'But I've spoken to the PM's secretary. He will not be giving you a call about your resignation yet.'

Chauhan stiffened and took a deep breath. Nagarajan was not so agreeable.

'How dare you put pressure on the PM?' he started. 'This government deserves to fall! They have been completely discredited. They are being controlled by some blackmailer!'

'So are you,' Vishnu pointed out.

'I am not part of the government!' Nagarajan said stoutly. He looked around to the other opposition members for support but found none.

'This government deserves to fall,' he repeated.

'Nagarajan, none of us wants to contest elections with this on our heads,' Kumar said dourly. 'Some of us actually have a chance to win.'

'You know,' Vishnu said thoughtfully, 'The presence of this Guardian will actually help all of you in the long run. It'll reduce the pressure.'

Kumar responded, 'Reduce the pressure? We have to answer questions about this from the voters. People will laugh at us.'

'Well, right now, yes. Elections right now will be humiliating,' Vishnu said. 'But over time, people will forget. But if somebody manages to actually implement a limit on funds, it'll reduce the pressure on you to raise money. I've seen how it affects you. The pressure eats into your heart. None of you can get a good night's sleep.'

'Mistryji, please be kind enough to let our sleep remain our business,' Kumar said harshly and the room fell into a silence, albeit an unsettled one. There was bleakness on the faces of the gathered, but their minds were scurrying for answers. Kumar looked especially reflective despite his words.

Kirloskar was still looking at the picture. 'I'm sure we can find this man. I've seen him somewhere.'

Suddenly Chauhan's phone rang. He picked it up and his manner got increasingly excited as he listened.

Finally disconnecting the call, he told the others, 'They've traced a call to Karad...from Mumbai; the same morning. They say it was from some guys in the Mumbai underworld.'

TWENTY-ONE

It was a seagull. She was sure of that. When her father had first got transferred to Mumbai, their living quarters had been by the sea. Sometimes, seagulls would come circling, swooping in on the garbage cans of Bengali professors in the colony.

Tara now remembered that she would spend hours just sitting by the sea, her small legs dangling over the breakers. She would feel the salty, comforting breeze wash over her, watch the birds and the skies and the sea and be reassured by the smallness of her existence. All her troubles were nothing compared to that of the sea.

She'd stopped this activity after her father's death. There just hadn't been much time for idleness. Not much time for oceans and smallness.

Around her, the rooftop canteen of the office slowly filled up as people came out for their breakfast. The increasing noise made the bird flutter away. She watched it go, a white fleck against the grey skies as the city closed in on her again. How had it come so far inland? A lost bird in a lost world...

The sky looked silvery white; a moment of respite from the rains with sunlight melting over the firmament. She leant against the railing, silent, and surrounded by her little bubble of silence. Nobody spoke much to her nowadays. With the vigilante story, she had become the most celebrated outcast in the organization.

She felt a little surprised then when she smelt tobacco next to her, though she wasn't surprised to find it was David. The old man leant in next to her, his cigarette smoke streaming out into the city.

'Nice scenery,' he commented, when she looked at him.

'I especially like that mouldy grey building over there,' he said, pointing at a crumbling edifice opposite their office. 'I can see why you are standing here.'

She laughed at that, adding, 'There was a seagull.'

David arched his eyebrows. 'You should buy a boat like I have. Out there you'll see more seagulls than pavement dwellers in here.'

Tara didn't reply.

David glanced at her and said slowly, as if choosing the right words, 'Though I have heard that your boat-buying days might be over.'

There was a glint in his eyes, but the smile on his face was more concerned than amused.

'It's his loss,' Tara said stiffly.

The snort he gave now was one of amusement, 'Let's be realistic here, heroine. The loss is all yours. You have to be old and have a moustache before you can buy a boat now.'

Tara's eyes flashed, 'He's pretty damaged too, you know. He's not as perfect as he seems.'

David took a long, slow, thoughtful puff. 'Yeah,' he said. 'Yeah, I know. I think that's why you love him. That's why he loves you.' He turned to face her and said, 'I think, in the end, he won't let you go.'

'I couldn't care less.'

David chuckled and shook his head. 'Listen, I wanted to tell you, that…' He paused, and then awkwardly patted her shoulder saying, 'You did good. I wanted to tell you that I'm proud of you.'

Tara stiffened and turned away. It suddenly occurred to her that she couldn't remember when she'd last heard those words. She glanced at him. Did he know that? Had he guessed?

She looked at the rest of the people in the canteen. Each table had a small cluster, a group of chattering people. In India, nobody ate alone. Not unless they were absolutely hated.

David stood beside her, following her gaze and said gently, 'You're thinking bitter thoughts.'

She could feel her lips trembling and her vision getting blurred. Tara took a deep breath. She wouldn't break down now—not in the canteen.

'It doesn't matter what they think,' David said, gruffly, 'Because you see, they aren't two hundred years old like I am. They haven't seen that much.' He glanced at her. 'Just keep being brave, like you have been so far. I have a feeling that terrible things are coming.'

~

The clinic was even worse than Navkar had imagined. It lay in a neighbourhood of buildings eaten away by monsoons, lying bare of paint. Their only decorations were tattoos of moisture streaking down their facades. There were a few families living on the pavement, under broad trees that sprouted out of the road and sometimes even on the walls of buildings. The clinic itself was a crude construction of naked bricks added on to the back of a building, right next to a covered well that lay in disrepair.

The place reminded Navkar of the old line about Mumbai being three cities and three hundred villages. He supported Salim as they walked past the well on the garden path made of moss and gravel and checked the name on the door for confirmation.

Pritam Chawla, it said.

They stepped inside the small space meant to be the waiting area. There were three plastic chairs and some *Stardust* magazines lying around. His eyes skimmed around to notice the paint peeling off the walls. A large woman seated behind a plastic table eyed them suspiciously.

'We're here to meet Chawla,' Navkar told her.

'Doctor Chawla,' she corrected him coldly.

Navkar remembered the gaunt, weather-beaten face of the man. His eyes skimmed around the camel-coloured peeling paint of the clinic. 'Yes. Doctor Chawla,' Navkar repeated with due deference. Each is a king in his own domain.

The lady glanced at Salim. 'You're both bleeding,' she said, unhappily.

'That's why we're here,' Navkar replied, irritated now.

His arms were gashed from the impact with the tree but otherwise, he felt fine. Salim had realized afterwards that a shard of glass had entered his side. He now sat with a spreading red stain on his shirt.

Just then Chawla came out of his room.

'What have you been up to?' he asked with a slight frown.

Navkar gave a dry chuckle and responded, 'Investigating those murders you wanted me to cover.'

Chawla's eyebrows rose to almost touch his receding hairline.

Over the next half hour, they bore the sweltering heat of Chawla's small office while he patched them up. Navkar recounted the events that had happened. Chawla got increasingly excited as the story progressed, his eyes glittering as he looked at Salim with a child's wonder. For the first time in his life, Navkar saw Chawla smile, though the maniacal grin that the man sported now was worrying in itself.

The shard hadn't gone too deep inside Salim's body so he was safe, but Chawla still had to pull it out with a hideous-looking implement and then stitch up the wound. Salim had gone very quiet, though the local anaesthesia removed any pain. He just lay back with dull eyes. Navkar sat on one of the plastic chairs, feeling adrenaline course through him even now. He could feel his blood pumping through his veins. He felt restless and angry.

'So casually…' Navkar said suddenly, his teeth gritted. He flinched as he looked at his grazed knuckles and fingers added, 'He took out a gun so casually, just like that, with no fear.'

'That's how these people are,' Chawla said, with a tinge of glee, as he stitched Salim up. 'Besides, what would he be afraid of?'

'I don't know. The police perhaps? He took out a machine gun in the middle of the city; in the middle of Mumbai—not just some small town somewhere.'

Chawla glanced at him. 'You've seen our police. If your dead body was found in that building, do you think they would ever be able to collect clues, investigate and find out who killed you, then trace him and arrest him?'

Navkar said nothing. His hands clenched into fists, unclenched, then clenched again.

Chawla continued, 'In a city like Mumbai, with thirty million people, half of them living illegally with no address?'

He got up and stretched, having finished the stitches, 'The only judgement these men need to fear is the judgement of God.'

Navkar looked up at him. 'It wasn't always like this, was it? What happened to this place?'

Chawla responded, 'Everything that should have happened was stopped. Look at this police reform proposal. Even the great Vishnu Rustomjee Mistry can't get it passed, despite all his efforts.'

Vishnu's name felt like a needle in Navkar's heart. He frowned as he suddenly thought of Tara. He wondered what she was doing now and how she would have reacted if he had been gunned down today. He wondered when she would have even got to know of it. Would she have cared?

He sucked in a deep breath and took out his phone, then kept it back in his pocket restlessly.

Navkar then noticed that Salim was sitting up now and staring into space, as if the world was invisible to him.

'You still can't believe he tried to kill you, huh?' Navkar asked him. 'Your Khurram bhai?'

Salim was quiet for a moment or two, then said finally, 'It's not that. Why did he want to kill me?'

His eyes were large in the dingy darkness of the room as he looked intently at Navkar. There was a sheen of sweat covering him. 'Why did he want to kill me?'

Navkar didn't understand. 'He'd threatened you in front of me, right? Maybe he just doesn't have any use for you now. Or maybe he realized that you're spilling the story to a reporter.'

Salim gave a ghostly smile, as if he knew some inside joke. 'It can't be that, you see. If he knew that he would've let everyone know what I'd done—everyone in the gang. He would want to kill me publicly in our basti, make an example of me. He wouldn't set me up in a remote part of the city.'

'He didn't want anyone to know he wanted you dead!' Chawla suddenly jumped in, his voice high-pitched with excitement. 'This is so great! This is the best day of my life!' he chirped, smiling like a child.

Salim stared at Chawla in disbelief, till his troubled expression sobered the latter down.

'It has something to do with my investigations. It has to be,' Salim said and sighed deeply.

Navkar could see he was struggling to utter the words.

'He's betrayed the gang,' Salim said finally. 'He's done some deal.'

'Deal? You mean…with the police?' Navkar asked.

Salim got off the bed, wincing with pain. He gingerly touched the bandages. The wound was no longer bleeding but he was clearly in a lot of pain.

'It won't be the police,' he said thoughtfully and added, 'If it was, then Khurram bhai would've asked them to have me killed in an encounter. That's easy for the police, because we always hesitate shooting at them. We always try to run. They always stop us in an encounter if we're messing up some plan. Khurram bhai wouldn't have got some amateurs to do the job.'

He came and stood in front of Navkar, 'So the question is, who did he get into a deal with? That's the key to everything.'

Salim started pacing the room now, up and down, restlessly, with furious concentration and for the first time

Navkar could see that he was what he had claimed. He was actually an investigator, even with his glaring red shirt and body odour. He realized that he'd never really believed it till now. Perhaps, somewhere in his mind, he'd always thought of all basti dwellers as the same. The idea of them actually having a profession, having a certain mindset and skills, took a while to sink in.

A sudden realization hit Navkar. 'Why did he want to kill you now? It must be something you did recently.'

Salim's eyes were flashing. He wheeled around. 'Exactly! Everyone knew I was investigating the disappearance of the boys in the gang. I'd been looking into that for months without any trouble. It must have something to do with the hawala people I've been talking to.'

They stared at each other.

'Call him! Call the Dubai guy you were going to meet!' Navkar said, jumping to his feet.

Salim tried the mobile for a few minutes but without success. 'His phone is switched off.'

'Do you know where he lives?'

Salim nodded. He took out his gun and hefted it in his hand, as if trying to make a decision. 'We should be safe. Khurram can't tell the boys in the gang to attack me. And the ones who take supari would never come into these territories because they belong to the gangs.'

'Ahh!' Chawla suddenly cried out, jumping up from the table. 'You don't have bullets? That's the problem? Here, here!' He ducked behind the table and rummaged in his cabinet and stood up with a polythene bag stuffed with cartridges and a gleaming, sleek, long, black revolver. 'I saved for ten years to buy this,' he said proudly, holding up the bag. 'One bullet at a time!'

Navkar stared at him, 'Why?'

'I-I like this stuff,' Chawla said sheepishly.

Salim took the revolver and loaded it and stuffed in bullets in both his pockets and then both of Navkar's pockets. Navkar could feel his pockets sagging under their weight but he didn't want to touch them.

As they were leaving, Navkar remembered something. He took out his wallet and gave Chawla his ATM card.

'Listen, I need you to do me a favour,' he said, taking Chawla aside. 'Can you get some jewellery delivered to my mother? Something nice.'

Chawla looked at him and nodded silently. Navkar whispered the ATM code into his ear and then called home. His mother was surprised to get the call.

'What happened, bete? Are you coming home for lunch?' she asked.

He smiled at the question. He never came home for lunch.

'No, ma, just called like that. But what are you cooking anyway?'

'Gobi,' she said, not sounding too enthusiastic. 'I think it has burnt a bit, but it should be okay.'

'I'm sure it will,' he said, quietly. 'I'll have it in the evening. I'll probably be home early.'

That cheered her up. 'I'll make kheer for you.'

Navkar grimaced at the thought. 'That's okay, ma. You don't have to. I'll-I'll see you soon.'

As he disconnected the phone, his finger couldn't help swiping downwards, his eyes looking for Tara's name on the list. He frowned to himself, and kept the phone in his pocket.

'Let's go.'

TWENTY-TWO

The lights were glaring bright, reflecting off every surface in the hotel lobby, from chrome-plated vases to glass tables and granite pillars. The blonde newscaster from CNN waited in her seat, adjusting her hair while her camera and lighting crew, who had taken over the lobby for this shoot, made the final adjustments to their set-up. They gave her the ready signal and she started.

'We have with us today, Vishnu Rustomjee Mistry, son of Rustom Mistry and the chairman of the Rustom Group, which controls more than fifty billion dollars in capital and has interests in sectors ranging from energy, retail, television to locomotion, healthcare and security. Mr Mistry, will you tell our viewers in the United States about this police reform bill that you have been pushing for?'

Vishnu pursed his lips thoughtfully before responding, 'Well, firstly, I object to that name. It is by no means a legislation focused on the police. It is a reform for the whole justice system, proposed by eminent members of Indian society, including a few parliamentarians, twenty-two Supreme Court judges and three erstwhile Chief Justices of India. So it's not a police reform bill per se, and I'm by no means the only one pushing for it.'

'Well then Mr Mistry, how would you describe it? We would like you to give our viewers a sense of the changes proposed.'

'The most important thing I'd like to stress is that no changes are being proposed in the laws or the system of justice in India. This legislation has been compiled by legal champions, and nothing about the workings of the judiciary—that is a free and fair judiciary—is being touched. However, we are suggesting immense changes in the organizations that are supposed to be implementing these systems. That is where we want change.'

'Why do these organizations need to change, according to you?' the journalist asked. 'What is lacking in them today?'

Vishnu gave a dry chuckle and responded, 'The question would be easier to answer if you asked me what *is* working today, because frankly it's a small list. Not much is working right. The only good thing to be said about the current situation is that the higher Indian courts, on the whole, give good and fair judgements and Indian laws and its court precedents are, on the whole, good and fair. They are progressive, unbiased and uphold the idea of a free and courageous society, more or less. There are few exceptions, but on the whole, that is decently done.'

'So what doesn't work?'

Vishnu gave a grim look and shrugged. 'Everything else. Pretty much nothing else really works.'

He sat up. 'Let's start with the criminal justice system. For the common citizen, the most important part of this system is the part that prevents crimes—that gives them security from crime, rather than justice afterwards. A just society stops most of its crimes. Now for this, you need the presence of beat cops patrolling streets and neighbourhoods. We have one policeman for every thousand Indians. One cop for a thousand! That is five times lesser than the number in developed countries. This is without counting the fact that most developed countries have a much deeper net of surveillance to help their police. That makes it easy to commit crimes here.'

'Well, thankfully our cities are densely populated, so it's naturally a bit difficult,' Vishnu said. 'But yes, the police ratio is certainly far below the necessary limit for citizens to feel safe. Moreover, you need these cops to be accountable and professional and unbiased. We're failing miserably there. There is a structural problem at the heart of it. Police personnel in India report to, and only to, elected ministers. It has been proposed for twenty years now that senior police officers should report to and be managed by a committee comprising elected ministers, members of the opposition and members of the judiciary. By no means should they be managed only by elected ministers.'

The journalist frowned and asked, 'But doesn't that speak of a lack of faith in the idea of democracy itself?'

'Anyone who believes that democracy by itself is the solution to all problems is living in a dream,' Vishnu said, before adding emphatically, 'There is no democratic country in the world which doesn't balance its elected representatives with nominated professionals forming the civil services and the judiciary. This is because everyone knows that elections create their own corruption. It is inevitable because elections need funding and political parties don't have legitimate revenue sources. This leads to corruption and a subversion of justice.'

Vishnu's voice grew heavier. 'What is tragic is that this subversion leads to a corrosion of law and order even where it is not linked to elections, even in normal day-to-day society, if elected officials are the sole controllers of the police. Why? Because for their own agenda, they would prefer a weak, disintegrated police. So politicians ensure that, if they have a chance. And once the police force is rendered weak, it is weak in all cases, even in the crimes committed by one common man against another.'

'And that has happened in India?'

'To an alarming degree! This weakening of the police has led to very low allocation of funds for their service. It has led to an almost complete lack of accountability, a complete lack of proper training, a lack of basic amenities, like housing, which affect the morale and dignity of its personnel. As a result, the police in India are completely and utterly incapacitated. Most of the time, they're thugs themselves, but even at their best, they are incompetent.'

'And this bill seeks to rectify those issues?'

Vishnu paused, choosing his words carefully, 'It also seeks to change the way police are hired and seeks to ramp up the number of personnel in a matter of months. But more importantly, it seeks to simultaneously step up the capacity of the courts to handle cases, so that the system, as a whole, functions.'

'So the courts in India also suffer from the lack of capacity? From having too few judges?'

'To an even larger degree perhaps,' Vishnu said. 'The whole court infrastructure is severely impaired. There are too few judges, there are too few building to hold them, there are too few specialized courts. And here, of course, we are crossing over from the criminal justice system to the civil one as well. While the problem exists in both, it is unimaginably worse in the civil courts simply because there are far more cases there.'

Vishnu sat forward and continued, 'The presence of free and fair civil courts is the very basis of a society. It forms the fabric upon which everything else is built. It implements property rights and business disputes, which underpin the entire economy. It decides the validity of various social behaviours with regards to the Constitution. It guards against the excesses of government power.

'If the civil courts take fifteen years to give a judgement, the country just can't function very well. It is the single biggest impediment to anyone trying to do business in India, or to own property, or to deal with the government. Just upgrading our court infrastructure to match the increased size of our economy will make India ten times more attractive than it is today.'

'So you're saying these reforms will have an economic impact in terms of growth and investment?'

Vishnu smiled, his perfect teeth sparkling in bright light. 'Absolutely! I'm a businessman myself and I can promise this. You can ask anyone who owns a business and who has thought of investing in India. Having courts that can give judgements within six months, coupled with the existing progressiveness of Indian laws and the fundamentals of a young population with increasing skills and education, will make India the most attractive investment destination in the world.'

The camera shifted to the presenter, who gave a smile before continuing, 'There you have it. The latest news from

India and our special interview with Vishnu Rustomjee Mistry, who many regard as a beacon of hope for a country that has seen dipping growth, falling investor sentiment and warnings of difficult times ahead.'

TWENTY-THREE

Chawla let them take his battered Maruti 800, a car which looked malnourished, with its ribs sticking out and its shoulders bony.

'I got it in my dowry,' Chawla said proudly.

'That's what it looks like. Must be fifty years old,' Salim muttered.

Salim had never learnt to drive properly, so Navkar took the wheel. The car took a few tries to start. Salim was nursing the gun he was carrying thoughtfully. Navkar slammed the accelerator down, the car lunged forward suddenly. He felt a sudden power, a sudden fury course through him. The dead lady, the bullets flying by him, the sounds of footsteps while hiding under the tarpaulin. He felt his thoughts marching up and down his head. And somewhere deep and secret, he felt Anisha watching.

Navkar gritted his teeth as he took the road, one hand permanently on the horn as he cut past cars and corners.

'How far is it from here?' Navkar asked.

'Eight or nine kilometres,' Salim said, glancing a bit nervously at him. 'There's no real need to hurry.'

Navkar's eyes were narrowed as he said, 'If they tried to kill you, they'll try to kill him too. Put on your seat belt.'

'There aren't any!' Salim said helplessly.

Navkar took the Western Express Highway, revving the old car to a hundred till the entire frame was shaking as if caught in a hurricane. The road was almost empty at this point and he recklessly swerved past the few trucks and cars that were ambling along.

Finally, Salim made him turn into a smaller road that led past a quiet neighbourhood engulfed by a forest of guava trees and then into smaller and smaller lanes and finally asked him to park the car in a pile of mud and step out into the rain. The journey had taken twenty-five minutes.

Salim tucked the gun in and asked Navkar to follow him into another series of winding lanes that opened up into a strange street awash with colour and slush. Bundles of yarns in every possible colour were hulked over the tiny shops, the threads being drained of their cheap dyes by the rain.

'What is this place?' Navkar asked, staring at the surreal sight, while ducking under overhangs of dripping loops of cotton and wool.

Salim had red and blue water running down his face, as if he had worn war paint. 'This is the only place in Mumbai where yarn is still handmade,' Salim said, as they walked over what were once cobbled stones, but now worn down by time and feet and covered in a thin layer of mud that loose earth forms when it rains. Every puddle had a tinge of colour, some green, some blue, some yellow.

'All these shops are under our protection,' Salim informed and added, 'I get my clothes from Malik Sahib over here.'

The crude wooden shop seemed to be held up by bales of cloth and unspun yarn—it seemed like it would explode into a flurry of textile any moment now. Navkar could see that most of the shops suffered similarly.

'This place has enough cloth to cover half of Mumbai!' Navkar grunted, though he doubted whether South Mumbai girls would like Salim's dress sense.

Salim laughed. This was clearly a place dear to his heart. 'Follow me. The hawala guy's office is at the end of the street.'

It makes sense, Navkar thought. If most of these shops were under mafia protection, then they probably doubled up as money-laundering fronts as well. Navkar wondered if Tara would want to do a story on this place next, once everything had died down. A small part of him grew perturbed whenever his thoughts turned to her. He knew he shouldn't think of her—she was above his pay grade. Hell, as long as she was dating Vishnu Mistry, she was above anyone's pay grade.

But then again, Navkar knew that. He knew he didn't have a chance with her. That didn't trouble him at all. Perhaps in a strange way, he just felt proud that he owed her.

His foot trampled on loose yellow threads and he saw the colour splotch on the already sorry state of his shoes. They stopped in front of a two-storeyed building at the end of the street. It was newly painted.

'Doesn't look like they've been here yet,' Salim said as they entered.

Navkar looked at the building in some surprise. The interior was brand new, as if all the furniture had been set up in the lobby only the day before. There was even a large, shiny plastic water container on the roof to collect the rain water. The place looked better than Channel 10's office, Navkar thought. The whole place had a lingering smell of newness.

'I didn't know that the hawala guys have granite floored offices,' Navkar said.

'They don't,' replied Salim as he made his way to the office.

'Sir, do you have an appointment? You can't just go in…' started the chubby secretary, trying to swivel out of her chair desperately.

'Appointment?' Salim sounded disgusted as he pointed her back to her seat with his gun. 'What is wrong with you?'

He pushed open the door to the office carefully. There was no sound from within. He urged Navkar to stay back and swung the door open with a flourish. There was only a man taking a nap on his chair, his head lolling on his thick neck.

Salim pulled Navkar inside and locked the door.

'Sharif Mian, you sleep well for a man about to die,' Salim said loudly.

The man caught himself suddenly as he woke up with a snort.

'Who…who are you?' Sharif grunted, his groggy eyes adjusting to the fright.

'That depends on what you tell us,' Salim said grimly. 'My name is Salim. I was supposed to meet you.'

The man looked from one to the other confused. 'S-Salim bhai? Yes, yes. But you were supposed to come day after.'

'I realized if I waited that long I would have to talk to a corpse,' Salim said nonchalantly, coming round the table and leaning on its edge. 'And corpses smell.'

'What are you talking about?' the man spluttered, looking up at Salim.

Salim leant over and said, 'Khurram bhai has betrayed us,' he said quietly. 'He knows that I've found out. He tried to kill me. You will be next.'

The man's eyes now threatened to pop out, his face had started to colour into an alarming mottled purple.

'Tell me about the money coming in from Dubai,' Salim said, gripping his face. 'Then I can protect you.'

'What Dubai money? I don't know anything!' the man gurgled. 'How did you get in here anyway?'

Salim frowned. His voice grew impatient. 'Don't you understand? Khurram has betrayed us. He's going to kill you. You're a dead man!'

The man didn't say anything. He didn't even seem to understand.

Salim was shaking him by the collar now, heaving that fat neck and big head.

'You fat piece of dung!' Salim roared and pressed the barrel of the gun to the man's temple, digging the metal in. 'What do you know about the Dubai money? Who's sending it?'

'I-I don't know! Honestly! I don't know!' the man cried out. 'I only handle collections at this end. I don't know who sends it from there!'

Salim gritted his teeth in frustration. He somehow knew that was the truth. 'Then who collected it, you idiot? Tell me something before I blow your brains out!' he shouted.

'Wh-what? It was one of your boys. He just came two days ago for the new shipment,' the man blubbered.'

'What was his name?'

'I don't know.'

'Who was he?' Salim grunted hitting him with the butt of his revolver before repeating, 'Who?'

'Wait…stop,' Sharif implored and fumbled around his phone and showed it to Salim, 'This is his picture. I took it secretly…in case, you know?'

Navkar tried to see the picture. It was too grainy to make out properly but Salim's eyes widened.

'This is Majid, chota Majid…he disappeared two months ago…he is supposed to be dead,' Salim cried out, his breath faltering.

Navkar looked at him, alarmed. 'Are you sure?'

Salim held the mobile screen close to his eyes for a moment and then threw it on the table to let out a deep breath.

'What does that mean?' Navkar repeated, confused.

'They're alive! They're alive. It's true. Khurram has sold us out.' Salim was looking at him. 'Khurram is recruiting for something else. He's been making the boys disappear. He's making a new gang!'

Navkar didn't know how to respond.

'A new gang…that's where these boys have been going…and the money, they are planning to attack us.'

He turned to Sharif again, waving his gun around madly. 'You…you know anything? Where is the money going? Are they planning an attack?'

'You're wrong. They aren't planning to attack you,' Sharif said, much calmer now. He wiped the sweat from his face and repeated, 'You can relax. They're not going to attack you.'

Salim slammed the gun back against his forehead. 'Then what, you fat cow? Tell me what you know!'

Sharif looked straight at Salim. 'I've heard…there have been people, trainers coming in…from the Middle East.'

Navkar straightened, moving to the table. He asked in a puzzled voice, 'Trainers? What do you mean? To train the gangsters? For what?'

Sharif didn't say anything.

Salim had gone very quiet. He was pacing the room again. Navkar could feel his thoughts racing.

'Money flooding in from the Middle East, boys going missing or dead; turns out they are alive. Where have they been, what have they been doing? Trainers brought in from outside to train the boys. For months now,' Salim muttered pacing even faster now. He stopped suddenly and turned to Navkar slowly. The latter could see now that he was scared; his hands were shaking.

Salim bit his lip and said finally, 'It's a sleeper… A terrorist attack.'

Navkar could feel his heart knot and churn. Slowly, painfully. He didn't know what to do or say. He felt around for support and found Sharif's table to lean on. It suddenly hit him that he had to tell someone. It was his responsibility now. Tara! He had to call her. That news had to be out!

There was a noise, a scuffle in the lobby. Sharif stood up immediately.

Salim patted Navkar's shoulder, breaking his thought.

'They're here.'

'What? Who?'

'Shooters,' Salim said grimly. 'Sharif mian's baraat.'

Navkar looked around wildly. 'What do we do? We have to make it out of here! If-if it's a terrorist attack we have to tell someone!'

Salim's face was gaunt in the afternoon light, his eyes feral. 'We will be fine. There will be one, maximum two of them outside now. I'm going to kill them.'

'How do you know there'll be only two?' Sharif asked, trembling. His hands were fumbling over the desk, picking up his glasses, his papers. He was trembling.

'This is our territory. There's no way more of them could've sneaked in without being discovered,' Salim said, positioning himself by the side of the door.

'So what do we do? We still have only one gun,' Navkar said, unconvinced.

Salim's mouth was a hard thin line, his eyes hooded as he responded, 'This time, surprise is on our side,' he said, his voice eerily calm. 'When I give the signal, jump through the window and run.'

Before he could finish, a bullet crashed through the lock of the door as Navkar and Sharif dived under the table. There was a small crack in it that allowed Navkar to see Salim. He was standing next to the door, completely still. Navkar said a quiet prayer under his breath as another bullet burst through the door; it sounded even louder than the last one. Navkar wondered if God could hear through gun fights.

A foot kicked the door. Again. The third kick broke open the door and a massive man jumped in with a gun. Before he could turn, Salim had sprung out and shot him, clean in the face. The man's expression didn't even change. Just a sudden spurt of blood and he fell backwards.

'Go, go!' Salim screamed and Navkar felt his body react.

He grabbed Sharif and with a deep breath, thrust him out and then followed him through the window. Salim rushed behind them but just as Navkar jumped out, he heard a loud thud behind him. He turned back, frightened, to see a man had caught hold of Salim. Navkar reached up, grabbing the man's arm as Salim slammed his face with the muzzle of his gun. The man's grip loosened. There was another entering through the door now, bringing his gun up, but hesitating as his partner blocked the window.

Salim kicked Navkar away and gripping the man's collar squeezed two bullets in his stomach and heaved him towards the other man. Then he turned and leapt to the ground and they both ran, the wind slapping their faces, rain hustling down on them and the mud slippery underfoot. They saw Sharif huddled behind a large metal trash container overflowing with a mountain of garbage. They knew they couldn't stop. Not even to turn and join Sharif.

Navkar felt like he couldn't breathe. The stink, the fear covered him, sank inside him. He felt like he would vomit, like he would vomit till he died. The gunfire hadn't started yet. The man was climbing out of the window. Salim turned suddenly and shot two bullets. There was a cracking sound, followed by an immense crash. Salim had shot the new Sintex water container sitting atop the building and water came cascading down. Navkar looked back, catching his breath for a second. The man had fallen under the weight of the water. He was scrambling for his gun.

'Run!' Navkar felt Salim's hand on his collar. 'Run before he gets up!'

Navkar found himself running again, but in the direction of the shooter. Running as fast as he could, through that blinding rain and the flying threads and splashes of colour. He felt rage course through him. Rage at the injustice of it all. At the callousness of violence he'd seen. Rage at everything that was broken. Everything that was lost. He found himself running straight at the shooter, even as the man found his gun. He was raising it now. He was going to pull the trigger. He was too late.

Navkar crashed into him bodily, slamming him back against the wall. The man'e eyes widened in surprise. Navkar was hitting him in a blind fury, gripping his head and smashing it back against the wall and kneeing his stomach again and again and again. The man tried desperately to push him away, but couldn't. Navkar's knuckles were bleeding, his fingers white with tension as he gripped the man's collar. His other hand had prised the man's gun away. The metal was heavy. It felt right.

Navkar remembered her face suddenly. Anisha's face. He could see her face after so, so long. She was sitting in front of him in class. She was turning back. She was smiling. He raised his arm and slammed the metal on the man's head. Once. Then again. Again. She was smiling. The man was bleeding now, his blood flowing down Navkar's arm. She was looking at him. The man gave a desperate lurch and Navkar slipped, falling back. The man's face was covered in blood. He took a step forward and then there was a crack. The man fell back.

Navkar looked up to find Salim standing over him. A tendril of smoke snaked up from his gun, sizzling in the rain. Navkar stared at him. He could feel the rain washing away the slush from on his face.

Salim took a deep breath, the air whistling in. He sighed, patting Navkar's arm and lifting him to his feet.

'What made you do that?' he asked, looking at Navkar with a strange expression.

'I have to call Tara,' Navkar said, shoving his arm aside.

~

The traffic on the road was an endless line of honking cars and trucks, impatient under the pattering rain. Tara leant back in her seat, watching the sketches the rainfall made in the air as it got lit by faint streetlight. She wasn't usually out of the office at seven and the endless traffic made her wonder why she'd even tried today.

She passed her music USB to the driver and asked him to plug it in and hand her the remote. She found the song after three minutes, a Japanese vocal that was the soundtrack of an animated movie released fifteen years ago. It was the first movie she'd seen as a teenager. It was her escape from reality.

However, her ringing phone interrupted the song, breaking through those words she loved and didn't understand. It was Prateek Sharma.

'Chauhan is holding an impromptu press conference at the Mantralaya. Chatterjee and I are out as we have programmes scheduled. Do you want to go?'

She sat up slowly, frowning. 'What is he going to speak about?'

'He'll probably issue some statement on your vigilante story. There might be a chance for a few questions.'

She thought for a moment before saying, 'Yeah, I'll go.' She motioned to the driver. 'Turn the car. You have to go a bit faster than this.'

The roads were clearer in that direction, but by the time she arrived, there was already a line of news vans creating a big jam on the road outside the Mantralaya. Her cameraman hadn't arrived yet. She gave him another call and then decided to go ahead. The guards gave her the same sordid look they always did and their eyes followed her to the wooden booth where the security lady would frisk her, and followed her when she exited.

There were two calls from Navkar while she was in security. She debated for a moment if she should call him back. She had been wondering what he was up to. She'd sent him a message in the afternoon but he hadn't replied. The last she knew he'd gone to meet an informer with that gangster he was following.

She frowned and slipped the phone back into her pocket. There was no time now. She rushed through the dingy, gaunt corridors of the building, past the blue-grey crumbling paint and the paan-speckled walls. She looked around once or twice at the high ceilings and pillars, even though she was in a hurry, and then averted her eyes as if she'd invoked misfortune. Coming here always made her feel uneasy and jumpy, a strange nauseous mixture that was part disgust and part something else—something she couldn't identify, though its presence was strong enough to be a lump in her throat and a drying of her lips.

Press conferences were always held in this one room on the third floor, with wood-panelled walls and a thick carpet that stank of moisture and neglect. There were plastic chairs laid out in uneven rows which were now filled with jostling, shouting reporters, screaming out their questions while the floor manager tried to silence them in vain.

Her eyes sought out the chief minister. He was dwarfed by the lectern he stood behind. He looked helpless.

For a moment his eyes met hers. She wondered if he recognized her; if he knew who she was.

Was there a widening of the pupils, a flicker of recognition? Surely he knew she would come.

As she took one of the few remaining seats in the last row, she wondered if the nausea was actually longing that she felt. Longing for the city she'd once thought she would live in when she'd first come to Mumbai.

She felt her phone vibrating and found a message from Navkar. She read it once and then again, her hand rising to her ear, involuntarily trying to shut out the noise.

We traced the mafia money to a hawala. Money has been flowing into the gangs from Dubai.

Tara began typing a reply, asking him where he was, but before she could finish, another message arrived.

The money has been used to recruit gang members, to take them away for some task. This guy says some foreigners have been brought in also, maybe from the Middle East.

She looked up, her eyes scanning the room and her phone vibrated again to signal another new message. Tara's fingers were shaky as she opened the last message. It had just one line.

Salim says they are planning a terrorist attack.

Tara found the words tumbling over in her mind as she sought to grip them, to pin them down and stretch them out, so she could take them in. It wouldn't happen. She couldn't feel it. It wasn't real.

She decided she would call Navkar. Once she spoke to him it would be clear. He could tell her exactly what had happened, exactly what the man had said, who he was, where they had met him. Then it would be clear.

She rose and made for the corridor to make the call. She glanced back at the room where pandemonium still reigned. She wasn't going to miss anything. Besides, her cameraman hadn't arrived yet.

The evening still hadn't turned dark. There was a mild drizzle in the twilight, and the scent of rain in the air. She leaned across the railing, bringing the phone to her ear but paused midway. There was some commotion downstairs.

She could hear loud voices and then she saw a few people run out of the building and out of the main gate. She stepped back and looked around. The corridor seemed just as it had ten minutes ago, mostly deserted, with a peon sleeping on a metal chair, his breath rising and falling with gentle snores. She looked down again and saw a few more people stumbling out of the building. She went over to the peon and woke him.

'Listen,' she asked. 'What is going on?' Is something happening?' She pointed out to the commotion downstairs and he leant over dutifully.

He scratched his head, looking confused and then called out to a babu in the room next to the conference hall. The man came over with another and the three of them peered at the scene.

Tara was growing impatient now. 'What's happening?' she asked again.

Before they could answer there was a sudden noise, repeated again and again. It sounded like a door slamming shut, or a loud clap. They stared at each other. Then the sound returned, but with a far greater frequency, different this time.

'It's a machine gun,' Tara said, hardly believing the words herself. 'It has to be. The others were gunshots too.'

'No, no, madam,' the babu said, frowning in confusion, turning this way and that. 'How could it be?'

The noise had increased downstairs.

'Look,' the peon said, pointing to a plume of smoke rising from the other wing.

Suddenly, they heard a loud patter of footsteps. Someone was running up the stairs. The sound made them all jump. She could see the realization dawning on their faces, the fear in their eyes. They stood there, tense, waiting, wondering whether they should run. Before anyone could stir themselves to move, the man appeared. He was one of the guards, breathless from running, a sub-machine gun slung over his shoulders.

'We have to go,' he cried out, panting. 'Where's the CM? We have to go now!'

'What's happening?' the babu asked, gripping his shoulders. 'Is that the sound of firing? Is there an attack?'

The man nodded, too out of breath to speak. 'Yes!' he said finally. His eyes were large with fear. She could see he was young, his moustache a thin, unsure line above his lips. 'Yes! Where's the CM?'

The babu didn't answer. He was still gripping him, staring uncomprehendingly.

'Inside,' Tara said, reacting. 'He's inside with the media people.'

The guard didn't say anything. He stumbled over to the room. The sounds returned, gunshots in rapid succession, faint and faraway. As soon as the guard opened the door, the noise of the chaos inside the room washed it away.

The guard started to wade through the crowd, shouting, but his voice was lost in the din. Tara and the babus stood by the door, looking inside and then out of the balcony and then, with fearful eyes, at the stairwell and then back again into the room, wondering what to do.

Finally, Tara stepped aside and dialled the police number. She got a busy tone and dialled again. She could feel her heart speeding up, the hollow feeling of fear spreading. The phone was still busy. She stared in the room. Everything was happening so slowly. The guard had reached the floor manager, who was now announcing that everyone had to follow his instructions. The guard had taken Chauhan by the arm and was trying to exit the room. The reporters were surrounding them, jostling, questioning.

Tara didn't see the second guard arrive, but suddenly he was there among the crowd. He was older, his voice louder.

'There is an attack!' he roared. 'We have to get the CM to safety!'

The reporters wouldn't let them go. They were shouting, confused and panic-stricken.

The floor manager was shouting over the mike, 'Follow them! They'll take us to safety!' The guards were finally out of the room. The younger one had Chauhan by the arm. The older one looked grim, frustrated, but he was waving at the media people to follow him. His expression made it clear that he didn't like the idea.

'In a line!' he yelled. 'Follow in a line!'

Tara found herself behind the pushing, panic-stricken crowd. Her legs felt oddly light, one foot following another blindly as she stumbled behind them. She couldn't stop trying the phone number. The tone was constantly busy.

The babus had pushed ahead. Tara could see them elbowing their way to Chauhan. The guard was taking him along at a sprint, the crowd following in a wave of confused terror. Some of them had crossed the guard, nearly trampling over Chauhan in their hurry, running blindly forward.

They were almost at the end of the corridor, down the opposite wing from where the plume of smoke now rose to the sky. But they could still hear the sound of gunfire. Tara was running now, behind the crowd. The sounds wouldn't leave her. She felt them getting louder as her fingers tapped the call button desperately. The tone began to ring. She felt the crowd break loose, break the line, running ahead of the guards and Chauhan, pushing past them, toward the stairwell at the end of the corridor.

She heard a bored nasal voice of a woman. 'Name and address?' the lady asked.

'Listen, there's a terrorist attack here!' she said breathlessly before continuing, 'There are gunshots! They're...'

'Wait!' the voice interrupted. 'First, please tell name and address.'

The sounds were closer now, impossibly loud! She could feel herself skidding to a stop. Screaming had broken out in front of her.

'Name and address?' the voice demanded once more.

People were pushing past her now. Tara almost fell, trampled afoot before she caught herself by pushing against someone else. She started running in the opposite direction. She could feel the phone call being cut from the other end as she failed to reply. The world was full of screams.

Suddenly she saw people falling, and spurts of blood. She fell to the ground, half by instinct, half in surprise. She could see others crouching now, hands over their head, trembling, crying in terror. She could see some running ahead, screaming out as they fell bleeding. She saw the older guard as he tried to dive into a room and his side exploded in red. She felt herself turning, not able to stop herself, not able to stop her need to see. The young guard lay in front of her, face down, eyes open and unmoving in a pool of spreading blood.

That is when she noticed the two masked men. One had Chauhan gripped by the neck. Their guns were aimed outwards. They were saying something. What were they saying? Her ears rang numbly. She knew they were speaking but the words wouldn't come through.

There was no one running any more. There were others beside her, they were kneeling. They had their hands behind their heads. Her ears began to quieten. The sounds were fading.

Someone was yelling,

'Kneel, all of you! Put your hands behind your head and kneel!'

TWENTY-FOUR

There was a green field, clumps of grass and wildflower and weed, beautiful, stretching out beyond her vision. She remembered running through them. There were blue butterflies dancing around each other, as if to tease her, and she was running after them. She remembered her father's face, smiling widely, as he picked her up. She used to be scared of his smile when she was little, since he smiled so rarely. It was a face she wasn't used to. It made him look like a stranger. He didn't let her go, but hugged her... How old had she been? Four? Five?

Why did she think of that now, here in the midst of death? Was this what they said happened—your life passed before your eyes?

She patted her hands over her body, checking for injuries. She was still unhurt. The man in front of her was bleeding. He'd left a bloody trail when he was pulled into the room. His face was glazed over, his eyes hollow with pain.

They weren't bringing too many injured in here. He must be someone important, Tara gauged.

She glanced over at Chauhan for his reaction. They had placed him right next to her, but he hadn't even given her a glance and he didn't look up now. He sat still in that same frozen, pensive pose, hands over knees, staring ahead.

She realized that most people weren't moving much. There was none of the fidgetiness that usually accompanies sitting around. Even the carpet here didn't stink. Or perhaps it just didn't register any more. They were bringing in more people, crying, screaming people who became quiet once they were brought here and made to sit.

This was their hostage room, on the third floor of the building—halfway up, halfway down.

They had gathered the surviving media people here, along with some officials and ministers. It was clear that they were not trying to occupy the entire building. They had just been looking for a few people. Chauhan. The principal secretary. Members of the cabinet. Once they were found, they were being dragged in here.

People were streaming out of the main exit on the ground floor. Tara remembered seeing them as she was being brought in.

There were about fifty hostages in the room and at least three gunmen that she could make out, coming in and out. They all wore identical masks and jeans. They'd put on black jackets over their shirts. She supposed they would have needed to wear different shirts in order to not stand out in the beginning. There were more of them stationed outside, all along this floor. She felt there must be around ten, and then she almost laughed at her thoughts. How did it matter to her now, whether there were ten or a hundred?

There was sudden screaming as one more lady was brought in. Tara realized it had been a while since the last person.

'Sit,' one of them told her. He had done most of the talking, all in colloquial Hindi, as was spoken on the streets of Mumbai.

Navkar had been right.

She was felt proud of him, sitting huddled here in this room of death.

'Where's the AC control?' one of the gunmen muttered. They seemed quite calm. They were right too; it was getting pretty hot. There were more people here than the room was meant for.

One of the hostages put up his hand nervously and the gunman gave him a questioning look. He pointed behind the curtain to the controls of the air conditioner.

'Maximum,' the gunman said and the man turned the knob till cold, dank air streamed in.

They must be hot in those masks, Tara realized. The gunman stepped aside and began muttering to himself in a low tone. She then noticed, for the first time, the telltale bulge in his mask; he was wearing a mobile headset. She looked around at the others and realized that they all had it.

What was the man saying? Tara strained her ears.

'We have two-and-a-half hours,' the man began to speak to the others. He seemed to be one of the leaders, a short, stocky man in a white T-shirt under his jacket.

He then turned to the hostages. 'Alright, now who is from the media here?'

No one answered. The man looked at the other gunmen and shook his head, as if he was just realizing how hard this was going to be.

He started again, 'We are going to voice our demands through the media. You will not be harmed. We just want you to call your offices with our demands.'

This time, there was interest. Several hands shot up. Tara almost laughed. Reporters could never overlook an opportunity for a story.

The man looked around. Tara put up her hand slowly. The man's eyes stopped on her. Slowly, he walked over and leant over her. His rough hands rose to her face and cupped her cheek, almost delicately.

'I've seen you on TV,' he said softly and his thumb ran across her lips, his eyes drinking in her face.

'You said you wouldn't hurt them,' a voice suddenly called out.

Tara realized with a shock that it was Chauhan.

The gunman seemed equally surprised.

There was pindrop silence in the room. The man straightened and walked over to Chauhan, glaring at him, but still unable to come up with a reply.

Chauhan looked up at him. 'You think you're the first gunman I've seen?'

The man slid the gun from his shoulder and pointed it at Chauhan dangerously, 'Shut up.'

Chauhan continued looking at him. The man raised the gun, taking aim. One of the other gunmen, in a chequered shirt, hurried forward and slapped Chauhan sharply across the face. Chauhan fell to his side, blood erupting from his mouth and a grunt of pain escaping him.

The chequered shirt now patted the other man on the back and looked at Tara, 'Make the call.'

She got out her phone and dialled Chatterjee's number. There was no scope for heroics. She just had to do what they said.

'I'm inside the Mantralaya,' she told Chatterjee when he picked up and heard his gasp in response.

'What? How?' he cried out finally.

'I was at the press conference when the attack happened.'

He groaned loudly. 'How is it always you, Tara? How?'

The gunman didn't let her reply. He snatched the phone and spoke rapidly. 'Listen to me carefully. Set up a recording. We will call back in ten minutes.'

He cut the call and looked at his comrades and then adjusting the earphone, stood still. He was clearly getting instructions. He stepped out of the room to talk.

'Is it ten minutes already?' he asked when he returned.

It wasn't, only four minutes had gone by. There was an awkward fidgety wait. The white T-shirt man was still staring at her. She wondered what would happen if they had too much idle time.

Her phone began to ring. The chequered shirt man picked up. 'Do you have the recording set up?'

'Yes,' Chatterjee said.

The man seemed to be listening intently to a message on his ear piece. 'Alright, these are our demands. We want a million dollars in cash and a helicopter. This should take us to the airport where a plane with 30,000 litres of fuel will be waiting. We want this within twenty-four hours or we will kill all the hostages.'

He paused, then continued, 'We also want this message to be sent to all media channels. Otherwise we will kill one media person here every hour, starting with this one.'

'No, no!' Chatterjee exclaimed. 'We'll send it out. Don't worry. We'll send it out immediately.'

The man didn't answer. There was a moment's silence. Then Chatterjee asked, his voice sheepish, 'Anything else? Would you like to tell us why you're doing this? Which group you're from?'

The man rubbed his head, as if he didn't want to say the words. 'We're not from any group.'

Before Chatterjee could talk again, the man cut the call. He looked up at his partners. 'Get their phones in a bag.'

They got a bag and went around collecting everyone's phones. After that they seemed to relax. The room had become really quiet. One of the gunmen sat down on a table, his legs swinging, his shoulders slouched.

The one in the chequered shirt went out for a while and came back and spoke to the others.

'No one has arrived yet. Let's do one more check.'

He called the others into a huddle and gave them directions. Soon they all left the room, except one who stood on guard at the doorway. Tara could see few others outside in the corridor.

She heard a dull groan of pain from Chauhan. He was gingerly rubbing his mouth. Perhaps a tooth had become loose. She kept her gaze straight ahead but whispered to him.

'Thank you.'

Chauhan didn't reply. The gunman at the doorway was looking outside. He hadn't noticed.

'You know,' Chauhan muttered under his breath, 'I don't know whether to like you or dislike you.'

Tara glanced at him, surprised, and then quickly looked ahead.

'You screwed me over,' Chauhan continued. 'But then you screwed over the others too. Kumar, Kirloskar, even Nagarajan.'

Tara couldn't believe he was talking to her about that. She felt like laughing. Laughing at this mad world, at the spluttering air conditioning and the masked gunman, and all the stories she'd ever done.

'It was good work, wasn't it?' she murmured.

Chauhan didn't answer but she could see the wry shake of his head with the corner of her eye.

'How could I resist a mystery like that? A secret vigilante? I had to do it.'

Chauhan gave a low muffled grunt and his voice had a calm, soft, edge to it as he said, 'He won't be secret for long. I will get out of here alive, and then I will find him and deal with him. No one beats Rajender Chauhan so easily. '

She frowned, surprised at his words and even risked a glance at him. She realized with a sudden shock that he was trying to reassure himself. That was the reason for his display of bravado, his tone, his words. She noticed he was shivering.

There was noise outside and the gunmen who had left the room earlier came back from their preparations.

Chauhan's eyes had narrowed. 'And I'll take care of these fools too. They're from this city. I can tell. They won't be able to hide.'

The chequered-shirted gunman shouted out angrily. He looked worried, his movements jerky and anxious. 'When will the fire brigade and police get here? The building is burning down already.'

'It's Mumbai. There must be a traffic jam,' Chauhan replied smiling, which only angered them more.

~

The Maruti 800 groaned unwillingly as Navkar turned the ignition one more time. The old machine had finally given up, refusing to budge for the last ten minutes. Navkar slammed the steering wheel in frustration.

'Try calling her again,' Salim urged.

Navkar knew there was no point. She would've replied to

his text by now. He took out his mobile again and pressed it to his ear. The same tune, the same monotonous drone. No reply! He defiantly thumbed in her number again. This time the call didn't even go through. At least he didn't have to hear her phone ringing again.

'No luck! We just have to make it to Channel 10 somehow', Navkar sighed.

'Well, we aren't getting anywhere in this thing. Let's get a taxi,' Salim said enthusiastically, trying to lift Navkar's spirits.

Navkar nodded as they both made their way to the main road. It seemed deserted. He checked his watch. It was 8.30. The sky had darkened. But at this time, Mumbai was usually a river of endless rush-hour traffic. Yet today, the flow of vehicles was a trickle, the wide roads almost empty and Navkar for the first time noticed with surprise how large they actually were. A flock of pigeons wheeled above, returning home. Where were the people?

'Is there a taxi stand nearby?' Navkar asked, pushing these thoughts away. Puzzles were for later.

'There is one under the bridge nearby,' Salim replied, hurrying behind him.

But there was no taxi there. They walked on down the unending road. Quickly, then slowly, and then fast again, for twenty minutes, without finding a taxi or an auto.

Suddenly, they heard a commotion from around the corner. They rushed over to find a large crowd gathered outside an electronics store, their eyes fixated on the large televisions displayed. Navkar couldn't make out what they were seeing. There was just a lot of noise, shouting, screaming.

He grabbed a boy standing near him, 'What's going on?'

'Terrorists!' the boy said, eyes wide. 'They've taken over the Mantralaya.'

Navkar felt a sick feeling sweep over him. It made his legs weaken and he stumbled back a few steps. It was happening already! So soon! Before he even had a chance! After all that he'd gone through, it was happening before he even had a chance.

He fumbled in his pocket and took out his phone and called the Channel 10 office.

'Navkar here,' he said urgently. 'Sudhir Navkar. Where is Tara? I have to meet up with her.'

The girl's voice was high-pitched, scared as she replied, 'She went to cover the press conference at the Mantralaya. It's so terrible! It's so…'

Navkar cut the call. He was staring at the TV, blind to what was being shown. He couldn't believe what was happening. He felt a hand on his shoulder. It was Salim. He brushed him off and tore away from the crowd, walking even faster than before, breaking into a jog.

Salim rushed behind him, 'Where are you going? What happened?'

'We are going to the Mantralaya.'

'How?'

'The buses are still running,' said Navkar without turning, as Salim suddenly noticed a big red BEST bus pull into the bus stop in front of them.

The bus had a row of empty seats, all proudly painted vomit green. Salim realized he had never noticed the colour before, probably because the buses were usually crammed with people. Today, however, it was just the driver and conductor.

'Which stop?' the conductor came striding over.

'Mantralaya,' Navkar muttered.

'Oh!' the conductor said, his eyes widening, 'You want to see the terrorists? It'll be my first time too. I've never seen something like this before.'

He rambled on, excited, 'Bollywood stuff!'

'Shut up!' Navkar roared at him.

By the time they reached, the Mantralaya had become a magnet of traffic and confusion. The bus wasn't moving any more. Nothing was. All the traffic in Mumbai seemed to have decided to rest in this spot—the most dangerous part of the city. People wanted a look.

Navkar and Salim decided that running would be faster. They ran past the police trying to cleave a way through the crowd. As expected, the police had arrived last on the scene. At the front were the hordes of cameras and busy news channel crews. Navkar tried to elbow his way through desperately, getting caught by a hand here, an accidental head butt there. Finally, they made their way to the front where the Channel 10 logo stood proudly amidst a bunch of frantic cameramen.

Navkar rushed to them, 'Where…where is Tara?'

He could hear shouts from behind him.

'Who is this?'

'Get out.'

'Saala, you're ruining my shot.'

A man grabbed him from behind, 'Stand back. It's not safe.'

'I'm from Channel 10,' Navkar protested. 'I need to see Tara.'

'Ma'am is not here. Now stand back,' the man said, pushing Navkar aside.

Navkar looked at him, 'What do you mean? Where is she?'

'Inside,' said the man grimly.

Navkar stared at the man, then at the building. He felt a deep hollow in the pit of his stomach and lurched a step back. 'Not again,' he said wildly. 'Not again!'

He felt a hand on his shoulder.

'Our super heroine has got herself into trouble,' a deep voice said.

He turned to find the bearded, grizzly face of David Agarwal. 'I thought I'd find you here,' the old man said.

Navkar didn't reply. He turned back to the building, looming like a giant curse over all of them. The bottom storey had a pillar of smoke rising from it, and a glow of fire from within. There was a fire brigade nearby, but the firemen hadn't tried getting near the building to put out the fire. Why would they? They were just minimum-wage forgotten labour.

David Agarwal stood next to him.

'Why did you come?' Navkar asked, glancing at him. 'You're not a field reporter.'

David scratched his white beard and replied, 'I was, when the last one happened.' He gave a dry chuckle, 'Maybe I don't want to get old. Or maybe I'm here for the same reason you are.'

Navkar noticed the glint in his eyes. Before Navkar could respond to that, he was suddenly shoved aside by a policeman. He looked around confused.

Large bulletproof vehicles had arrived and policemen marched in front of them, using their batons to part the crowd. Navkar jumped back as one of the constables took a wild swing, catching his neighbour in the ribs.

'Everyone move back. Move behind the perimeter set by

the police,' a voice boomed through a loudspeaker from the lead vehicle. 'This is for your safety. Please move back.'

'Saala, you come late and are telling us to move?' screamed the Channel 10 cameraman hit in the ribs. The constable kicked him in the stomach.

People started moving back, some hurling abuses, most just turning their cameras, mikes and phones towards the armoured vehicles and the battalion of police-bearing shields.

Navkar felt himself being dragged back by Salim. His mind was a whirl, still processing the facts. Tara was inside as a hostage and he was outside and completely helpless.

The men with shields started forming a line in front of the public, preventing them from going near the Mantralaya building beyond which the vehicles had to stop. Everyone was standing on their tiptoes, trying to catch a glimpse of what would next happen.

The vehicles stood next to each other. One by one, powerful floodlights on their roofs were switched on, covering the entire building in an eerie, dazzling light. They were part of the anti-terrorism protocol after 2008, meant to blind the terrorists and hide the police.

The lead vehicle opened its doors and khaki-clad men in bulletproof vests and helmets stormed out, each carrying a large combat rifle.

Navkar hurriedly climbed atop the Channel 10 van. He was just in time.

Madhav Rao Shinde stepped out of the lead vehicle. He was a large man with a deliberate walk. He too, was belted up in a vest and wearing a helmet.

He stood beside his vehicle with a few bodyguards, his back to the crowd and his chin raised, as he addressed the gunmen within the building, with his voice booming through the mike he held in his hand.

'We would like to speak to the leader of your group,' he said. 'Talk to us and perhaps we can all leave this place alive.'

There was no answer for a long time. The floodlights were searing white and burning hot. Shinde stood in the shadow and waited.

Suddenly there was a loud crack and the man next to Shinde fell to the ground.

'Take cover!' Shinde yelled into the microphone as he ran behind the vehicle and repeated, 'Take cover! They have snipers!'

Everyone was running now; away from the line of shielded police and hiding behind the news vans, buses and other vehicles.

Navkar, too, slid down and crouched behind the Channel 10 van. Salim was already there.

'I saw the shooter,' he muttered. 'They don't just have snipers. They have goggles.'

~

The police were firing like madmen now. Tara could hear their gunfire. The terrorists seemed calm. Three of them were crouching inside the room while three others were behind the wide, square pillars outside. She wondered how much ammunition the police had and how much they had already wasted.

The firing stopped suddenly. She assumed that the police, too, must have figured that out. She heard the same booming voice again. Was this Madhav Rao Shinde? She couldn't be sure; she'd never interviewed him. He'd always been elusive, known for his practicality and incorruptibility. They said he'd taken on a whole unit of naxals single-handedly once, when he was part of the special attack force sent to Chattisgarh. Some said he always had his gun with him, even when he slept.

It reminded her of someone else. It was a memory she didn't want.

'I am here to talk to you,' the voice on the megaphone said. 'Let me come in and talk. We can reach an understanding. Why shed blood unnecessarily?'

The chequered-shirted gunman was talking on the earpiece. His shoulders were slumped, as if disheartened. With an effort he straightened himself and barked out a curt command.

'Cut the lights now!'

The sniper was on a higher floor. She'd sensed that. There were four loud cracks and the sound of glass shattering. The blinding white light that had flooded into the room abruptly ceased.

The gunfire resumed, with even greater frenzy.

Shinde, in the meanwhile, was crouched behind his vehicle, half-rising in fury even as his officers held him down, in case he got hit by the snipers. He was shouting hoarsely, but even his voice was lost in the maddened firing that the men had started.

'Stop! Stop!' he yelled.

The bullets flew like rain, with as much effect. Shinde looked up, wondering if they were even reaching the fourth floor. He raised the microphone to his mouth, realizing that this was the only way to stop his own men.

'Stop, you bloody fools!' Shinde roared and his magnified

voice rolled like a wave over the whole street, till finally the guns hesitated and spluttered to a stop.

'Hold your positions!' Shinde snapped and switched off the microphone.

He fumbled in his pockets and retrieved his mobile phone. It was an old model. His daughter kept telling him to get one of those new 3D ones but he'd never felt the need. She'd told him it was because he was getting old.

'Murali, it's me,' he said on the phone.

'Madhav Rao! They killed your lights!' the man answered, his voice high. 'Do you have more? What's the plan now?'

Shinde's voice was grim as he answered, 'Murali, these terrorists know our procedures. Even the hostage and anti-terror procedures. They're really well trained.'

'Wh-what do we do now?'

'We need commandos, Murali. When are they coming?'

'We're talking to the army right now,' Murali answered weakly. 'The home minister is looking into it himself!'

Shinde frowned and his hands gripped his phone tighter. 'He's still looking? They haven't been released yet? There was supposed to be a unit ready in Mumbai, right, after 2008!'

'We got them removed five years back, Madhav Rao,' Murali said slowly. 'The department felt they were adversely affecting the prestige of the police. You also kept telling us that you could handle any attack, Madhav Rao. Everyone did.'

Shinde looked around him. His men had their guns ready but they were waiting for his command. They stayed behind cover, alert. Each of them had combat gear, new rifles. Most of them were fit, far fitter than anyone in the cadre a decade back. They were looking at him, waiting.

'Can you just hold out till then, Madhav Rao,' Murali was saying. 'They're not running around shooting like last time. They're just sitting with the hostages. Just hold your positions and wait.'

Shinde cut the call.

He called over Karat, the SSP of this Special Ops squad. The man had been the running champion of the state when he was younger. He'd only stopped when a bullet had shattered his thigh in Chattisgarh. He was still stronger and faster than most men Shinde had seen.

'We're going to pincer them, like the Jonamgarh operation,' Shinde whispered to him. 'I don't think they have enough men to hold more than the landing they're on. They're guarding the balcony and I think they'll cover the stairs and some of the corridors. There are a lot of entrances on the other side, a lot of rooms. I'm going to open fire here. You have to take ten people and slip away and come up behind them. We'll charge at them simultaneously.'

Karat was a man of few words. He saluted, as you'd do in the army, and moved from vehicle to vehicle, speaking to the men. When he was ready, he gave a thumbs-up signal and Shinde ordered gunfire.

When Karat gave the order, two men from each vehicle slipped back into the crowds. They started driving the crowd away, closing down the live cameras and phones, using batons and rifle butts to smash the devices and pushed through the crowd, creating a visible ruckus, and then slipping out, they made their way to the lane on the other side of the Mantralaya. It took five minutes of sprinting to circle the building.

'We're in the building,' Karat said on his phone, and Shinde ordered two of the vehicles to load up.

Karat's team then moved through the dimly lit corridors of the first floor, past old wooden tables and untidy piles of paperwork and small rooms that led to the bigger rooms of the sahibs. The whole floor was deserted. It made the rooms seem larger and the corridors longer. Silence lay thick, magnifying each step they took and every rustle of their clothes. Each amplified sound seemed to echo through the building, making it difficult to believe they hadn't been heard.

They seemed to be safe, however. They took the stairs, stopping and clearing every landing. The second floor seemed deserted as well. They reached the third and Karat stopped and updated their status. Some of the men spread out along the corridor as Karat spoke on the phone. That is when the screaming started.

The door of one of the rooms slammed open. The policeman next to it jumped, his gun swinging up and his finger squeezing the trigger reflexively, shooting an old lady in the chest with three bullets before he stopped. The rest of the people still waded forward, hugging him, crying and screaming in desperate relief. They spilled out into the corridor, almost forty of them.

'We thought we were going to die! We never thought you'd come,' one of them said.

The policeman pushed them aside, reaching for the dead lady and holding her up, trying to shake her, his khaki getting soaked with her blood.

Karat came over and wrenched him away. He then began to direct the crowd downstairs.

'Are there more people?' he asked them.

They didn't know. They didn't want to go down by themselves. They wanted the policemen to take them to safety.

Karat glared at them.

'The terrorists are on the fourth floor,' he growled and added, 'Go downstairs. We'll stop them here.'

The words didn't convince them, but the tone made them run. Their feet thundered down the stairs, deafening in the silence of the building, but as their footsteps faded, Karat became aware of other sounds. There were shouts and cries from deeper in the building and from that very floor. There were more people trapped here, waiting for rescue! There were other sounds, too. Sprinting footsteps above, on the fourth floor.

'With me!' Karat screamed and started to run. His thigh felt a jolt of pain with each step, but he would never let that stop him at times like this. He could hear the cries of the people ahead as they rushed forward. The footsteps above them were speeding up too and from the change in the sound, he knew when they took to the stairs.

He took out his phone as he ran and called Shinde. Breathless, he barked just one word, 'Engaging!'

A young man was running towards him and several others were following him. Some were peons, some bureaucrats. They were running loose, the younger men leading. Karat's eyes focused on a white-kurta-clad man stumbling forward at the end of the crowd and recognized him as Anand Kumar.

Karat's shoulder caught the young man in his face as he rushed passed him, shooting in the air and slamming through the crowd, with his squad following him. The confused, anguished cries of the people filled his ears. He couldn't make out any other sound. He couldn't hear the footsteps of his enemy. Three breaths more, he counted. Three breaths more and they would appear in the stairs.

Karat stretched his arms, bringing up his gun. The men around the white-kurta-clad man tried to shield him, thinking that Karat would shoot him. Karat lunged, slamming into Anand Kumar, pushing him to the ground, bringing his gun up and squeezing the trigger as the first gunman rounded the stairwell and spat gunfire.

The bullet caught the gunman in the chest, but he was wearing armour. The man stumbled back with the impact and ducked behind the stairwell. Around Karat now, six people lay bleeding, two of them policemen.

'Take cover! Get the people into cover!' Karat screamed.

He stumbled to his feet and helping Kumar up and pushed him towards a door on his right, 'Into the room.'

There was a metallic sound of something being thrown and bouncing off the floor. Karat tried to jump towards Kumar in a desperate effort but he had no chance. The grenade exploded right in front of them, throwing their charred bodies against the rest of the crowd.

It had been fifteen minutes. Shinde knew he had no time left. With each passing second he was wasting hundreds of bullets. Karat had not replied. He had said he was engaging the enemy three minutes back. There had been no communication since. Shinde now wondered if they'd run into trouble. He didn't understand how it could've got this bad. He had sent ten of his best men. He didn't think there were that many terrorists, probably eight or nine of them. The squad should have been able to take cover and put pressure on them.

Shinde's eyes searched the balcony of the fourth floor once more. He couldn't see any any movement. He looked at his watch again and realized that he had no option. He looked to the vehicles and gave the command to charge.

The two vehicles that had been loaded revved up and began to move. Immediately, there was firing from above, but the armour held. The vehicles built up speed towards the gate, swung in and skidded to a stop, even as gunfire from the floors above sprayed them. The back doors of the vehicles opened upwards, thick armoured doors providing cover as Shinde's squads leapt to the building, with their bulletproof shields held over their heads. The squads huddled in the corridor of the ground floor—under its natural cover—safe from the gunfire from atop, and contacted Shinde.

Shinde still couldn't get through to Karat. He tried the deputy's number and heard a breathless, panic-stricken voice.

'Manjrekar! Where is your squad now? Where is Karat?' Shinde asked.

'We-we're on the first floor. I…we…sir, Karat sir is dead, sir!' came the man's voice. 'They used grenades. Anand Kumarji, the minister was there, sir. He's also dead. There were lots of people, sir. Karat sir told us to get them to safety. We're bringing them out from the back, sir!'

Shinde stared at his men now making their way to the stairs at the end of the wing. The terrorists had grenades. They'd used grenades to kill Karat.

Suddenly there was an explosion near the stairs his men were climbing. Shinde felt himself jolted back. He knew what was going to happen, what would happen right now. There was no way of stopping it.

There was another explosion as more grenades were rolled down. Four men had already been killed, ripped apart. The rest of them turned, ran and leapt into the first vehicle. It had started moving when there was a sound of a rocket and the entire vehicle exploded, rising off the ground, tearing apart, a coffin of melting metal and fire.

The rest of the men just ran for it. They didn't even try to get in the remaining vehicle. They didn't even get till the gate before they fell, one by one, mowed down by the gunfire.

Shinde stared in horror, transfixed, not knowing what to do. His eyes caught a smoke trail for a split second.

Suddenly there was a deafening, numbing sound as one of the vehicles next to him exploded, blasting back into one of the press vans, tearing it into pieces.

The bastards had bazookas, Shinde realized to his horror! They hadn't used them so far!

It was the final blow. Shinde could see his men running now, abandoning those new, unused vehicles, the sign of the revamp after 2008, the pride of the force. He could see them leave all sanity behind, run blind and mad, like rabbits. Everyone was running, the remaining media people, his men in khaki. Some of them fell as the sniper took them. Shinde looked around, frozen in horror. The vehicle he was taking cover behind was still standing. He could do nothing else. He lunged inside, and retrieved the biggest weapon he could find, a grenade launcher. He stepped back, far back, setting his sights, squeezing the trigger.

The grenade didn't reach the fourth floor. It's range was too low.

But he felt a sudden pain in his shoulder, a blinding, disorienting pain. His hand rose to it. It was wet. He felt the world tilt as the pain spread through his back and shoulder. He was looking at the sky now and could see people's legs as they ran past him. He had been shot. He had been shot and he was lying there without cover, open to the sniper.

Suddenly he saw a face, that of a young man. The man held his shoulder and he felt his pain increase, tenfold, till it made him scream. He saw the sky move and now the back of a van loomed large next to him, invading his sky. The pain dulled. The man had let him go after dragging him behind the van.

'Who-who are you?' he asked feebly, a disoriented curiosity gripping him.

'Sudhir Navkar, sir,' the man said adding, 'I'm a reporter.'

'I hate reporters,' Shinde found himself saying. His lips opened and closed, without words. His throat felt parched. 'But you saved my life. Yes. Yes, you saved my life, I think.'

The man seemed to be hesitating, as if he wanted to say something but didn't know if he should. His face was turning red, blue. No, the whole world was. The whole world was changing colours.

'I know how they were trained, sir!' the man said suddenly. 'I know who these men are.'

Everything was tinted now. The man was looking at him intently. 'Tell me,' Shinde said, weakly.

The man's face was grim. There was fury in his eyes. Fury at what, Shinde wondered? He had to keep his eyes open. He had to listen. But the world was swimming now, darkening. He felt darkness overcome his senses.

TWENTY-FIVE

The chai had a mouldy smell to it. The man was used to it. Airport control never had good tea. He didn't drink it for the taste, it just helped calm his nerves.

It hadn't been a good day for him. He had found out just this morning that his wife was having an affair, and now this. The channels had been running the same scenes over and over for an hour now, but he still found it frightening. The police had reached late as always. They didn't even look prepared, the bastards! One couldn't trust them to get anything right. Couldn't trust anyone these days. Everyone was just out for themselves. Lying, cheating, stealing to get ahead.

He wondered how much each of these policemen had stolen in their lives. And the ministers being held hostage? He wished they would all just die in this attack, burn and die. Who took ministers hostage anyway? Nobody wanted to save them. He remembered his wife's face from the morning. He spat out his chai in disgust. The TV was still better.

He gave the radar a quick check. Headquarters had called him a couple of times to check if everything was okay. The airport was closed. They'd just kept one person on duty, in case any stray flights turned up. He'd volunteered. He didn't want to go home any more.

He got up to get another cup, wondering if the samosa boy was still working tonight. He doubted it but decided to call and check anyway. His mobile was next to the radar. As he went to retrieve it, he noticed a funny thing. That couldn't be right—there was a big rectangle on screen. An airship? He nearly spilled his chai in surprise. He checked carefully. The rectangle only grew clearer. It was approaching fast. It was an airship! He fumbled for the communications switch. The samosa could wait. He needed to get headquarters, quick!

'I think an airship has entered airspace,' he screamed over the mouthpiece, tipping his chai all over the controls in his agitation. Damn it! Nothing could go right today. He didn't hear anything for a moment, as if the guys at the other end were still processing their disbelief. He tried to dry the controls with his sleeve, which only made his sleeve wet. Damn! They still hadn't answered.

'Hello, this is control tower. Did you hear me?' he yelled again. Damn these bastards! Sarkari idiots! They would sleep through the end of the world.

'Are you sure?' came back the reply.

Why were they delaying? He needed instructions. It could be more terrorists. They might need to scramble air force jets. Before he could reply though, he heard a crackle on line one. The airship was trying to contact him.

'Wait,' he yelled into the mouthpiece as he turned on line one. 'Control tower, this is Vishnu Rustomjee Mistry requesting entry into Mumbai airspace,' a calm voice came over the line.

Vishnu Mistry? The billionaire? What was going on?

'Sir,' he started nervously. 'Are you in the aircraft?'

'No. The call is being routed through a satellite. But the

aircraft is mine. I'm bringing in help for the Mantralaya situation.'

He was bringing in help? What was he talking about?

'Sir, you do not have permission. This airport is closed today. If you're out of fuel, we can allow emergency landing,' he said slowly.

'Listen to me,' came the voice, firmer this time. 'The home minister has just given his approval for the paramilitary to be released. They will be getting the orders in Pune within a few minutes. They will get ready, find a plane, fly here, land. It'll take them three hours more. Many more people will be dead by then.'

The plane was not slowing down, or flying lower. It was going to shoot overhead. That would be a violation of air space.

'How do I know it's you?' the man said into the mike. It sounded like Mistry, though he had only heard the voice on TV a few times. But even if it was, he couldn't let Mistry in. The only possibility was a forced landing.

'Airport control, do you read us? What plane is it? Do they have permission? Should we inform the air force?' came a voice from the headquarters.

He stayed quiet. If he told headquarters, they would have to scramble fighters. Those were the orders, the rules.

'I cannot prove to you that I'm Vishnu Mistry,' line one crackled again, 'Not right now. And I'm afraid this is not the time to wait. Every minute the Mantralaya goes without help, more people will die.' There was an urgent conviction in the voice. 'You'll have to have faith tonight, and you'll have to be brave.'

'I can't. I'll lose my job,' the man he heard himself say.

He wondered if he needed it now, actually. His wife had left him anyway. Maybe he just wanted some people to die today.

The voice on the other side was calm, 'At our difficult moments, we must trust each other to do the right thing. I trust you, Kapoor. You must trust me in turn.'

Kapoor caught his breath, surprised. Mistry knew his name. Akhilesh Kapoor, born in Vistrapur village, thirty-four years old, married fourteen years. A nobody.

And here was a plane that shouldn't be there and on the line was Vishnu Rustomjee calling him by name, asking for his help, depending on him.

Kapoor looked at the TV again. The first police force had been decimated.

'Let the plane through, Kapoor, and you would've done your part.'

Kapoor looked at the radar, the big red blip of the airship. If he let it go he would be trusting an unknown voice, a possible threat. If anything went wrong he would be kicked out, discredited. Maybe the media would get to him, make stories about the controller who let a terrorist plane in. Maybe he would be put in jail.

He turned to the carnage on TV now; the exploding vehicles, the chaos, dying policemen and the commissioner getting shot.

The plane got ever nearer. It would fly over the airport within minutes. If he informed HQ they would get jets to shoot it down or force it to turn around. The Mantralaya would burn. There would be no hope for it.

The way his day was going, it would probably be the biggest mistake of his life, but then, how did he care? Life could go screw itself.

'Good luck, sirji,' he said quietly, and cut off the connection to headquarters and tore off his headset.

~

The noise had died down—the gunfire and the screaming. The night had become strangely, eerily quiet, only broken by the sirens of ambulances that were making the rounds.

It was a new-moon night, Navkar realized. He was sitting on the pavement in one of the lanes opposite the Mantralaya, smoking listlessly. His face was lit by red and blue lights as an ambulance stopped beside him and took away a few of the remaining policemen who'd been hit.

A shadow fell on him, cutting off the light, and he looked up to see Salim, mud-caked, blood-splattered. He supposed he looked much the same. He hadn't thought about it till then.

'What're you smoking?' Salim asked.

Navkar held up his cigarette before taking another drag. His phone beeped with a message from his parents and he replied that he was safe, far away from the action.

Salim sat beside him and fumbled in his pocket to retrieve a half-smoked rolled beedi. 'I keep one for tense situations.'

Navkar didn't look at him. 'I'm not tense.'

Salim lit the beedi and handed it to him. The burning smell wasn't of tobacco.

He glanced at Salim, who shrugged and said, 'For tense situations.'

Navkar felt the smoke sink into him and leant back against the lamp post beside him. It was an old one, its form ornamental, quaint.

'It was a brave thing you did,' Salim said, after a few minutes. 'You could've been shot.'

'I could've been shot many times over the last few weeks,' Navkar muttered and added, 'Ever since I met you.'

Salim winced visibly. 'It's been the same for me. It's not that I'm always running around getting shot at. It's these last few weeks.' He paused before saying, 'It's what we were investigating, you and I.'

'You and I, huh?' Navkar handed him the joint. 'What good was it anyway? We didn't change a thing. It was all a waste.'

Salim frowned as he took a drag. The sirens of the ambulance faded away, only to be replaced by another.

'They got massacred,' Navkar said quietly. 'The damn stupid fools, they got massacred.'

'I'll tell you something,' Salim said finally. 'Something that we in the basti know better than you middle-class types, because we have to live with this truth every day.'

He frowned and looked at Navkar. 'We can't change everything. We can't make everything go our way. The best we can do, is follow our karm. That's as good as it gets.'

It was then that they heard the sound. A faraway sound, a whir and a rustle, like a sound of a distant thunderclap, or that of a giant bird.

Salim looked up, surprised, the beedi slipping from his fingers. He then stood up and started running, following the sound. Navkar watched him go and then with a grunt, rose himself and followed him. They ran out of the lane and towards the mess of cars and vans and wreckage outside the Mantralaya.

Above them, an airship appeared, a large, bulky aircraft of military design with monstrous propellers louder than thunder. It was flying so low, they could see the rivets in its undercarriage. They ran below it, following it, their hearts in their mouth.

The plane swooped low enough to brush tree tops. Rockets fired from it—one, two, three—whooshing through the air and slamming into the fourth floor of the building. They noticed smoke from this impact. The plane then rose above the building. A hatch opened behind it. Even from here, they could see the bloom of parachutes as people jumped out of it, gliding to the top of the Mantralaya.

TWENTY-SIX

Tara was feeling tired, her calves were getting a cramp but she didn't have the will to spread them out. She wanted to sleep in that comfortable bed in the tower, with a view of Mumbai shining in the moonlight. Peaceful, safe and in his arms. She sat up straight with a jerk, catching herself. She was thinking of him again. Looking around her, she noticed one of the terrorists looking at her with a kind of undisguised yet hopeless desire.

They'd brought in the one who'd been shot by the police in the skirmish that had just taken place. Most of the bullets were embedded in his jacket, but the last one had torn through his jugular. He'd bled to death.

She could see that tension was beginning to show. The eyes of the terrorists stared in hollow anxiety from behind those black masks. One of them, in a blue shirt, had switched on the TV in the room and was now scanning through the Hindi news channels intently. The media had captured most of the massacre. The horrifying images seemed to cause a strange anxiety in him. He hugged his knees, rocking to and fro, taut as a bow string.

The leader, in the white shirt, had gone quiet as well. His face was solid, looking ahead gravely, nodding a couple times to instructions. He took out a cigarette slowly.

Tara wondered when the paramilitary forces would arrive. The last time, they'd taken nine hours. The government had not become any better in the last ten years.

But a part of her knew it was good that they weren't coming. It was better if they just didn't turn up at all. She knew what would happen once they did. Everyone knew.

There would be death.

There was a strange sound that was building, starting from the edges of her consciousness but growing stronger and stronger till she looked up. It was a deep rumbling, a throbbing of the air.

It was a plane, she realized suddenly.

She looked out the doorway. There was a bright yellow glow around it—the fire downstairs had started to flare up. She noticed something, some small black thing flying towards them. A stone? It came right at them, and suddenly it was whistling through the room, smashing into the wall opposite. Was there an explosion? The whole room was filling up with smoke. There must have been an explosion. The smoke was strangely coloured, it filled her lungs, it burned. She felt her eyes closing against the acidic sensation, tearing up even when they were closed. She was coughing, everyone was coughing.

'It's a tear-gas shell!' yelled the blue-shirted terrorist near her.

Tara looked up, the room was covered in smoke and fear. A few of the hostages were shrieking in pain, rolling on the ground, trying to escape the burning smoke. She had to escape too. She had to. She couldn't breathe, her lungs and insides were burning away. She desperately tried to crawl her way to the doorway. The tear gas was everywhere, in her nose, her eyes, her mouth.

'Retreat, retreat to the other room!' she could hear the terrorists screeching to each other. The blue-shirted one stepped on her hand as he tried to reach the doorway, but she couldn't even scream, as the pain burned through her eyes. She could hear the sounds of a machine gun go off. It was one of the terrorists in the room firing out into the passageway. There was no returning gunfire. She couldn't hear footsteps either. Nobody was there. The smoke was clearing a bit and she could make out the silhouette of the stocky white-shirted man standing firmly in the centre.

'We must retreat,' said the chequered-shirted man, going up to him.

'No!' he barked back. 'We are not moving anywhere.'

'I don't want to die!' the man in the blue shirt yelled, his voice cracking.

Tara could make out that he was young, maybe eighteen or twenty or so.

'Stand your ground,' the leader turned fiercely to him. 'Those are our orders!'

'No, no!' the blue-shirted boy screamed. 'Listen,' he said, gripping the other man desperately, 'Listen, maybe we can use the hostages now! Maybe they'll actually give in to our demands? Right? It's possible! We can take the plane and the money and run away! We can be free!'

The leader looked him in the face and asked, 'And what of our families? What happens to them?'

'We'll get them with us! Once we have the money we can bring them over. Once we have the money, we can do that!'

'They will be dead before we leave Mumbai. You know that.'

The boy's chest was now heaving with ragged breaths. He

was looking around with maddened eyes. 'I-I don't care! What did they ever do for me? What have they ever done in their lives? They'll just waste it all!'

'You have responsibilities,' the other man said coldly. 'Get a grip on yourself.'

'No, no, no, no! Why should I die? Why should I die and they enjoy?' the boy screamed, his hands on the trigger of his machine gun.

'Hey!' the chequered-shirted man jumped in to calm him down. 'Let the enemy come first. Don't lose it now.'

'I don't care, I don't care. I don't want to die here!' the boy cried, pressing the trigger as the bullets streamed out. One barely missed Tara but she saw blood fly out behind her. He was going to kill them all! She heard sickening thuds behind her as bodies collapsed on each other.

The chequered-shirted man tried to jump him, but the boy pushed him aside with a kind of manic strength.

'I'm not going to die here,' he cried out. 'You can't make me!' He brought his gun around. 'Stay away. Stay away! Or I'll kill everyone!'

His gun swung in an arc, towards her.

Tara shut her eyes. This was it. She wouldn't even see the morning sun, the beautiful monsoon sun she loved so much. This was it.

There was a loud crack of gunfire.

It felt ok, death didn't hurt so much. In fact, it didn't hurt at all.

She heard a soft thud.

'Who else doesn't want to follow orders?' she heard someone growl.

Tara opened her eyes and saw the blue-shirted boy on the

ground, his head turned away from her. The leader had shot him.

She was alive.

Suddenly, she heard dozens of loud thumps on the ceiling.

'They are here. The commandos,' hissed the chequered-shirted man, 'What do we do now?'

The leader was quiet for a bit, then readied his gun and let out a grunt. 'We do what we came here for.'

~

The satellite phone rang again.

It was the board of directors, calling for the fifth time in the past hour. They were getting slow at keeping track of him. Vishnu had always suspected that they meticulously tracked him whenever he left the tower. The slow old men, they had probably been distracted by the TV.

It kept ringing. They wouldn't let it go. They never did, when it was about money. He could pick up now, though. They didn't have the time to stop him.

Vishnu leaned over to grab the satellite phone, as the pilot let out a sigh of relief to finally hear it stop wailing.

'It's Cowasji,' a cold voice sounded through the phone. 'You better have an explanation for this, boy.'

'I'm not a boy any more, Mr Cowasji. That's the best explanation,' Vishnu replied before he could stop himself. There was no reply. Cowasji was obviously controlling his temper.

'Do you know how much this is costing the group, this little expedition of yours?' said a sterner voice this time. It was Irani. The man should've died decades ago but his old claw-like fingers had held on for dear life.

Vishnu realized that they had put him on speaker phone.

'Each of them costs ten thousand dollars an hour. It's my personal capital investment in our group,' Vishnu said.

'And who exactly are these people?' asked Irani, unimpressed as expected.

'They are mercenaries used to guard the Kandahar uranium mines,' Vishnu replied flatly. He knew saying it plainly would infuriate Irani more.

He heard the old man take a deep breath before he asked, 'And you're flying them into the Mantralaya?'

'Yes'

'This boy is mad! Crazy!' Irani sighed. 'I can't talk to him! Vakil, put some sense in him.'

Vishnu checked his watch. He didn't have time for this.

'Vakil sahib,' Vishnu started. 'This goes beyond money, but you will profit from this in the long term. Let me save this city tonight.'

Vakil was still quiet. Vishnu could hear them murmuring amongst each other. He heard Vakil clearing his throat and knew what they had decided.

'We cannot authorize that,' Vakil stated, his voice definite.

'People's lives are at stake, Vakil sahib,' Vishnu said, his voice clipped. 'It isn't something I can let the board of directors control. Your cooperation is expected.'

The directors weren't happy with that. Vishnu could hear them arguing over the line. Irani was yelling. They were grappling over the phone.

'Your father didn't leave this company to do as you please!' Irani screeched, losing his temper.

'My father didn't have a choice but to leave this company to me,' Vishnu corrected.

He cut the line swiftly. *The work of men is always to thwart the goals of the great*, his father had told him that once. He looked down at the dark waters below him and the Queen's Necklace straddling it. This was the time for conviction.

~

They hugged each other, the kind of hugs Tara had seen in families when someone was going away for a long time. The chequered-shirt man ended with a fist bump with the leader—an American gesture that had travelled on airwaves to the ends of the world.

'Do you think it exists?' he asked the other. 'The other side?'

The white-shirted man laughed. 'A bit late to ask that question.'

The chequered-shirted man then turned and left. Everyone, except one man and the leader, joined him. They slung their backpacks, rattling with metal, and turned, past the balcony outside, to the corridor leading straight into the heart of the building, where a stairwell led up to the roof.

The thin man beside him ruffled through his backpack and picked out a grenade. It had worked against the police beyond their wildest expectations.

'Be careful,' the chequered shirt warned. 'We do not want to die at our own hands.'

The thin man didn't answer. His hand was clenched tight around the grenade, his steps jerky. Suddenly the lights around them flickered, once, twice, and then all went out. The men froze. The thin man's arm swung, throwing the grenade instinctively, and the metal clattered off the wall and floor and the end of the corridor in front lit up in a red blaze for a moment.

'Don't waste the next one,' the chequered shirt said tersely.

There were sounds of footsteps in front of them and he raised his hand, gesturing them to take cover in the doorways of rooms alongside. They waited there, as the footsteps got nearer, hideously loud in the silence. Their enemy wore heavy boots.

'It's raining outside,' said the thin man quietly, pointing to the window in this room. It was true. There was a soft patter of rain against the glass, the gentle fall of a million drops under the unearthly halo of a streetlight.

'Open the window,' the chequered shirt said. 'I'll keep guard. Go open it.'

The thin man hurried to the glass, lifting it, and the smell of rain entered the room, dancing its way into the dank air-conditioned atmosphere.

'They should make perfumes of this,' the chequered shirt said. 'It's the best smell in the world.'

There was a sudden explosion of wooden splinters and the chequered shirt fell back, his arm and side bloody. The battle had started. Pain shot through his flesh, burning. He saw his men in the other room return fire. The thin boy rushed to the door, picking out another grenade, throwing it and ducking back in a smooth motion. The chequered shirt stood up painfully, looking at his men in the opposite room. They'd taken cover as well. The enemy's gunfire had stopped. They must be running, lunging for safety, he thought. The explosion would happen any second now.

Moments ticked by. There was no sound, no blast.

The thin man couldn't resist. He peeked out and when he ducked back his eyes were large, confused.

'There's frost,' he said hoarsely and repeated, 'There's frost covering the whole corridor.'

The chequered shirt stared at him. A memory slid into his mind—that of a video of the American military. They'd been showcasing their latest weapons. They called them nitrogen guns—a weapon made out of liquid nitrogen.

'Th-that's impossible!' he stammered. 'How can they have that?'

His eyes jerked up at the sound of a rocket and then there was an explosion in the room opposite. It filled with white smoke and through it he could see the covering of frost, the veil of cold death. He could see the frozen look of surprise on the faces of the men and then their legs crumbling into fragments.

'Bite the pill!' he screamed, as they fell to the ground, pieces of their body shattering, their eyes screaming.

He could hear the footsteps of the enemy get closer and looked around frantically. There was a door at the other end, leading to the next room. He pulled the thin man behind him and ran through the door. It led out to the corridor through another room.

They ran through the corridor, their footsteps echoing, and rounded the corner and stopped, hunched, breathing hard.

'How can they have nitrogen guns?' he repeated in horror.

The thin man was squatting, holding his gun, staring at him. 'Wh-what do we do now?'

He leant back against the wall. 'We have to try and hold them as long as we can.'

'Why?' the other man asked quietly as he took off his mask.

The chequered-shirt man sighed, and also threw away his

mask and breathed deeply, wiping the sweat on his skin. 'That feels much better.'

'Why?' the thin man asked again.

'Those are the orders,' he said, shrugging.

'How long?'

His companion looked away.

The thin man asked, 'Till we die?'

The other man looked inside his bag and then examined his gun. 'It won't be long. They have those rockets.'

That was true. It might not be long at all. He heard a door slam open, the first door. They'd advanced. They were coming.

He straightened and checked his ammunition.

'I want to kill some of them…before I go,' the thin man said suddenly.

His companion looked up, surprised.

'I don't want to die like a loser,' the thin man said.

Another door had been opened.

The chequered shirt took his position, raising his gun. 'We'll try to kill them,' he said.

'No!' the other one cried out. 'I want to make sure! I want to make sure I do.'

The chequered-shirt frowned. The smell of the rain had drifted in behind them, faint but unmistakeable. It was just the beginning. It would rain for months more. Festivals would come. People would dance. He remembered that. There was plenty to remember, plenty that he would remember till the moment he died.

But each moment of remembrance would only make it harder.

He replaced the magazine in his gun and nodded to the

thin man. When the next door opened, they charged with their guns blazing, the pins on all their grenades removed.

~

Chatterjee wore a grim, earnest expression and too much powder as he glared at the camera. 'We have already seen responses pour in over social media from around the country and the world. Hundreds and thousands of prayers and messages are being sent over this tragic event. Our reporters have been talking to people around the country for their reactions.'

The feed cut to a bespectacled man with a thin moustache. 'Here we have Mr Kholwade, here in Mumbai, speaking to us,' the reporter said. 'Tell us what you're feeling, Kholwadeji.'

'I just feel that if our politicians and bureaucrats worked properly, these things could be prevented.'

The reporter asked, 'And what do you think of Vishnu Mistry's actions? Was it right for him to fly commandos into the Mantralaya? There are a lot of hostages whose lives have been put in danger.'

The tall guy next to Kholwade answered, 'The police charged in before him anyway. Besides, it's not always about laws. Someone has to take responsibility. Someone has to take some action.'

The camera cut to a college campus with the same question.

'And where is the army anyway?' a girl put in. 'Where is everyone who's lawfully supposed to be there?'

A large youth stepped forward saying, 'Vishnu Mistry has done something heroic! Anyone who doesn't think so is a traitor to this country!'

'Yeah, we all salute him,' his friends joined in, 'We salute his courage! He's a total hero!'

The news shifted back to the studio. Chatterjee glowered at the camera. 'Vishnu Mistry's helicopter has just arrived at the Mantralaya. It's circling above the building now. We had seen that an airship was flown in earlier, for which Vishnu Mistry has claimed responsibility. Now we see him braving the bazookas that the terrorists used against police vehicles. One of those could destroy this chopper, so he is taking a terrible personal risk here. We bring you the latest images.'

The camera was far away from the building. No reporter was that crazy, no one was going near any more. The faint sound of the chopper was heard in the distance, it was a small blip in the sky, it's fog light scurrying over the ground.

The reporter was a young woman, her hair in disarray, an ugly bruise blossoming on her face. She was screaming at the camera.

'He's here! He's actually here!'

~

The white-shirted man was quiet as he hunched over a large black box, unpacking what looked like an advanced version of a megaphone. The other remaining gunman was fidgeting by the doorway, heaving in dry coughs and wiping his eyes continuously. The loud whirring of the helicopter invaded the room filled with coughing, crying people.

The white-shirted man assembled the megaphone and slung it around his neck, then removed his earpiece, snapping it into two.

He looked up. 'It's time,' he said.

He walked through the sobbing captives and Tara thought

for a frightening moment that he was reaching for her. She was wrong. He grabbed Chauhan's collar, lifted him up and gripped his neck in an arm lock. Then he dragged him away, pressing his gun to Chauhan's temple when he struggled too much.

A strange bright glow was framing the door and the man walked out, with Chauhan as a shield to find a strong beam of light from the helicopter framing him, pinning him.

He tightened his grip on Chauhan and when he spoke his words were picked up by the megaphone, boosted and delivered across the street and square.

'I will kill the chief minister right now, unless my demands are met!' his voice boomed. 'I will kill him right now.'

Chauhan felt the metal tip of the gun digging into his skin. His eyes were blinded by the light and his scanty hair was flying in the whirlwind caused by the helicopter. What was it doing flying so low, so close to the building?

'I want the commandos to be pulled back,' the man yelled. 'I'm talking to you, Vishnu Mistry! I want your commandos out!'

It was drizzling and Chauhan felt trickles of water running down his face and neck. The helicopter was Vishnu's. His soldiers had stormed the building. The thoughts made Chauhan's head swirl. They had done what the police couldn't. They'd done what should have already gotten Chauhan killed. If it were him, he would've shot the hostages long back, the moment the tear gas hit.

'I want this helicopter!' the man continued. 'Pull your men back and take me on this helicopter and everyone lives. Otherwise I'll first put a bullet through the chief minister and then my partner will blast a grenade in the room.'

The helicopter began to lower further, coming almost at level with the balcony. Its light glared at them and their shadows grew long and fierce on the wall.

Chauhan felt the man's grip tighten around him, almost choking him. He struggled, his face turning and he saw the man's red eyes. Red, wet, streaming eyes. He was crying. Chauhan stared at him, at the gun, at the face.

Out of the corner of his eye, Chauhan saw something impossible. The gunman blinked and the gun was removed from Chauhan's head and pointed straight ahead. The door of the helicopter had opened. The light was blinding. All Chauhan could see was a silhouette hanging to the side, casually, as if stepping out of a car. It took him a couple of seconds to register that it was Vishnu Mistry hanging outside, looking at them. Was he mad?

'Pull back your men!' the man yelled again. He then shot at the helicopter…once…twice. The bullets ricocheted off the metal. He pressed the gun back against Chauhan's temple. 'Pull back or I kill him.'

Chauhan could see those eyes now, even in the light. Those unblinking, terrifying, glittering eyes. Vishnu was looking straight at him. He was a madman. Chauhan could see that now. That was why he'd always been so unsettling. He was crazy. Vishnu looked away, turning his attention to the rotors and then at the rainfall. He seemed to be thinking.

'He won't do it,' Chauhan hissed to the gunman. 'He won't do it. Go back to the room. Take me back!'

The gunman didn't move. Vishnu's eyes had found them again. Chauhan grabbed the arm around his neck.

'We're going to die,' he cried out.

Vishnu's arm rose, a blur in the darkness, and there was a crack of a gunshot.

Chauhan stared at him, feeling the grip of the gunman loosen. He turned and saw his captor falling back. There was a red bloom on his mask.

The beating sound of the chopper drowned everything out. It all felt like a dream. Chauhan stood there, frozen.

The only remaining gunman rushed out, his gun ready, about to shoot. The bullets hit him on his head, neck and chest and he crumpled, his gun clattering away, sliding to Chauhan's feet.

He could hear a faint voice, lost in the sound of the rotors. He heard it again, like a ghost calling out to him.

'Is she alright?' Vishnu was shouting. 'Is she hurt?'

Chauhan looked back at him, at his form silhouetted in the glare of the chopper's light and nodded slowly. The helicopter began to rise and Chauhan's eyes rose with it, till that shadowed form was lost to his eyes.

Chauhan looked down. There was still a crowd. It was getting larger. People were running in from all sides. The helicopter began to descend in the middle of the empty road. People were shouting , cheering, forming a circle around it.

Chauhan leant over the balustrade, shaking.

It was all over. He was safe.

He stared at the crowd forming below the helicopter as a ladder was thrown down from it and Vishnu began to climb down.

It suddenly occurred to him that not a single person was looking in his direction, looking to see whether he was dead or alive.

TWENTY-SEVEN

The next day broke dull and rainy, with whipping winds straying in from the sea. The area around the Mantralaya wore a look of desolation and weariness. The charred remains of the police vehicles had not been removed. The ground floor of the building lay wet and soot-covered. A barricade had been put around the building and workers were clearing it of debris and weapons and the dead.

In the pavements lining the road outside, in the unseemly quiet of this morning, street vendors rolled in their carts, poured oil on their pans, and the greasy sizzle and spicy scent of their wares floated over the wasteland.

The day passed in mourning and accusation. A consensus was reached on the number of people who had died. There were forty-six overall, twenty-one of them policemen, eight from the media and seventeen were attached to the Mantralaya, either as part of the government or political parties. A hundred and thirty-six others had been wounded.

Blood lay crusted on the tiles of the road, colouring trickles of rain water, slowly washing away.

No one was very sure who was responsible for the attack. Some reports blamed the Lashkar-e-Taiba, some the Indian branch of ISIS and some the renewed Taliban regime in

Afghanistan. Not a single attacker had survived. There was no one to answer questions. The police claimed that two of them were part of the Nawab Khan gang that was a significant part of the Mumbai underworld, though no details could be found on this. Three of the members were clearly of Middle Eastern or Central Asian ethnicity.

One newspaper carried the headline that it was an international act of terror and the same line was carried around the world. The defence secretary of the United States expressed his deepest condolences and his strong feeling that India needed to increase the depth of their strategic partnership. He called for a joint presence in securing freedom in the Afghanistan International Region and containing regional terror elements.

Many news channels focused on the Indian presence among the attackers. They said several hostages had heard the attackers speak in Hindi, with the kind of accent common in Indian cities.

People agreed on only two things. First, that the unthinkable had happened. The shameful, the horrendous. When a prominent minister who hadn't been in the Mantralaya made the mistake of commenting that the attack had been far less devastating than the 2008 one, it became the last day of his career.

The second was on the visible and pathetic vulnerability of the government, contrasted with the incredible heroism shown by Vishnu Mistry.

'I wouldn't have risked my life to save those bastards', tweeted activist and singer, Saranya Subramaniam, and in five hours, the sentence was retweeted sixty-three lakh times.

Chief Minister Rajender Chauhan spent the day visiting

the bereaved families, his cavalcade blocking roads throughout the city as he travelled to and fro. Outside each household, a chaos of reporters and onlookers waited for him. His guards had to push their way through. It seemed to become more difficult with each stop.

Finally, under an orange-red sunset sky lined with streaks of purple clouds, it happened. Chauhan and his entourage were outside a large chawl that was a relic of the days when Mumbai was a mill town. It was home to a peon who'd died in the machine-gun fire, but the crowd didn't let him in. They shouted and pushed and charged his guards; a thousand grappling, angry hands outstretched. They cursed him and his lineage, their fingers, hooked into talons, gripped his clothes, his arms, yelling for his blood. Someone hurled a rock, he felt it hit his back, the pain shooting through his body. His guards fired in the air to disperse the crowd, but that only made them angrier. The guards somehow managed to drag him back to his vehicle in one piece.

'I don't understand,' Chauhan yelled in bewilderment, 'Why are they doing this? I was there! I was a hostage too!' His voice shook, hoarse and raw.

The rest of the day had several sporadic incidents of people roughing up the police or getting into deliberate altercations. The public seemed to have lost faith in those responsible for law and order. If a heavily guarded government office could fall to terrorists, what chance did the common man have?

The evening seemed to come upon the city suddenly, the winds dying away like tide, leaving the roads and its people unmoored. The rains, too, had stopped for the day, their sheen covering the roads like a carpet of mirrors. The dark visage of the Mantralaya loomed over its surroundings.

The first vehicle stopped with a screech when Chauhan saw the marchers. The one behind it didn't stop in time, it's plastic groaning as its bumper moulded inwards with the impact.

There were nearly three hundred marchers, each carrying a waving, flickering candle, each dressed in white. At the head of the column some carried placards, all saying the same thing:

STOP MAKING US VICTIMS.

The people settled outside the Mantralaya, stopping all the traffic around it. The handful of people who had come to work in the building found they were unable to go home.

Chauhan found himself sitting in his office staring at the gathered pinpricks of light, his stomach roiling in hunger. He wondered if he should order a lathi charge to disperse them, but decided against it. The police wouldn't agree anyway. For the first time in thirty-four years, he slept on an empty stomach, curled up on the sofa in his room.

But a sound sleep evaded him.

Twice that night, he woke up to the memory of cold metal against his skin, the memory of staring into a loaded gun, not knowing what would happen. He remembered his boastful words to Tara. He'd said he would deal with them, with the letter sender, with everything. It felt strange now, in the shiver of this hungry night. Under the thrall of his dripping, malfunctioning AC, the idea of those thoughts when faced with death seemed so ridiculous. He hadn't realized it then—perhaps he hadn't wanted to. He could actually have died that night. It could actually have happened.

He could have died the moment Shinde charged.

He eventually drifted into sleep, but it remained troubled,

twisted, and it was broken at first light as his phone began to ring insistently. He sat up blearily, his reddened eyes blinking, remembering those of the gunman. Around him the pale of the morning spread over the firmament and the rise and fall of the sea.

It was Anand Kumar's wife, Nandini. 'They failed us, Chauhan sahib, they failed us,' she said between hoarse sobs.

'People are right! We've let things slide too long. The police have become useless! They let him die, right in front of them, Chauhan sahib. We've let it go on too long.'

Chauhan didn't answer. He remembered her. A quiet woman with a dignified presence.

'We need to pass the bill now, Chauhan sahib. We need to renew our police. People are demanding it. They're right.'

He could hear her trying to rein in her voice, cut out her sobs, but she failed. She was crying now.

'M-my…hi-his party will support you!' she said. 'We have to do something!'

Chauhan felt the age in his knees as he stood up and walked to the window.

At ten o' clock in the morning, the third day after the attack, it was announced that the Justice Renewal Bill would be passed in an emergency session of the parliament.

The bill had three segments.

The first dealt with structural reforms of the police department and personnel. The police would now answer to a board comprising members of the government, judiciary and civil society. Their transfers and promotions would be decided by a majority in the board. There would be no single minister in charge. Police training would be intensified and a formalized system of performance review would be put in place. Induction into the police service would no longer be an assurance of life-long employment. It would be for a term of five years, at the end of which their performance would determine their continuation.

The second dealt with upgrading the police force, both in terms of infrastructure and numbers. The most important changes would be with regard to housing and physical infrastructure. Each police chowki bigger than 200 square feet would be rebuilt to a multi-storeyed building of at least ten floors, with the higher floors providing housing for the personnel. All police quarters would be rebuilt into buildings at least thirty storeys high. The housing capacity would thus be upgraded from the current twenty thousand to sixty thousand employees, which would be the new strength of the Mumbai police.

Five urban security training institutes would be opened, each admitting eight thousand students yearly. Hiring would begin within a month.

Finally, the third section of the bill would focus on increasing the strength of the state judiciary by fifteen thousand members over the next four years. There would be a new high court building built in Mumbai, which would be thirty storeys high, which would make it possible for two hundred cases to be heard simultaneously every day. A law institute would be opened in the Mumbai-Pune intersection which would admit five thousand students every year, along with ten state-of-the art legal colleges affiliated with various universities in the state. These would be built using the PPP model and each would admit at least two thousand students a year. Every court in the state would be rebuilt to be housed in a ten-storey building with the capacity to hear fifty cases at the same time. The high court would appoint a project management team to track and eliminate court lag in three years.

Nagarajan's party opposed the bill, calling it a militarization of the police. Kirloskar pledged his support, maintaining that it was the current government's incompetence that had delayed these important reforms in the first place.

The prime minister flew down in the afternoon, visiting the Mantralaya and Padmavati Hospital, where many of the wounded had been admitted. He gave a short statement to the media, promising to bring justice, and admitting that these reforms should be looked at by the centre, and perhaps be adopted at the national level.

In the evening, as dusk gathered around the cloud-worn tree in the middle of Vishnu's garden and its leaves shuddered with raindrop tears, a throng of people gathered in the hotel below to listen to him. He stood on an elevated dais, above the crowd, speaking through a microphone, his voice enhanced by speakers. He said he had just done what had to be done, whatever was in his power in the situation. He said that it was what his father and grandfather would have done. This city was in his blood; it was tied to his family from birth to death. He expressed his gratification that the country's leaders had come out of this tragedy with a commitment to change systemic problems. We shouldn't have to rely on crazy billionaires every time, he said with a smile.

Someone asked him how he had known he wouldn't hit the chief minister when he fired the shot. He shrugged and said he had known that the bullet would hit a terrorist either way.

KARM

The crowd laughed, even though they knew they shouldn't.

Towards the end, one old man asked him if he had done it all simply to get contracts for his security services company. The crowd grew silent, glaring at the man.

Vishnu Mistry's voice was solemn. 'When I was twelve years old and my parents were murdered in front of my eyes, I became the twelfth richest person in the world at that young age.' His eyes bore into the crowd. 'Do you think I need to risk my life for money?'

The crowd was silent. They looked at him and listened. They all knew the story. The whole world knew. But no one had heard him talk of it before.

Vishnu's voice grew sombre. 'In fact, this brings me to an announcement. I am creating a fund, which I call the India Future Fund, with ten billion dollars of my personal wealth. It's a small amount for this vast country, but I have faith that if we focus on changes that can reform the fundamentals of our country, the fundamental promises that it was founded upon, we can rebuild our nation.'

His words fell upon the assembled in murmurs and whispers, hurrahs and confusion. How would he change the fundamentals of the country, someone asked? Did that mean he would enter politics, came another question.

Vishnu Mistry looked right and left, at the shifting, restless men and women. 'Only if you trust me,' he said quietly. 'Do you?'

TWENTY-EIGHT

The day dawned bright, with a cool breeze fluttering through the city. Sunlight skittered into the room, lighting Navkar's face, and he woke up groggily. He tottered over to the living room, stumbled over to the window and drew the curtains to let Mumbai creep in. He waded to the attached kitchen, made coffee in his tiny coffee machine and added a pinch of cinnamon.

As he sipped his coffee, he frowned thoughtfully, remembering that first day when he'd spoken to Tara. That day, so long ago, when she'd sat on his motorbike. It had been a bad day. He would finally be seeing her today. He hadn't got a chance when the hostages were being brought out and she hadn't come to office since then. Her phone was switched off and he hadn't had the courage to go to her home. Besides he didn't know where she lived and it would be awkward to ask his colleagues.

He arrived early to work. Some of the others were bringing in cakes and candles and streamers. There would be a welcome party for Tara.

She came in by 9.30, wearing a white top and formal pants, just like she would on any other day. She had her sunglasses perched atop her hair, as usual. Everyone gathered around her when she entered. Navkar found himself at the back of the crowd. He could hear the shrieks of welcomes, the cheers and hugs. There were sniffles too. Some people were crying in emotion.

He returned to his cubicle when it was over, feeling a hollow in the pit of his stomach. He synced his slate with the screen and started work.

Some ten minutes later, Navkar felt a tap on his shoulder. He turned and found himself staring at Tara's face.

'Breakfast?' she asked.

On the rooftop canteen, she hugged her coffee mug close to her chin as usual and he munched on a plate of pakoras. She sat silently, with a dreamy, faraway look in her eyes, breathing in the fragrance of the coffee between small sips. Her feet were up on the ledge and her hair fell in a tumble down her shoulders.

'How does it feel?' Navkar asked. 'Now that…it's over.'

She shrugged and smiled. 'I don't know. Calm, I suppose. Everything feels slow. In a good way.'

They sat there for what seemed like ages. She told him how it had been, about the gunmen, what they did, about Chauhan. She told him how she'd felt as she waited. She spoke in bursts, a few words, then a long silence, then a few words again, and all through it, he watched her and felt her voice tap dance in his head. His pakoras lay forgotten, cold and soggy in their accompanying chutney.

'I couldn't believe when I heard what Vishnu had done!' she said finally. 'I'd never even imagined something like that.'

The words made Navkar look away. He shifted in his seat, remembering the sight of the airship swooping low and the hissing rockets, the lurch of his stomach as Mistry's helicopter arrived with its fog light.

'He was incredible! A hero!' Navkar said, quietly.

'He's a madman,' she said, but she giggled like a schoolgirl.

'Perhaps they are not so different,' Navkar said. He tried to smile.

Tara finished her cup and deposited it on the table. She smacked her lips and looked at him. 'You know, we need to get more evidence for what you found. Otherwise these lazy bastards will just keep running *Vishnu is Our God* for a week.'

He stared at her then laughed. 'You're thinking of work? You almost died!'

She leant over, and her eyes bore into him, her voice lowering, 'But I didn't, you see.' She glanced around once, before continuing, 'It was all wrong, Sudy. It was all wrong. It doesn't make sense.'

Navkar blinked and shook his head. 'You're mad too,' he said with a sigh. 'You two are perfect for each other.'

Tara stiffened and sat up straight, her eyes scanning the drab, grey houses across the lane. He could see her lips curl in a smile. 'He called me today. He's going to show me his old home, the one he grew up in. He never shows it to anyone.'

'Maybe he's going to propose,' Navkar said and immediately regretted it.

Tara turned sharply, her eyes wide and large. He could see a flush creep up her face. Then she shook her head, as if shaking the thought off and laughed.

'Tell me how it goes, when you meet him. I am sure there will be celebrations,' Navkar said abruptly as he got to his feet.

Tara smiled and picked up her mug and stretched as she got up. As they left the canteen, she asked, 'By the way, you never told me how you found out that an attack was going to happen.'

KARM

He shrugged. 'It's a long story. I'll tell you the next time we talk.'

He couldn't be near her any longer.

~

Tara left office early, around five in the evening, when most people were just getting their third cup of coffee. It was a long drive to Vishnu's home. First she took the expressway towards South Mumbai, then the sanguine arc of the sea link, past the dargah of Haji Ali with its white walls twinkling in the sun and sea, and finally, the curving sea road of the Queen's Necklace.

They'd finally started redeveloping some of the squares of four-storeyed houses that overlooked the road. Giant cranes loomed over half-broken buildings, scattering the old, promising the new. The road was still uneven though, still a criss-cross of irregular slabs and lumps of tar joining them.

The other end of the Necklace narrowed into a small lane that curved past a corner looking onto the sea. It then snaked past a solitary streetlight, blocking traffic that had once been known as Teen Batti, and then into Malabar Hill.

She could see snatches of blue-green between old residential towers with peeling paint and clumps of trees, as the car snaked its way up the hill and towards its far end.

The old Rustomjee bungalow was right at the last bend of the hills, at the furthest point from the rest of Mumbai, where there was nothing but the slope and the sea. The driver had to ask a few people on the street before he found his destination.

At long last, the car turned into a shaded, unpaved path, shadowed by swaying palm trees and made of red earth. The house was in a clearing, hugging the edge of a sheer drop to the sea, a construction in rock and red tiles, just two storeys high.

Tara stepped out of the car, and the salty breeze blowing in from the sea slapped into her face and made her smile. It was sunset now. The orange-red expanse of the sky loomed over them, unhindered by concrete residences or towers. She could see black specks of wheeling birds returning to their homes against cream swirls of cloud. And below them she could see his tall frame and restless stance. He was smiling.

'My great grandfather built this, back in 1880,' he said. 'I have heard that he blew up a bit of the cliff to create this patch of level ground.'

She wouldn't run to him. She'd told herself that. She walked as slowly as she could make herself, and stopped a few paces from him. He was still smiling, but it was a tired, distracted smile, not that of a revelling hero. She wondered what he was thinking. She wondered if she should hug him. His hand reached out and cupped her chin and she decided she had shown enough dignity and hugged him tight.

His arms moved around her, surprising her with their strength, as always.

'When I heard you were in there, I thought I'd never see you again,' he said.

'So did I,' she said into his shoulder.

She felt his arms dig into her and suddenly she was up in the air, the sky spinning as she was twirled around.

She tottered when he let her down. 'Come,' he said, laughing, 'I'll show you the house.'

They went past the porch and the doorway hand in hand, into a large, airy living room. It was sparsely filled. The furniture was old but practical rather than ornate. The sofas and curtains were faded.

An old man was waiting for them, bent with age, dressed in a starched white shirt over grey trousers. He wore thick glasses. An old, golden pen peeked out of his shirt pocket.

'Munimji,' Vishnu said, with a stiff smile, 'This is Tara.'

He turned to her. 'Munimji has taken care of me for a long time now. He's all the family I have.'

Tara stared at the man, not knowing how to greet him. Part of her wondered why she'd never met him before. Munimji didn't seem very pleased to meet her. His eyes seemed to be glaring at her from behind those glasses, his wrinkled face not yielding even a token smile.

Vishnu helped her out. He nodded to the old man, and without a word, pulled her behind him to show her the other rooms.

'This was my room as a child,' he said, showing her a large, empty room with a small bed, wardrobe and a wooden floor. 'I used to insist that it be kept empty. I used to arrange all my toys on the floor. It was my battleground.'

She looked at him as he spoke. 'You didn't tell me about,' she paused, 'about him before.'

He shrugged. 'How did you think I grew up?'

'He doesn't come to your tower? To the penthouse?'

Vishnu looked away, and she could see him frowning. 'He doesn't like my new life.'

She leant in the doorway and looked at that polished, glazed floor. She imagined him as a small child, a chubby little kid, lining up his toys. 'You've kept a lot of secrets from me.'

He didn't reply. He took her hand in his and led her to

the next room. This one was different. This one looked like it was still in use. It was preserved perfectly, as if the covers had been set just this morning. It was filled with knick-knacks and the many little day-to-day objects, each of them cleaned and polished.

'This was my parents' room,' he said, and his voice was hollow.

He moved into the room, his hands straying over objects. He wasn't looking at her any more, his attention was completely focused on the room. It seemed like he had gone miles away, years away.

'This porcelain elephant was given to my mom by my grandma,' he said quietly. 'I had chipped off a piece once and my father helped me fix it in secret.'

He then pointed to a clock kept on a side table, saying, 'And this clock was made by hand by my father. He liked technology. He liked tinkering.'

| 243 |

She looked at the clock. Her footsteps seemed loud in here, as if she was intruding. Her eyes fell on an old Sony walkman cassette player, carefully arranged, with its headphones kept beside it.

'My mother's walkman,' he said. 'She would wake up every morning and put it on and listen to songs. Only after that would she get up from the bed.'

She stared at him. His eyes were catching the sunlight, green-gold, like an open field on a winter morning.

'You remember so much,' she said.

His fingers ran over the wooden back of a chair set before the dressing table. 'Yeah,' he said slowly, 'I remember everything. I remember it all the time, every day. I can't forget a thing.'

KARM

There was a sudden sound from the doorway causing her to jump. It was the old man. He had a phone in his hands.

'A call for you. It's important.'

Vishnu went out of the room to take the call. The old man stood there in the doorway, silently regarding her.

'Thank you,' she said finally, his gaze making her nervous. 'Thank you for taking care of him. He means a lot...to everyone.'

The old man glared at her. 'Go away,' he said finally, his voice like brittle glass. 'Go away and forget that you ever knew him. Forget everything about him.'

He turned on his heels and walked out before she could stop him. She stood there, watching his shuffling steps, wondering what he meant. She looked around in the room and felt herself shiver. She could see why Vishnu didn't stay here any longer, why he didn't show it to anyone. It wasn't a home any longer. It was a mausoleum.

She could see Munimji standing by Vishnu from here, watching him intently, like she caught her mother watching her sometimes. It must be heart-breaking for him, she thought slowly, to meet a girl he cared for.

The thought brought a flush to her face. She wanted to leave this room, go to him, but she resisted. She took a few steps inside, but couldn't bear to sit on that impeccably kept bed. Her heart was beating fast; she could hear it in the silence of the room and it surprised her.

Vishnu returned soon after. His face wore the distracted stiffness of anxiety, but he put on a fake smile for her. 'Come let's go sit in the living room. Munimji has made sherbet.'

They sat at the dinner table, which was covered by a chequered cloth and had a vase of yellow flowers in the middle. The sherbet was blood-pink, shimmering beneath ice and sunlight. It tasted tangy-sweet.

'Sherbet-e-rivas,' Vishnu said. 'It's made from rhubarb.' He sat back and looked at her. 'Tell me about it; about what happened,' he said after a while.

Too many people had asked that of her today. She'd found a way out most of the time. It didn't feel right, going over those hours so casually. It felt disrespectful.

But it was different this time. Everything came out in a rush of words, everything she'd thought and feared. She told him how she'd felt it was strange, how they seemed to be getting orders, how they almost avoided killing anyone. She clutched his hand and leant forward, excited and lost. She said how they seemed to know they were going to die. They didn't seem to have any real hope of getting their demands fulfilled. They didn't even seem to have any real demands. It was like they were just saying something because they should.

She shook her head, wondering. 'The only thing they seemed to care about was holding that landing, and killing the police when they attacked.'

Vishnu gave a wry look. 'That's hardly believable.'

The sherbet stuck to her mouth and throat. Why was her heart beating so hard? She could feel the old man's shadow across the table. He didn't sit with them. She glanced at Vishnu. He was still listening intently, waiting for her to talk.

She shrugged. 'Then your commandos came. It happened pretty quickly after the police fled. And even then, the terrorists didn't do anything. They just hugged each other.' She looked at him, feeling strange just saying the words. 'It was as if they knew their end had come.'

He nodded. His gaze met hers. 'You have great eyes,' he said suddenly. 'You see everything. You're probably the best reporter in India today.'

She blinked, surprised by the compliment. Her phone started to buzz. Navkar had sent a message along with a picture. The message said that he'd asked Salim for a picture of Khurram bhai, the head of their gang who'd made the deal for the terrorist attack.

She peered at the photo. She felt she'd seen him before. She frowned, concentrating, and then jumped in realization.

'What happened?' Vishnu asked.

She looked up at him. It was the man with the sword. The man who'd attacked Chauhan at his rally in Karad. It was Khurram bhai.

'Everything okay?' Vishnu asked again.

She nodded slowly, thoughts racing through her head. Vishnu had stopped with his sherbet half-raised to his lips. Somehow, she sensed she shouldn't tell him.

'Just some work stuff.'

She noticed with a start that he was still carrying his gun. It was tucked into his belt, as always, its lines visible under his shirt. 'You know,' she said quietly, 'I knew you were a shooting champion, but I never imagined you could do something that amazing. I mean, the guy had Chauhan held in front.'

'He didn't hold him properly,' Vishnu replied.

'They were very sloppy in a lot of ways,' she mused. 'It was so stupid to go out to the balcony and make those demands.'

'He was probably desperate.'

'Yeah,' she said, watching the ice cubes dance in her glass. She remembered the white-shirted man's manner, his calm hands holding the megaphone, his level voice. He hadn't seemed desperate.

Vishnu's eyes were watching her. His gemstone eyes.

She realized she was sure of this fact—the gunman had gone out to die.

She took a long sip of the sherbet, down to its last drop. Khurram had helped organize the terrorist attack. He'd also been behind the attack on Chauhan by the vigilante. There was only one real possibility. She couldn't ignore it any further. There was only one way this made sense. They were both done by the same group. Or the same man.

'I just need to go to the restroom,' she said, getting up abruptly and nearly toppling her chair.

'You can use the one in that room,' Vishnu pointed.

She felt his eyes on her as she went and walked faster. She needed someplace alone to think. She entered the room again, the ghost room. She realized it had large, open, French windows. The curtains were flying in the wind. The last rays of the sun lay over every surface, colouring everything.

As she was closing the restroom door, her eyes fell on empty photo frames on the mantelpiece. She blinked thoughtfully. Vishnu must have removed the photos. He'd removed the photos but kept the frames. He couldn't bear to remember but he didn't want to forget!

She splashed water on her face, again and again. She rubbed it into her eyes and her skin. She stared at the mirror. Her make-up was running. She splashed more water, washing it off.

The vigilante arranged this attack on the Mantralaya. She remembered David Agarwal's words, his explanation behind the vigilante's threats, the enforced ceiling on corruption. The logic was undeniable. The vigilante had wanted to stop corruption. He had a strong sense of justice. He had a lot of money to pull it off.

There was a rap on the door and she jumped.

'Are you alright?'

It was Vishnu. He was trying the handle.

She turned to the door, staring at the handle turning and the vibration as he knocked.

The terrorist attack helped Vishnu. It helped him get that damned bill passed—the one he'd been obsessed with for so long.

The door shook again. His voice came through cold and clear. 'Open the door, Tara!'

Someone rich. Someone with a strong sense of justice. Someone who wasn't averse to violence. Her hands shook as she took out her phone and began to type a message to Navkar.

Suddenly, the door jerked violently, once, twice. She found herself trembling, her back to the basin. The latch came loose, the nails pulling out of the woodwork as the door slammed open. Vishnu was looking at her, his face betraying no emotion.

'What're you doing?' she screamed.

'That's what I wanted to ask you,' he said, almost casually.

She brought her phone up and pressed send. 'I just had to send some email for work,' she said, trying to keep her voice level.

He took a step inside. 'Show me,' he said.

She stared at him. 'What?'

His expression didn't change. His face seemed as though it was hewn from rock, his tone insistent. 'Show me what you sent.'

It was all over. She was right. She was right and it was all finished. She felt tears rising in her eyes. Stupid useless tears. She blinked, staring into his eyes.

'Alright,' she said and held out the phone.

He took a few more steps, moving past the door towards her, his hand reaching out.

Tara felt the hot trickle of her tears on her cheek as his fingers brushed against the phone. She looked into his eyes. One last time. She could look one last time. His fingers closed, but she'd pulled the phone back. She ducked and slammed elbow first into his abdomen. It was like walking into a pillar. But she had taken him by surprise. He stumbled back a few steps but recovered to reach out to catch her.

But she was past him already, past the door.

Tara jumped onto the bed, stumbling. One step, two, and then she swung her arm with all the strength she could muster, throwing the phone out beyond the balcony, beyond the sheer drop, into the sea. She felt his weight ram into her. Her breath left her as she collapsed on the bed, pinned down beneath him. The impact shook the bed. The porcelain elephant fell off the side table, shattering into a thousand pieces.

She was sobbing now; deep, wracking sobs that made her whole body shudder.

He was breathing hard.

'Why?' she asked, and let herself mourn.

TWENTY-NINE

Tara's feet slid along the soft gauze of the bed cover. She sat hugging her knees, her face covered by the fall of her hair. Vishnu was leaning by the French windows, staring out at the red-purple sea engulfing the sun, and the thousand mirrored waves that rose with the tide.

Munimji came in with snacks on a tray. His old eyes fell on her and looked away. She saw a pained sadness there. She hadn't recognized it before. Vishnu sent the man and the snacks away. She didn't mind. The last thing she wanted to do was eat.

'The police caught the wrong guy,' Vishnu said, his eyes fixed on the horizon and memory. 'Some poor guy they could beat into confession out of.' He glanced at her. 'The court did better. They let him go. But I spent the six years waiting...and so did his family.

'It kept gnawing at me. It wouldn't go away.' He turned away from the window.

She brushed her hair away from her face and stared at him, illuminated by the last rays of the day.

'I thought I had to become strong,' he said, frowning. 'Strong enough to fix things. It...it seemed right. You see, they had left me with everything I could possibly need. To stop things like this from happening.'

He shrugged. 'It sounds crazy, I know, but it felt right. It feels right even now. It gives some…reason to what happened.'

He started pacing to and fro, idly picking up the empty picture frame. He ran a hand through his hair. His voice was agitated, jerky, like a young boy trying to talk to a pretty girl. She felt his halting words spread through the room, through her. How had they met? She didn't even remember clearly. She couldn't remember anything right now.

'I thought about it a lot: what were the reasons that things like this happened? Could they be stopped at all? I did a lot of research, spoke to policemen, judges, people in the government and in politics. I spoke to…Munimji.'

Tara glanced at the door. The old man had disappeared. She realized there must have been a time when he was different, when they were close.

Vishnu's voice brought her attention back to him.

'It was surprisingly simple,' he said. 'It could all be traced to three problems. Just three, though they were difficult to solve.'

Her sobs had stopped, her tears had dried. She sat still in the aftermath of her sorrow. It was never meant to be. It never had been. It had always been a hopeless dream, a folly of her mind and her eyes. She found her voice as she felt surer of that.

'The first was about elections,' she said. 'That one we figured out.'

He nodded in agreement. 'Elections need money and more money than your competition increases your chances to win. This is inevitable. But political parties cannot genuinely make money—they provide no commercial services. So how can they make any honest money?'

'So they steal,' she said, 'and they fight and win elections with stolen money.'

'Yes. And it never ends. Everyone tries to match the winner, and it becomes an ever-increasing spiral of corruption. Once it starts, it never stops.'

He paused and smiled at her, probably encouraged by the fact that she was talking. He looked almost pitiful at that moment, like a lost child looking for approval. She realized he needed to tell someone. He had probably been craving this for a long time. Perhaps in a small corner of his heart he'd even wanted to get caught. Perhaps that's why he'd been attracted to her, a journalist who was willing to do anything to get her story.

'The second problem,' he continued, 'is the presence of organized crime. The underworld. It seems cliched, but well, if crime is organized it can never lose to law-enforcing agencies. It's a typical problem of asymmetric warfare. It's much easier for the underworld to observe, target, encircle the police than the other way, because overall, they always have the element of surprise.'

'The third seemed the simplest, though it was probably what hurt people most. It was what I had to face, and I'm not the only one. People face it every day. Basically, our system has become designed to fail. Our courts have become impotent, unable to handle their duties and our police have become incompetent and unaccountable.'

He gave a wry grin. 'I thought that would be the easiest to handle, but once I started planning I realized I'd got it upside down. It's the first two that were easy, because they were illegal. The third was changing a whole set of interlinked laws. It was a completely legal issue, and it seemed impossible.'

The light outside had faded. Darkness fell from the sky and the sea turned into foaming black ink. The breeze grew colder. She listened to him almost in disbelief, though she knew it was all true, every word. That is how he had thought. That is what he had decided. She pulled the bed cover up around her and gripped it tight.

'You hired people from the underworld yourself,' she said quietly.

He nodded. 'It's easy to hire thugs in India. It's a thriving industry. If you're willing to pay the right amount you'll find men in Mumbai who'll do anything you ask. They'll kill their own kin. So that is how I started. I paid for specific killings, betrayals. It started creating rifts, a thinning of trust, an atmosphere of uncertainty. In the underworld, uncertainty is fear. A thinning of trust is the same as a thinning of the gangs themselves.'

'The more they worked for me, the more they needed to work for me, since they needed a way out of the gangs. I realized I could use them for other work quite safely.'

'That's when the letters started,' she said.

'A little earlier. The one you uncovered was the fourth letter,' he said and smiled. 'The first one was just an introduction. But that was when I found how easy it was to control politicians. They're basically like businessmen, just with a more feudal mindset. The basic principle is the same— carrot and stick.'

He crossed his arms. 'I wasn't going to give them a carrot, so stick it was.'

'The blood price,' she said, looking at him.

'The blood price,' he echoed. 'Money doesn't work. You can always steal more money.'

~

The man's limbs were numb by now. It had been a long journey in the hold of the cramped boat. He stank of fish. He was sure this stink would stay a while. A bath or two wouldn't make much difference.

He swayed on the deck of the boat when they finally let him out, stamping his feet and feeling the tingling sensation of the blood flowing back. It was dark but he could see a flickering light in the spreading darkness. Someone was holding up a lantern on the dock. The boat slid closer noiselessly. There was silence everywhere. No one used this fisherman's dock in the monsoon.

The man holding up the lantern helped him onto the rickety wooden jetty.

'Khurram mian?' the man asked. He was wearing a white shirt stained with sweat, jeans and new sneakers.

Khurram nodded and the man grinned; yellow teeth in the yellow light. 'I'm Faizal. I thought you'd be hungry.'

He held out two rolls wrapped in greasy, translucent paper. 'Lamb or beef?'

Khurram stared in delighted surprise. He was famished. He could see meat shining with oil and spice, surrounded by pickled onions. He took the lamb one and beamed happily. 'It's true what they say. This is the home of hospitality.'

Faizal laughed loudly and then bit into the other roll. 'I've been waiting for you. Let's eat. I'm hungry too.'

They sat side by side on the jetty, their legs over the side, eating hungrily, with no need of conversation. A cool wind blew. There was lightning on the horizon, over the sea.

Khurram took a deep breath. He felt free now, finally. Free of everything, of that cesspool of a city. He would buy a farmhouse here, near Karachi. He would settle down, raise kids like they should be raised.

He turned to Faizal. 'Where are we going now?'

Faizal wiped his mouth, rolled up the paper and threw it into the water. 'I'm going home,' he said pleasantly. 'God only knows where you're going.'

He took out a gun, shot Khurram in the head and then got up and walked away.

~

The cutlery was silver. Tara twirled her fork in her fingers; the metal glimmered white under the neon light. Her food lay untouched. Munimji stood beside them silently. Vishnu sat opposite her, eating with delicate movements of his hands. She raised her wine glass to her lips and took another long draught.

It was old wine, thick and bitter on her tongue. 'When did you decide on *staging* the Mantralaya attack?' she asked.

Vishnu chewed thoughtfully and swallowed. He didn't want to speak with his mouth full, she realized.

'I tried to avoid it,' he said finally. 'If nothing else it was too risky for me, would make me too visible. The problem was that the last people who wanted this reform were the politicians. Their business would be one of the first to be affected. Yet, they were the ones who had to pass the bill. Even small police reforms have been rotting on the shelf for decades. Something this big would never happen.'

The cutlery clinked as he took another bite.

She glanced down at her plate. The thought of tasting

anything made her nauseous. She felt as though she was carved out of sorrow. 'You couldn't think of any other way?' she said quietly. 'Do you know how many people died?'

He frowned. 'For a while I thought that the threatening letters would work. Perhaps if Chauhan and the others felt scared enough, personally, they might give in and strengthen the police. I tried to get close to Chauhan, fund him, convince him, make him feel I was on his side.'

'That's what everyone thinks,' she agreed.

'He was really terrified of what was happening and was quite willing to support the bill, at least most of its clauses.'

'So what happened?'

Vishnu sat back and sipped his wine. 'It wasn't enough. He's not that powerful. His own party would have disowned him, forget the allies. I realized that things would not move without a dramatic demonstration of public opinion.'

'I had to show them how bad the situation was, something that would shock them—something so brutal, so big, so devastating that they would take to the streets in protest.'

It made sense. She knew that. It made perfect sense. A pure flow of logic. A mathematical problem, where the equations were people's brains and the outcomes, their lives.

'It would have to be riots or a terrorist attack,' Vishnu continued. 'The latter would kill lesser people. The enemy would be projected beyond the country's shores. It was an obvious choice. I started preparing the best way to do it. Then, one day, you forced my hand.'

She'd known that was coming. It almost made her smile. 'The vigilante story. You had to distract the media.'

He wiped his mouth with the napkin, folded and kept it aside neatly. 'I had to distract everyone. I had to stop people's questions. I had to finish everything before the questions brought down the government.' He looked at her. 'You're not going to eat, are you?'

She shook her head. He rose and came around the table, his hand outstretched to help her up.

Tara slid her chair back, and looked up at him. 'Your parents' death unhinged you,' she said simply. 'You're a madman.'

He didn't seem surprised by her accusation, though his hand dropped away. 'You have to understand,' he said carefully, 'that what is madness for most people is just a choice for me. Things that people can't dream of doing, what they will call insanity, are just specific expenses and risks for me. That is the gift my parents left me when they died.'

She didn't know what to say. There was nothing left to say. She knew what had to happen next. She knew what she had to do. She lunged up, stabbed the fork into his stomach, threw the chair between him and her, watched his beautiful, terrible eyes widen in pain, and ran.

She didn't get far. The old man caught her by the door, just for a moment before she threw him off, but it was enough. It took away even the slightest chance she might have had. Vishnu reached her and she felt his iron grip on her arm, then a monstrous pull that nearly wrenched her shoulder off, till she was pinned against him, locked in the cage of his embrace.

'I loved you,' she screamed. 'How can you do this? I loved you!'

His voice was a whisper in her ears, his tears wet against her face. 'That shall always be my greatest regret.'

'Please!' she wailed, flailing against his arms. 'Please let me go! I won't tell anyone! Please! My mother will be left all alone! You met her! You met her, damn you! Please!'

'I cannot,' he said, his voice shaking.

She felt her legs kick in the air as he lifted her and dragged her inside.

The old man was still on the ground, sitting, watching them, weeping openly.

'Munimji!' she cried out. 'Please! Stop him! Stop him, please!'

The old man stumbled to his feet. He walked towards them, coughing, crying. He stood before Vishnu. 'Listen carefully, Vishnu Rustomjee Mistry. Listen to me and save your soul.'

THIRTY

Navkar stared at his screen mutely. The Word document was blank, as it had been for the past hour. He hadn't written a word.

He checked the time again. Where was she? It was already ten o' clock in the morning.

He checked his mobile again, reading the last message she'd sent last evening. A short sentence… *Vishnu is behind everything. Run.*

He'd called her at least twenty times since then, but her phone had been switched off. He hadn't known what to do. He spoke to Salim, who had advised him to wait till today morning.

'He's a big man,' he'd said. 'Everyone knows she went to his house. He won't risk anything. She'll be back tomorrow morning. Then we will figure out what to do.'

He'd tried calling her again early this morning, but her phone was still off. He swirled his chair once more, hoping against hope that he would see her approaching, see her smile as she asked about breakfast.

No, she wouldn't smile today. Even if she turned up, she wouldn't be smiling.

Suddenly, the door to the room for the reporters opened.

Navkar rose from his work station, almost forgetting to breathe, stumbling forward to get a look.

It wasn't her. It was Malhotra, his henna-red hair uncombed, with a stubble and red eyes. He shuffled into the middle of the room and clapped his hands to get people's attention.

'I have an announcement to make,' he said loudly. 'Tara Verma has resigned this morning. She said she's going abroad for a long holiday and won't be coming back anytime soon.'

'What?' Navkar shouted and people turned towards him, surprised. He walked towards Malhotra, his steps unsteady. 'What're you saying?'

Malhotra glared at him. 'She's not coming back, hero. You want to leave too?'

He felt the room spinning. His hand grabbed at the wall for support.

It was raining heavily. A downpour. Thunderclouds rolled overhead. The park was empty save for a family huddling under a canvas sheet. Navkar could hear the child sniffling quietly.

Salim sat on the bench next to him. He was trying to pass Navkar his beedi, shaded by a protective palm. It wasn't enough. Even in the fraction of a second that it took Navkar to cover it, a raindrop fizzled it out.

Navkar felt like laughing.

'A girl died,' he said, leaning back. 'A long time back. A girl from my class.'

Salim played with the lighter idly, watching the flame get extinguished again and again. 'A sweetheart?'

'No,' Navkar said. 'Not really. She smiled at me sometimes. I smiled back. We were just kids.'

Trees were waving to and fro, buffeted by the violence of the wind. Navkar could feel the rhythm of the rain all around them.

'I wanted to know her,' he said. 'But then suddenly, she was killed. Just suddenly, one day. Just like that.' Navkar's fingers intertwined and he cracked the joints distractedly. 'We held a two-minute silence in assembly for her,' he said quietly. 'I'd never understood what powerlessness meant before that.' They sat in silence for a while. Navkar could see skyscrapers in the distance, ghostly behind sheets of rain. The silent watchers of Mumbai. The chroniclers of its streets.

'You checked Tara's home?' Salim asked.

'Yeah,' Navkar said, his voice flat. 'I found her address and went there. The house was locked. Neighbours said she and her mother left in a taxi. They said they were going to Mauritius.'

Salim looked at him intently and asked, 'You think she's still alive?'

Navkar had known that question was coming. It was inevitable. He'd prepared himself for it. 'I'll find out,' he said, his shoulders hunched. 'If she is, I'll find her.'

'If she isn't?'

Navkar ran his fingers through his hair. His jaw was tight. He'd prepared himself for this too. 'I'll get her justice,' he said.

Salim shook his head in disbelief. 'You'll get yourself killed.'

Navkar found himself shaking. 'I don't have a choice,' he said raggedly, 'I have to do what I can.'

Salim frowned. 'What can you do? Vishnu Mistry is too big. Who will even help you?'

Navkar looked up. 'Shinde,' he said quietly. 'I saved his life.'

'Shinde's gotten suspended,' Salim said. 'He's dishonoured.'

'Exactly.'